EVERYTHING WE KEEP

EVERYTHING WE KEEP

a novel

KERRY LONSDALE

This is a work of fiction. Names, characters, organizations, places, events, and incidents are either products of the author's imagination or are used fictitiously.

Published by Lake Union Publishing, Seattle

www.apub.com

ISBN-13: 9781503935310
ISBN-10: 1503935310

Cover design by LEADesign

Printed in the United States of America

For Henry, who traveled five thousand miles to find me.
I love you.

PART ONE

Gem City of the Foothills
Los Gatos, California

CHAPTER 1

JULY

On our wedding day, my fiancé, James, arrived at the church in a casket.

For years I'd dreamed of him waiting for me at the altar, wearing that smile he reserved just for me. It never failed to make my insides flip. But instead of walking down the aisle toward my best friend, my first and only love, I was at his funeral.

I sat beside my parents in the sanctuary filled with friends and relatives. They should have been our wedding guests. Instead, they'd come to pay their respects to a man who'd died too young and too soon. He'd just turned twenty-nine.

Now he was gone. Forever.

A tear trailed down my cheek. I captured it with the shredded tissue in my hand.

"Here, Aimee." Mom gave me a clean one.

I crumpled it in my fist. "Th-thanks." My voice hitched on a sob.

"Is that her?" a voice murmured behind me, and I tensed.

"Yes, James's fiancée," came a whispered reply.

"The poor dear. She looks so young. How long were they engaged?"

"I'm not sure, but they'd known each other since they were children."

A surprised breath. "Childhood sweethearts. How tragic."

"I heard it took weeks for them to locate the body. Can you imagine? The not knowing?"

I moaned. My lower lip quivered uncontrollably.

"Hey! A little respect here," Dad whispered harshly to the ladies behind us. He stood, shuffling past Mom and me, bumping our knees, and then sat, bookending me between himself and Mom. He pulled me into his side, becoming my shelter against the whispered gossip and curious stares.

The organ blared as the funeral ceremony commenced. Everyone surged to their feet. I rose slowly, my entire body feeling achy and aged, and gripped the pew in front of me to keep from collapsing back into my seat. All heads turned to the rear of the church, where the pallbearers hoisted James's casket onto their shoulders. As I watched them process behind the priest, I couldn't help thinking they carried more than James's remains, his body too decomposed for an open casket. Our hopes and dreams, the future we had road-mapped, also rode on their shoulders. James's plan to open an art gallery downtown after he quit the family business. My dream to start my own restaurant when my parents retired from theirs. The little boy I imagined standing between James and me, his small hands linked with ours.

Everything would be buried today.

Another sob tore free of my lungs, reverberating off the church walls, the sound louder than the organ's withering notes.

"I can't do this," I wailed in a harsh whisper.

Losing James. Feeling everyone's pitying stares burning my back as I stood in the second pew. The air was stifling, a stale mixture of sweat and incense wrapped in the sweet, syrupy scent of the orchid bouquets artfully displayed throughout the mission-style church. The flowers had been purchased for our wedding, but Claire Donato, James's mother, had them delivered for the funeral. Same church. Same flowers. Wrong ceremony.

My stomach pitched. I covered my mouth and tried to move around Dad toward the aisle. Mom snagged my hand and gave it a squeeze. She wrapped her arm through mine, and I rested my head on her shoulder. "There, there," she soothed. Tears rained unhindered down my face.

The pallbearers lowered the casket onto a metal stand, then moved to their seats. Thomas, James's brother, slid into the front pew beside Claire, who was dressed in a black suit with her silver hair coiled as tight and rigid as her posture. Phil, James's cousin, moved into the pew to stand on her other side. He turned and looked at me, dipping his head in acknowledgment. I swallowed, inching back until my calves pressed into the wood bench.

Claire twisted around. "Aimee."

I jerked my attention to her. "Claire," I murmured.

Since the news of James's death, we'd barely spoken a word to each other. She'd made it quite clear my presence was too much a reminder of what she'd lost, her youngest son. For both our sakes, I kept my distance.

The funeral progressed with a predicted lineup of rituals and hymns. I half listened to the speeches and barely heard the readings. When the ceremony ended, I slipped out the side door before anyone could stop me. I'd heard enough condolences to last me two lifetimes.

Guests spilled into the courtyard. I could see the hearse as I moved through the breezeway, hoping to leave unnoticed. I glanced over my shoulder and locked gazes with Thomas. He marched through the arched passageway and looped his arms around me. He gave me a hard hug. The coarse material of his suit scratched my cheek. He looked like James: dark hair and eyes, olive skin. A broader, older version, but he didn't feel like him.

"I'm glad you're here." His breath wove through my hair.

"I almost didn't come."

"I know." He moved me away from the crowd gathering around us until we stopped under the blooming trumpet vine at the edge of the breezeway. Lavender blossoms danced in the July afternoon breeze. The coastal fog that had blanketed Los Gatos in the predawn hours had burned off with the rising sun. The day was already too warm.

Thomas leaned away and gripped my upper arms. "How are you doing?"

I shook my head, pressing my tongue to the roof of my mouth to stifle the sob threatening to be heard. I stepped from Thomas's arms. "I have to go."

"We all do. Come, ride with me. I'll take you to the burial and reception afterward."

I shook my head again. He'd driven to the church with Claire and Phil.

Thomas sighed heavily. "You aren't coming."

"Only to the burial." I twisted my fingers in the tie of my wrap dress. I'd driven there with my parents. I planned to leave with them, too. "The reception's your mother's affair. Her relatives and friends."

"They were also James's and your friends."

"I know, but . . ."

"I understand." He reached inside his suit and withdrew a folded piece of paper. "I'm not sure when I'll see you again."

"I'm not going anywhere. Just because James is . . ." I swallowed and studied my shoes, black wedges. Not the white satin open-toe pumps I was supposed to wear that day. "You can call me. Or visit," I offered.

"I'll be traveling a lot."

I lifted my head. "Oh?"

"Here. This is for you."

I unfolded the paper he handed me and gasped. It was a personal check from Thomas. A very large check. "What—?" My fingers trembled as my mind absorbed the value. $227,000.

"James was going to update his will once you married, but he . . ." Thomas rubbed his jaw, then let his arm fall to his side. "I'm still the beneficiary. I haven't received the funds from his bank accounts yet, but this is everything you would've received, except his ownership at Donato Enterprises. He wouldn't have been able to will that."

"I can't take your money." I held out the check.

He slipped his hands in his pockets. "Yes, you can. You were going to be married today so it would've been yours."

I studied the check again. It was so much money.

"Your parents are retiring soon, right? You can buy their restaurant, or start your own. James had mentioned that's what you wanted to do."

"I hadn't decided."

"Then travel, see the world. You're what, twenty-six? You've got your whole life ahead of you. Do what makes you happy." He smiled tightly and glanced beyond my shoulders, his gaze fixed across the courtyard. "I have to go. Take care, OK?" He kissed my cheek.

I felt the soft brush of his lips, but his words barely registered. The din in the courtyard had risen, and my thoughts were far from there. *Do what makes you happy.* I had no idea what that was. Not anymore.

I looked up to say good-bye to Thomas, but he was already gone. I turned around and found him across the courtyard with his mother and cousin. As if he felt my gaze, Phil cocked his head and met my stare. His brow lifted with deliberate purpose. I swallowed. He leaned over and whispered in Claire's ear, then started walking toward me.

Air sparked like oil in a scalding pan. I heard James's voice. An echo from long ago. *Let's get out of here.*

I tucked the check into my clutch and turned to go, slipping away toward the parking lot. I walked away from my past, unsure of my future, and with no idea how I'd be able to leave. I had no car.

I stopped at the curb, debating if I should return to the courtyard to find my parents when an older woman with pixie-cut blonde hair approached. "Ms. Tierney?"

I waved her off. I couldn't bear hearing one more condolence.

"Please, it's important."

I hesitated at the odd tone in her voice. "Do I know you?"

"I'm a friend."

"A friend of James?"

"Yours. I'm Lacy." She extended her hand.

I stared at the arm hovering midair between us, then raised my gaze to hers. "I'm sorry. Have we met?"

"I'm here about James." She lowered her arm and peeked over her shoulder. "I have information about his accident."

A tear beaded in the corner of my eye. I inhaled a deep breath, my lungs rattling from all the crying I'd done these past weeks. James had told me four days only, a quick business trip. Fly to Mexico, take a client fishing, negotiate contracts over dinner, and come home. The boat captain had said James cast his line, and after the captain checked the motor, James was gone. Just like that. Gone.

That was two months ago.

For weeks James was missing, and eventually he was presumed dead. Then, according to Thomas, James's body washed up on shore. Lacy probably hadn't heard his body had been found. Case closed.

"You're too late. He's—"

"Alive. James is alive."

I stared at her, dumbstruck. Who did this woman think she was? I pointed at the hearse. "Look!"

She did. We watched the driver slam the back hatch and walk around the side of the vehicle to sit in his seat. He closed the door and drove away, heading out of the parking lot toward the cemetery.

I looked at her with a warped sense of satisfaction. But she kept her eyes on the black sedan and spoke in a hushed tone loaded with fascination. "I wonder what's inside the casket."

"Wait up!" Lacy trailed me as I weaved through the parking lot. "Please, wait!"

"Go away!"

Tears rimmed my eyes. Saliva thickened my tongue. I had to vomit, and Lacy wouldn't leave me alone. I glanced toward the street. My house was less than a mile away. Maybe I could walk home.

Bile swiftly rose. *Oh God.*

"Let me explain," Lacy pleaded.

"Not. Now." I clamped my mouth and ducked behind a large van. Heat flashed across my body. Dampness soaked my armpits and the undersides of my breasts. My insides pitched and roiled. I hurled forward.

Everything I'd held back broke free, spewing onto the sunbaked pavement at my feet. The voice mail from James that never came. The lonely nights awaiting word he was still alive. The call from Thomas, the one I had dreaded receiving. James was gone.

Then there was Claire, who'd insisted the funeral take place on our wedding day. Her church had already been booked and her relatives had travel reservations. Why should they have to cancel or reschedule their plans?

Another shudder racked my body. I retched until my heart ached and stomach emptied. Then I wept. Gut-wrenching gasps tore through me. Heavy tears plunged to the asphalt, splattering in the acidic stew.

In some remote part of my brain, I understood I'd reached my limit. If only I'd shattered at home, hugging James's pillow. Not here, in the parking lot, with a crowd of people thirty yards away and a stranger hovering beside me.

I sagged against the van and sat on the bumper. Lacy offered a bottle of water. "It's new."

"Thanks." My hands trembled and I couldn't wrap my fingers around the narrow cap, so she took the water back and unscrewed it for me. I drank a third of the bottle before taking a breath.

Lacy tugged several tissues from her shoulder bag. "Here." She watched me clean my lips and wipe my nose as she fiddled with her purse strap. "Better?"

"No." I stood, wanting to go home.

Lacy's forearm disappeared again into the mouth of her bag. She shifted around the contents and pulled out a business card. "I need to talk with you."

"I'm not interested in what you're selling."

Her cheeks flamed. "I'm not selling anything. There's something—" She broke off, searching the parking lot behind us before looking back at me.

I blinked, shocked by the intensity of her lavender-blue eyes. Instinct flared. She knew something.

"I'm not selling anything and I'm very sorry about *how* I said what I said, but it's the truth. Visit me as soon as you can." She snagged my free hand and slapped the card in my palm. Then she retreated and disappeared around the van.

Footsteps approached, the click-clack of heels running on pavement. "There you are," Nadia gasped, out of breath. "We've been searching all over for you. Your parents are looking for you." Waves of auburn hair spilled around her shoulders. Her updo had come undone, probably in her rush to find me.

Kristen stopped beside her, chest heaving. A run in her sheer stockings trailed up the side of her calf.

They should have been my bridesmaids.

"What're you doing over here?" Kristen asked, her voice pitched high, strained from running.

"I was . . ." I stopped, not wanting to explain I was hiding, had been chased by a stranger through the parking lot, and then vomited on my shoes.

"You were what?" she prodded. Nadia nudged her with an elbow and motioned toward the ground by my feet. Kristen grimaced at the evidence splattered across the pavement like a toppled can of paint. "Oh, Aimee," she moaned.

My cheeks burned and I ducked my head. I read the card in my hand.

Lacy Saunders
Psychic Counselor, Consultant & Profiler
Murders, Missing Persons & Unsolved Mysteries
Helping you find the answers you seek.

A chill nipped at my core. I jerked my head in Lacy's direction. She was gone.

"What's that?" Nadia asked.

I gave her the card and she rolled her eyes. "Sheesh, the wackos are coming after you already."

"Who?" Kristen peeked over Nadia's shoulder.

Nadia quickly folded the card, tucked it away in her handbag. "Don't be naive, Aimee. People will take advantage of you."

"Who will?" Kristen asked again. "What was on the card?"

"Nothing worth Aimee's time."

Nadia was right, I reasoned. Lacy was wacked. The nerve of her, approaching me today. She probably stalked funeral announcements in the paper's obituary section.

Kristen twined her arm with mine. "Come on, honey. We'll take you to the cemetery. Let's find your parents and tell them you're coming with us. Nick's waiting by the car."

Nick. Kristen's husband. James's best friend. James.

I let Kristen tug me along. "I was going to walk home."

She eyed my four-inch wedges and popped a trimmed brow. "Sure you were."

~

After the burial, Nick dropped us off at my house. Kristen and Nadia followed me inside. I stopped in the doorway between the entry and the front room of our three-bedroom bungalow and looked around. There were the caramel leather side chairs and taupe chenille couch. A flat-screen TV propped inside the walnut armoire, doors ajar from the last time I'd watched, whenever that was. Three of James's framed paintings adorned the wall above the sideboard by the front door.

Everything was in its place except the man who lived there.

I tossed my keys and clutch on the sideboard.

Nadia walked through the dining area into the kitchen, the click of heels on hardwood echoing through the house. "Do you want something to drink?"

"Tea, please." I slipped off my shoes, spread and stretched my toes.

Nadia pulled out the blender. She scooped ice cubes from the freezer's tray and dropped them into the pitcher. They crackled, adjusting to the pitcher's warmer surface.

"How about something stronger?"

I shrugged. "Sure. Whatever."

Kristen looked up from where she'd removed her shoes by the coffee table and frowned. She sank into the leather chair nearest the fireplace, tucking her feet underneath her legs. As I retreated to the master bedroom, I felt her eyes on me.

I went straight to the closet James and I had shared and opened the beveled doors. My clothes hung next to his suits. All charcoal, black, and navy. Some with pinstripes, but most solid. Power suits—that was what he'd called them. So different from the casual plaid shirts and jeans he'd wear at home.

Looking through his wardrobe, one would think the clothes belonged to two different people. Sometimes I'd felt I was living with two different men. The man who worked for Donato Enterprises was formal and polite compared with the free-spirited artist with sleeves rolled and paint splattered on his forearms.

I loved them both.

I pressed my nose against the sleeve of his favorite blue shirt and inhaled. Sandalwood and rich amber, his cologne, mixed with a hint of turpentine from cleaning his paint supplies. He'd worn this shirt the last time he painted, and behind my closed eyelids, I saw him, shoulder muscles rippling under the faded blue cotton as he wielded the brush.

"Do you want to talk?" Kristen softly asked behind me.

I shook my head, untied the knot at my waist, and unwrapped my dress. It slid down and pooled at my feet. Reaching into the closet, I snagged James's shirt and the sweatpants I'd had since high school and put them on. Warmth surrounded me as I tugged on the shirt. It felt like James giving me a hug in the pull of material across my back.

I'll never forget you, Aimee.

My heart cracked a bit more. I choked on a sob.

Behind me, the hardwood floor creaked and the bed moaned. I shut the closet doors and faced Kristen. She'd propped herself against the paneled headboard and pulled a pillow across her lap. James's pillow.

My shoulders dropped. "I miss him."

"I know." She patted the space next to her.

I crawled across the bed and lay my head on her shoulder. She rested her cheek on my crown. We'd sat this way since I was five, snuggled against each other as we whispered secrets. We'd also been sitting this way a lot during the past two months. Kristen was two years older, and she'd filled the sibling void of my only-child youth. She draped her arm across my shoulders. "It'll get easier. I promise."

Fresh tears spilled over. Kristen fumbled for the tissues on the nightstand. I snatched several and blew my nose. She brushed damp curls off my temple and grabbed her own tissue, dabbing the corners of her eyes. A watery chuckle escaped, and she smiled. "We're a mess, aren't we?"

Soon we joined Nadia in the kitchen, and over margaritas we shared stories about growing up with James. Several hours and too many cocktails later, Nadia crashed on the couch and started snoring within seconds. Kristen was already asleep in my bed. I felt isolated in the darkened house, the only light coming from the candles Kristen had lit earlier. I lifted Nadia's feet and sank into the couch, dropping her feet in my lap. It was ten o'clock, and I should have been in James's arms as he guided us across the dance floor at our wedding, leading me in a gentle sway to our song, "Two of Us."

Nadia grunted, shifting on the couch. She stood and shuffled to the guest bedroom, dragging the throw blanket behind her.

I took the spot she vacated and let my mind drift. I thought of James and why he'd gone to Mexico when he did. Why not wait, or let Thomas handle the client? He was Donato Enterprises' president, and overseeing the company's furniture import/export operations was his job. As the finance executive, James's responsibility was handling the books, not contract negotiations. But he'd insisted he was the only one who could manage this particular client. He'd left the day after I mailed our wedding invitations.

My eyes grew heavy and I drifted to sleep, my thoughts twisting. I dreamed about the woman in the parking lot. She was dressed from head to toe in black, and her eyes radiated an iridescent glow. She raised her arms over a prone form, and her lips moved. The melodic chant of her incantation vibrated the air around her and the body resting at her feet. A body that was now moving. That was when I realized the body wasn't just any man. It was James. And Lacy was bringing him back from the dead.

CHAPTER 2

"What are you doing here?"

Dad's baritone boomed in my ears. I jerked and stared at him. He stared right back. His arms, peppered with freckles, hung at the sides of his barrel chest. The door separating The Old Irish Goat's kitchen and dining room swung behind him, hinges creaking with each pass through.

It was Monday, two days after James's funeral, and like every morning since I started working at my parents' pub, I'd risen at five a.m. And like every morning since James disappeared, I rolled out of bed and dragged myself into the bathroom. I poured coffee from the brewer I didn't remember filling the previous night, shuffled to my car, a burnt-orange New Beetle, and drove to The Old Irish Goat, an upscale pub house my parents had purchased before I was born. I grew up in the restaurant, mopping floors and stocking shelves. Eventually, I moved to the kitchen and worked alongside Mom, the executive chef, and Dale, her sous chef. Dale had trained me to be a pastry chef. Breads were my specialty. After I graduated from the culinary academy in San Francisco, I stepped in as Mom's sous chef when Dale took an executive chef position at one of the oldest eateries in Cambridge, Massachusetts. The opportunity of a lifetime, he'd once told me.

As I gradually became aware of The Goat's interior space around me, the stainless steel commercial ovens and ranges, walk-in fridge and adjoining freezer, pots and dishes within reach, I felt as though I were waking for a second time that day.

Fluorescent lights buzzed overhead like a bee swarm. A nearby radio, volume turned low, whispered a local station's morning show. I could barely make out the host's words, but the cadence of his tone was smooth and rich. Everything was familiar. Just a typical morning that wasn't typical at all.

Dad looked askance at me, growing wary of my silence. I stood at the pastry station surrounded by loaves of rising dough, my fists jammed in a mound of the cool substance dusted in flour. White powder covered the entire counter surface.

"What time is it?" I croaked.

Dad moved farther into the kitchen. "Nine."

Three hours since I had left the house.

Images flashed through my head. Parking the car, disarming the restaurant's alarm, gathering supplies, assembling ingredients. Those memories could have been from any of a thousand mornings.

I extracted my hands from the dough. They made a loud sucking noise. Gooey chunks stuck to my fingers and filled the space underneath my nails. I roughly rolled my palms together, but the sticky mess refused to budge.

Usually I treasured these mornings of solitude—craved them, actually—kneading the day's dough. It was a rhythmic distraction I'd had since childhood, when Mom taught me to bake in our kitchen at home. The repetitive task allowed my mind to drift, to plot the day's events, plan for the future, think of the past. But not today. The dough clung to me like a wad of gum stuck to the bottom of my shoe. An irritant. It was as unwelcome as the reminder that all those hours I'd spent planning the future were a waste. That future no longer existed.

I wiped harder, using my nails to scrape off the dough.

Dad appeared at my side with a wet dish towel. He started cleaning my hands. The gesture was gentle and loaded with fatherly concern. He was cautious not to further irritate my skin, dabbing softly along the angry marks I'd left on my flesh. His tenderness incensed me further. I didn't want to be treated as if I were about to break. I tugged my hands from his and yanked the towel from him. I rubbed hard at my skin.

"Go home, Aimee."

"And do what?" I threw the towel on the countertop.

Dad didn't say anything further. He watched as I rolled the dough and added several loaves to a large metal tray. I slid the tray onto a rack and wheeled the loaves and rolls aside to bake later.

Mom strolled into the kitchen carrying two brown paper shopping bags. Her trimmed salt-and-pepper hair was chicly spiked, showing off the sterling silver earrings that corkscrewed below her lobes. Her eyes darted sideways to Dad before she smiled at me. "I saw your car outside. Why are you here?"

"Baking bread. Same thing I do every morning, five days a week." I cringed at the bite in my tone.

"I've already suggested she go home," Dad said.

"He's right. You need to rest."

"I need to work," I said, grabbing a wooden spoon. "You need my assistance, and we need bread for today's lunch and dinner."

They exchanged glances.

"What?" I asked.

"I called Margie." She gave me a square smile that exposed both top and bottom teeth. She used Margie only in dire situations, like when I called in sick, or when we had a large private party to host. Margie owned the bakery around the corner and supplied many restaurants in the area.

I inhaled and drew in the warm, moist scent of freshly baked bread. Bread I hadn't made. My eyes narrowed on the paper bags Mom had brought. MARGIE'S BAKERY & ARTISAN BREADS.

"Our customers love my breads," I whined. "You can't replace them. *Or* me!"

"We're not replacing . . . *you*," Dad stammered.

I huffed, slapping the wooden spoon against my thigh. I hadn't meant to say that last thought aloud.

Mom rushed to my side. "It's nothing like that. We made arrangements with Margie because we thought you needed time off."

"But I don't need time off." Mom pursed her lips and I groaned. "How long?"

They exchanged another one of their looks and Mom rubbed my arm. "As long as you need."

"There's going to be some changes—"

"Not now, Hugh," Mom interrupted.

"What changes?" I looked at Dad. He scratched his cheek and glanced at the floor. "What aren't you telling me?"

"Nothing, dear," Mom said.

"Tell her, Cathy. She's going to find out sooner or later."

Mom locked eyes with Dad. "Your father and I are retiring."

I clutched the spoon. "You're retiring? Already?" I gave them a wild look. "Jeez, I just buried James. I'm not ready to buy you out. I can't operate The Goat on my own."

"You don't have to. We've sold the restaurant," Dad said.

The spoon clattered on the counter. "You *what*?"

Mom groaned and tossed me an apologetic look.

"The deal should close in ninety days," Dad added.

Mom smacked her forehead. "Hugh!"

"What did I say?"

"What *didn't* you say? We agreed to break the news to her gently."

My gaze ping-ponged between them as I waited for one of them to tell me this was a joke. They both looked back at me, faces riddled with a mixture of apology and concern.

"Why didn't you discuss this with me?" I asked.

Mom sighed. "You've known for some time we've struggled to stay open. A buyer came along and offered to take the restaurant off our hands. He has big plans for this place."

"I had big plans for this place. Why didn't—*Fuck*." I rubbed my temples. "Why didn't you let me buy you out?"

"And saddle you with our debt?" Mom shook her head. "We couldn't do that to you."

"How bad can it be? I could have handled it." A traffic jam of ideas bumped around my head. I didn't have much in my savings, and the only joint account James and I had was the one we used to pay the mortgage and utilities. His contributions to that account ended when he'd been pronounced dead. The cash in his personal bank accounts went to Thomas, who gave it all to me in a check at James's funeral. A check I couldn't stomach cashing. I didn't feel it was my money to spend.

Maybe I could refinance the house. Or sell it, move back in with my parents temporarily.

"The Goat's too far gone to salvage." My thoughts skidded to a stop with Dad's confession. He dipped his head, took a deep breath. I thought he was disappointed until he raised his face and I realized he was ashamed. "You'd be scraping pennies to pay for flour to bake bread. The last thing your mother and I want is to watch you file for bankruptcy."

"Bankruptcy?" I exclaimed.

Mom nodded. Her eyes sheened. "We mortgaged this building and took a second on the house, and we still couldn't make ends meet. We also owe some of our suppliers. They've been generous enough to waive interest fees, but we still have to pay them. The new owner has agreed to assume our debts, except the house mortgage."

"I hadn't realized it was that bad," I said.

Dad put his arm around Mom. "After the shopping center across the street was remodeled and those two franchise restaurants opened, we all watched them take away our customers."

"I had ideas to bring them back. I was going to expand our dinner menu, brighten the dining area, add live music on Thursday and Saturday nights—"

"All ideas we've considered, which aren't enough to repay the loans and make a profit."

I twisted my apron. It was a pretty good guess the buyer was a developer who would level the building. There had to be a way to keep The Goat. I'd already lost James. I couldn't lose this, too. So many memories existed within these walls, tangled inside with scents of rosemary roasted potatoes, and whiskey-glazed corned beef. "I wish I would have known sooner. I could have helped."

"We'd planned to say something, but . . ." Dad scratched his head. "Well, James died and there never seemed to be a good time to explain. No parent wants to be a burden to their children. You were already . . . um, well . . ."

An emotional mess.

I let go of the apron I'd been worrying and smoothed the wrinkled material in long, tempered strokes. I felt edgy, without direction and purpose. I felt lost. "What am I supposed to do now? The Goat is all I know." Fear of the unknown weighed heavily in my voice.

Mom latched on to my hands. "Think of this as an exciting new opportunity. You can try something different."

"Like what?" I pulled my hands from hers and tore off the apron. Their news was starting to sink in.

Mom stole a glance at Dad. "Well, your father and I feel that now more than ever is a good time for you to figure out who you are and what you want to do."

My eyes widened. "What do you mean 'now more than ever'? Because The Goat's been sold, or because James is gone?"

Dad cleared his throat. "A little bit of both."

I gawked.

"You and James had been together since you were what, eight? You'd been inseparable."

"Are you accusing me of being too dependent on James?"

"No, not exactly," Dad hedged.

"Yes," Mom said simply.

I stared at my parents.

"Look, Aimee, we all miss James very much. Your father and I feel as if we've lost a son. But for the first time in your adult life it's just you. You have the education and experience to do what you want. Start your own restaurant if you really want to run one."

How could I even think about starting a restaurant from scratch when I could barely process the news about The Goat? I wadded the apron and tossed it onto the counter. A flour cloud rose and expanded. White flakes dusted the floor. I grabbed my purse and keys.

Dad's brows pushed up in the middle. "Where are you going?"

"Out. Home." I shook my head. "Somewhere." Confusion twisted inside me. I couldn't think straight. A huge weight pressed hard on my chest and it hurt to breathe. Walls were closing in. I left the kitchen.

Mom followed me to the parking lot. I fumbled with my keys. They dropped on the ground and my chin dropped to my chest. I sucked in a ragged breath and exhaled. My shoulders trembled, my chest tight with sobs straining to be released.

Mom's arm curved around my back. She pulled me into her chest. I tucked my face into the curve of her neck and cried. My fingers clawed at her back until I finally held on. She gently rocked us and stroked my head, urging in a soothing tone to let it out. To just let go.

"I don't know how."

"You'll find a way," she said.

"I don't know what to do."

"You'll figure something out."

"I'm all alone."

She leaned away and clasped my face, wiped my tears aside with her thumbs. "You're not alone. We're here for you, honey. Call us. We'll help, whether it's references for a new job or a shoulder to cry on."

I appreciated her offer, but it wasn't what I wanted to hear. Not yet.

I was eight when I met James. He'd moved to Los Gatos from New York and was Nick's new neighbor, two blocks from the ranch home where I grew up with my parents, Catherine and Hugh Tierney. On a midsummer Saturday morning, Nick and Kristen brought James over to introduce us. I remember details about that day more clearly than any others at that age, from the way James topped off his wave with a smile, revealing he was as nervous meeting me as he was eager to make new friends. He wore his hair longer than the boys at school, and I couldn't stop looking at the thick, brown waves curving around his ear lobes under the rim of his New York Jets cap. He combed his fingers through his hair as though trying to flatten the unruly strands.

Like most Saturdays in our neighborhood, the air was heavy with the scent of fresh-cut grass. The neighbors' sprinklers droned on, white noise in the background. I heard the gentle hum each time Dad cut the engine to his mower. And like many summer Saturdays, I'd set up a lemonade stand to raise money. I was saving to purchase a pouch of Magic Memory Dust from the toy store downtown. The sales clerk had told me if I sprinkled a pinch over my head each night before bed, I wouldn't forget where I'd put my shoes or when to do my chores. After hearing that, I had to have a pouch.

But this particular Saturday morning was different from others, and not because Nick and Kristen were coming over with their new friend.

Robbie, the kid across the street, and his cousin Frankie had seen me set up my stand. Robbie was enough of a bully on his own, but the two of them together meant hair-pulling and name-calling, damaged toys and angry tears.

They'd just finagled a cup of lemonade from me, offering up shiny quarters that I wanted more than I wanted them to leave me alone, when Kristen and Nick arrived.

"Hi, Aimee," Kristen said. She motioned to the new kid standing beside Nick. "This is James."

I poured Robbie his lemonade and smiled at James. "Hello."

He grinned and gave me a short wave.

"Lookie who's here," prodded Robbie. "Icky Nicky and Sissy Pants. Is that your new girlfriend?" He thrust his chin at James.

James stiffened. Nick took a threatening step toward Robbie. "Buzz off, loser."

"Ugh!" Frankie moaned. The cup slipped from his hand. He gripped his neck with both hands and weaved. "She's poisoned me. I'm dying."

"Stop messing around!" Embarrassed, I tossed James a panicked look. He scowled at Frankie.

"Let me try." Robbie downed his lemonade and the cup flew from his hand. "Oh no! It *is* poisoned." He pitched forward across the table. Plastic cups rained onto the ground. "She's killed us, Frankie."

"No, I didn't!" I shoved Robbie. He wouldn't budge. "Get off!"

"Move it!" Kristen tugged Robbie's arm.

"Good-bye, cruel world." Robbie rolled to his side, dragging Kristen. She fell hard to the sidewalk and burst into tears. As she tried to stand, Frankie pushed her back down.

Nick punched the air two inches from Frankie's nose. "Get lost!" Wide-eyed, Frankie ran across the street into Robbie's opened garage.

The table collapsed under Robbie's weight. He grabbed my shirt, twisting as he pulled me down, landing on top of me. My ribs burned and back throbbed. James yanked off Robbie, who came up with fists flying. He punched James in the mouth, splitting his lip. James grunted and popped his left fist into Robbie's right eye. Robbie burst into tears and ran home.

I slowly stood, James helping me up as I dusted off my clothes. His eyes zoomed over me.

"Nice left hook you've got," Dad said from behind me. "That should keep Robbie and his weasel cousin on their side of the street for a while."

I looked over the disaster on the sidewalk and my lungs deflated. Kristen wiped her nose and sniffled. Her knees were scuffed and blood trickled down one shin. "Sorry about your lemonade stand," she said.

My chin quivered. "Now I'll never get the Magic Memory Dust." James gave me a funny look.

"Kristen, come inside and Mrs. Tierney can fix up your knees," Dad offered.

"I want to go home," she whined, gingerly touching the raw skin.

"I'll take her." Nick tugged Kristen's elbow. "We'll catch ya later," he said to James.

As they walked away, Dad looked down at James. "What's your name, son?"

"James, sir." He wiped his palms on his shirt and extended a hand. "James Donato."

Dad grasped his hand. "Nice to meet you, James. Come inside so we can clean you up."

James took a quick glance at me. "Yes, sir."

"Aimee, take James into the kitchen. I'll tell your mother to get the Band-Aids."

By the time Mom retrieved the bandages and ointment, James's lip had stopped bleeding. His mouth was swollen, so he sat on the kitchen stool beside me holding a bag of frozen peas to his face.

I rattled off questions. I wanted to know everything about him. Yes, he would attend the same school as me. Yes, he loved to play football. No, he had never punched another kid before. Yes, his hand was sore.

He held up five fingers twice and then one more for eleven years when I asked his age.

"Do you have any sisters?"

He shook his head.

"Brothers?"

He held up two fingers before shaking his head harder and changing two fingers to one.

I laughed. "Robbie must have hit you hard if you can't remember how many brothers you have."

He frowned. "I have one brother. And Robbie punches like a baby."

I laughed harder and slammed both hands over my mouth to quell the giggles, afraid he would think I was laughing at him and his miscount rather than Robbie's expression after James pummeled him. I'd never seen Robbie run home so fast.

James glanced around the kitchen. Mom's apple pie for her bunco party baked in the oven. Classical music floated into the room from the radio my dad had taken outside. James shifted in his seat. "I like it here."

"I'd like to see your house." I hoped he wanted to be my friend because I really liked him. He had a nice smile and was very brave. He'd punched Robbie, something I'd wanted to do for a long time but had been too afraid. Robbie was much bigger than I was.

"Yours is better." His eyes skirted back to me. "What's Magic Memory Dust? It sounds cool."

My cheeks flamed as I recalled James's face when I'd whined about the dust earlier. As we leaned on the countertop, I told him about it, keeping my face ducked. I admired how dark the skin on his forearm looked next to mine. I shrugged over the dust. "Doesn't matter now. My lemonade stand is ruined and I'll never raise the money I need."

James reached across the countertop and dragged the sugar bowl toward him. He pinched raw crystals and raised his hand above my head.

I looked up. "What're you doing?"

"Close your eyes."

"Why?"

"Trust me. Close your eyes."

I did and heard scratching overhead. My hair rustled and scalp tickled. My nose itched and it felt like raindrops were landing on my cheeks, but they weren't getting wet. I blinked and looked up. Sugar crystals rained on my face.

"What was that?" I asked when he finished and wiped his hands.

"James's Magic Memory Dust." The unbruised corner of his mouth lifted. "Now you'll never forget we met."

My eyes rounded and his face heated. He slapped the peas against his mouth and winced.

"I'll never forget you," I had promised, crossing my heart.

Over the years, James had made promises, too. It would always be just the two of us. There would never be anyone else; we loved each other that much. We'd grown up together and made a promise to grow old together.

I couldn't imagine wanting anything else than the life we'd planned together.

CHAPTER 3

Nadia and Kristen were inside my house when I arrived home after leaving the restaurant. Kristen rushed over. "We used your spare key. Your mom called, said you could use some company." She paused and took a breath. "She told us about The Goat. I'm so sorry."

I nodded, tight-lipped, and tossed my keys and purse on the sideboard.

She eyed me cautiously. "Are you going to be OK?"

I shrugged. After leaving The Goat, I'd driven aimlessly around town, thinking about the restaurant, and then I thought about James. Instead of driving home, I went to the cemetery and visited his gravesite. He'd been buried at the Donato family monument next to his father, Edgar Donato, who'd passed from lung cancer earlier in the year. A flat granite slab marked James's plot: **JAMES CHARLES DONATO**. Underneath his name were his birth and death dates. Thomas and Claire weren't sure of the exact date of death, but the coroner placed it two to five days after James had left. So they'd settled on May 20. A nice round number.

I'd spent an hour lying in the wet grass, my cheek pressed to the grave marker, thinking about the days leading up to the day he left. He had been adamant about going to Mexico. It had to be him and not Thomas. I didn't want him to go. It was too close to the wedding. We had too much to plan and prepare. But with words and kisses he convinced me he wouldn't be gone long. When he returned he would quit Donato Enterprises and pursue art. Painting was his passion, so I relented. Looking back, I should have been just as adamant as he was, insisting he stay home. Then he wouldn't be dead. We'd be married and on our honeymoon in Saint Bart's.

My mind wandered to the days after James had gone missing. I'd visited Claire, hoping to spend time with someone who grieved for James's disappearance as much as I did. I should have known I'd been expecting too much from her. Claire was more interested in the wedding invitations that had already been mailed than the possibility our worst fears could come true. She wanted me to notify our guests that the wedding might be off.

I blanched, facing her on the opposite couch in the Donatos' formal living room. I wasn't anywhere close to giving up on James or our future. The couch's silk fabric under my thighs felt cool and stiff through my skirt. The room's modern furniture had been shipped through their import/export business, Donato Enterprises. All the pieces had sharp, hard angles like the bones in Claire's face. There was nothing soft about any of them.

"I can't call people. Not yet." I couldn't bear telling our guests the wedding might be postponed, or worse, cancelled. It made James's ordeal too real.

Claire stiffened. "But you must—"

Movement in the doorway drew my attention. Phil came into the room, his gaze on target with mine like a hunter looking through a rifle's scope. Soundlessly, he sat beside his aunt. He draped an arm across her shoulders, looking too relaxed and at ease for a man who might have lost his cousin.

Claire patted his thigh. She let her hand linger as she kissed his cheek. My stomach curdled.

"Aimee." Phil dipped his chin.

I shifted restlessly on the couch. I hadn't seen him since last summer, and I'd had no idea he was visiting.

Claire rubbed Phil's thigh. "I don't know what I'd do without Phil. It's been a terrible year for our family. I'm so thankful he's moved in to keep me company. Phil gets me through the day."

I jerked my gaze to Claire. Phil was living here? I dug my fingernails into the cushion. My knees knocked and I pressed my legs together as they trembled, the vibration moving up my torso and outward to my arms like a ripple in water.

Claire's brows furrowed. "Are you all right?"

I shot to my feet. "I'm sorry. I have to go."

She stood. "If you must. Give me a moment. I have something for you." She left me in the room with Phil.

He didn't bother to stand, but I felt his eyes slide up my body.

"It's been a long time, Aimee. Have you missed me?"

His voice was barely above a whisper. I heard every word as clearly as if he'd bellowed in my ear. I stared at the wall behind him.

He sighed. "Ah, well. I've missed you. You look good . . . considering."

Fabric rustled as he shifted on the couch. *Don't get up; please don't get up.*

"It is unfortunate about James."

He almost sounded remorseful. I glared at him.

He chuckled. "There it is. I've missed that fire."

He'd crossed his legs, both arms extended across the couch back, leaving his starch-white oxford shirt exposed underneath the suit jacket. I felt exposed the way his gaze perused my length. Good thing a look couldn't scald flesh. I'd have blisters.

"You understand Claire's occupying herself with the mundane, frivolous things like your wedding. She worries about the guests because it's too difficult for her to worry about James."

"It's difficult for all of us."

He rubbed his upper lip. "Yes, well . . . I suppose it is. I'm sorry."

Everything inside me froze. I looked down at him.

"About James," he clarified.

Anger burned deep inside me. "You have a lot more than that to be sorry for."

Claire's heels echoed in the hallway. She entered the room, holding a manila folder. She motioned for me to take it.

"What's this?"

The folder shook within her grasp. "Phone numbers and e-mails."

I frowned. "For who?"

"James's wedding guests. You already have their street addresses. Now you can call or e-mail, tell them what's happening. It'll be quicker than mailing another letter."

Was she serious? I debated arguing, but the longer I stayed, the more time I would be stuck here. I doubted Phil had plans to leave Claire's side, not with me here.

"I'll call them." I took the folder and said good-bye.

Phil stood. "I'll walk you to the door."

"No," I snapped.

Claire's eyes rounded. Phil had always been her favorite, more so than her own sons. And she was a stickler for manners.

"No, thank you," I said in the most polite tone I could manage. "I'll see myself out."

I left before either could object.

Kristen rubbed my arm, yanking me back to the present. I blinked at her. "Come sit down. I'll get you something to drink."

I followed her into the kitchen and dropped into a chair.

"We brought lunch and groceries," Nadia explained. She aligned dry goods on the counter that separated the kitchen from the front room. Kristen poured lemonade and handed me a glass.

I drank greedily, and after wiping my mouth, burst into tears.

Kristen and Nadia stilled and stared. It took a second, but Kristen recovered first. She set down the pitcher and sat in the chair across from me, handing over a napkin so I could wipe my nose. "This has been so hard for you, Aimee. Please talk to us, tell us how we can help. Did something remind you of James? What has you so upset?"

Everything, I thought. James. The restaurant. My career, or lack of one as of this morning.

Nadia retrieved plates from the cabinet and busied herself mixing a salad. "You need to eat something. You look pasty."

A watery snort escaped. "Thanks a lot." I laughed into the napkin.

She smiled. "That's better."

Kristen rubbed my forearm. "Please talk to us," she beseeched again.

I groaned into the napkin, nodding. I needed to tell them, but not everything. Dabbing my eyes until they were somewhat dry, the surrounding skin tender, I confessed to something else altogether. "I'm just feeling guilty, that's all."

Nadia brought the salads to the table. "How so?"

"Just thinking about James and wishing I'd tried harder to convince him to stay home." I pushed the salad around with my fork. "We'd be on our honeymoon right now."

Kristen pushed out her lower lip. She rubbed my forearm. "You have a terrible habit of holding things inside. You shouldn't do that. And you shouldn't blame yourself either. You know how stubborn James could be. Whether you pushed harder or not, he would have still gone to Mexico, so there's no point to feeling guilty."

"Why shouldn't she?" Nadia objected. "A little bit of guilt is OK."

Kristen's mouth went slack. "How the heck do you justify that?"

Nadia shrugged and stuffed arugula in her mouth. "Grief stages," she said after she swallowed. "Moves her one step closer to getting on with her life."

"She's barely started grieving," defended Kristen. "James was buried only two days ago."

I waved my hand. "Guys, I'm still here. You can talk to me."

"Technically, he's been dead for almost two months," Nadia pointed out.

Kristen gasped. "Oh my gosh, you're unreal." She stood and took her plate to the sink, muttering under her breath.

Nadia raised her eyes toward the ceiling before giving me a look of understanding. "I did the same thing when my dad moved out. Blamed myself." She'd been thirteen when her father left her mother.

"It was right after he found my makeup stash, remember? He grounded me and sent me to my room. When I came out for dinner, he was gone. Once again I had disobeyed him and that's why I thought he left. Mom told me later about Dad's affair and I think he'd used the punishment to get me out of the room. He and Mom were having one of their screaming matches."

"Why didn't you tell me this before?"

"Same reason as you. I felt guilty so I held it all in. I didn't learn about Dad's affair until after I graduated from high school. For five years I blamed myself." She reached over and squeezed my fingers. "Feeling guilty is natural. Just don't hang on to it as long as I did. You'll only get depressed and there isn't a damn thing you can do to change the past."

That was easier said than done.

"What am I supposed to do now?" I asked.

She arched a brow. "About James?"

"No, work. I need to find a job." I needed to cook and bake . . . create. That was where James and I were alike. Where he painted to relieve stress, or think through an issue, I baked. A lot. My fingers itched to dig out ingredients from the cabinets. To mix a new batch of dough unlike the one I'd made this morning. Lost in my thoughts, I'd added too much water. The dough was too sticky. Clingy.

"You can find work. Or," she paused for effect, "you can travel."

"That's what Thomas suggested." Because of our honeymoon plans, I had a passport, but I'd never been anywhere without James. It would be strange traveling alone. He was the spontaneous one, always veering off the plotted course to venture onto side roads. "You never know what surprises you'll find," he'd once told me.

Nadia smiled. "I like his line of thinking."

I shook my head. "No traveling. Not yet."

"Then open a restaurant."

"Did my dad tell you to say that?"

She laughed. "No, but I think it's a great idea."

"So did James. He wanted me to open a café. Said I could brew a mean cup of coffee."

"It's something to consider."

Starting a restaurant from scratch without James by my side was an overwhelming prospect. I glanced over my shoulder at Kristen. "What do you think?"

She held up her hands. "Hey, I'm on Team Aimee. Whatever makes you happy."

James and The Goat made me happy.

Nadia took her plate to the sink. Kristen peeked inside the fridge and opened cabinets. I watched them both, recalling today was Monday. "Shouldn't you be working?"

"I have a sub, so you have me all day." Kristen was an elementary school teacher and taught year-round. She had only a few weeks left in the summer session before the new school year started. She and Nick had married last year. They wanted to start a family soon and we'd planned to raise our kids together.

So much for that idea.

Nadia put her plate in the dishwasher and dried her hands. "I'm free only until two."

Kristen looked around a cabinet door. "You said you had all day."

"I received a call on my way over about the retail space downtown. The new lessee accepted my proposal and wants to meet ASAP."

"The space on North Santa Cruz Avenue?" I asked. "The one between the dance studio and wine bar?" It was the only available spot I knew about. And I knew about it only because of James.

"The very one. It'll be an art gallery."

I balked. "Are you kidding me?"

Nadia gave me an odd look. "Um, no. Is everything OK?"

"You're designing a gallery in the very spot James had planned to rent for his gallery."

She cringed. "I'm sorry."

I waved her off. "Not your fault."

Kristen poked her head into the fridge again. "Where did you put the wine, Nadia?"

"There wasn't a bottle with the groceries?" Kristen shook her head and Nadia shrugged. "It probably didn't get bagged."

"There should be a few bottles chilling in the garage fridge," I offered in a tone heavy with emotion. My thoughts were still on the gallery space downtown. Its lease was hard confirmation that dream would never transpire.

Kristen gave me a wary look and went into the garage, the door slamming behind her. She returned a moment later with a bottle of chardonnay. "When did you clean your garage?"

"Does it look like I've cleaned?" I waved an arm to encompass the open living space. Unanswered mail piled high on the countertop. Unread newspapers stacked on the floor. Dust bunnies mingled and multiplied in the corners.

"Whatever." She popped the wine cork and poured three glasses. "The garage looks good."

We drank the wine and talked about Nadia's new design project. Soon her appointment alarm buzzed on her phone. She glanced at the screen. "I have to go. I'll call you tomorrow." She kissed my cheek and grabbed her hobo bag. The handle snagged on the chair back and everything dumped. Lipstick, pens, mints, and papers skidded across the tile floor.

She swore and I bent to help her. "I've got it." She waved my hands aside and scooped up her belongings. "Gotta run." She rushed to the door.

I waved good-bye and launched a playlist on the stereo, wondering how long Kristen would stay. She poured another round of wine. Good. She planned to stay for a while.

We danced and talked, and watched a chick flick on pay-per-view. The doorbell rang around ten p.m. Nick had come to pick up his wife.

"I'll call you tomorrow." Kristen pushed off the couch.

I walked with her to the door. She bear-hugged me. "Night, night, sweetie."

Nick wrapped his arm around her, tucked her into his side. They were a perfect fit. I watched him brush aside wisps of his wife's blonde hair with his fingertips. He kissed her on the forehead, eyes briefly closing. Their caress was intimate. My heart twisted. I'd lost my opportunity to have that with James.

"Will you be OK tonight?" Nick asked me.

Did I have a choice?

"I'll be fine."

"Call if you need anything."

"Thanks." I shut and locked the door after they said good-bye, listening to Nick drive away. I slid to the floor, my back to the door, and my eyes drifted close. I felt myself floating from the wine. Sounds and smells penetrated my foggy mind. Ticking from the mantel clock. Humming from the air conditioner. Scents of lemongrass and coconut from burning candles.

My eyes flew open. I needed to blow out the candles.

I eased up and a small scrap of paper underneath a kitchen chair caught my attention. It was bent in half and propped like a miniature tent. I went over and picked it up, peered at the text.

Lacy Saunders.

The psychic from James's funeral. I'd almost forgotten about her. Nadia must have left the card when the contents of her purse spilled. I stared at the card.

James is alive.

Lacy's words whispered through my head.

What a nut job. I tossed the card onto the countertop and moved through the house, blowing out candles, locking doors, and turning off lights. I double-checked the garage, and sure enough, Kristen had left on the single overhead light. I flicked it off only to flick it right back on.

Behind my VW Beetle was a large empty space where there should have been eight boxes loaded with James's bubble-wrapped canvases. They were gone.

I walked around my car and gazed stupidly at the bare cement floor. Only one box remained. Where were the others? How long had they been gone? I'd been so out of sorts these past months the boxes could have disappeared at any time. Maybe James had wanted more space in the garage and had moved the paintings to his company's warehouse.

Thomas might know where they were. I should call him. *Tomorrow,* I thought, yawning.

I returned inside and crashed in bed.

CHAPTER 4

OCTOBER

Days came and went, each blurring into the next. Endless nights out with Nadia, dinners with Kristen and her husband, and countless evenings alone watching movies from the couch. When there wasn't anything interesting to watch, I baked.

Every so often I drove to The Goat and worked my shift, but the certainty it would close soon only served as a reminder that I'd have to figure out what to do with my life. So I stopped going.

Mail piled higher. Newspapers stacked taller. Dishes collected in the sink. Glasses littered any available surface through the house. Casseroles, cakes, and cookies sat uneaten on the kitchen table. The washer and dryer were used only when my situation was dire. Like when I'd run out of underwear.

I packed my days and crammed my nights until I crashed. When I woke, my mind and body dragging, I got creative with espresso. I mixed exotic beans and syrups to keep me wired, and then I baked some more. My house was a mess. My life was a disaster. I was a wreck.

Until the day I woke up.

It was to the sound of a lawnmower. I peeked through the front window blinds and saw Nick move back and forth across the lawn. The front door opened and Kristen gaped at me. "You're awake?"

"I thought I'd join the human race." I thumbed out the window. "He's got to stop doing that."

Kristen shut the door. "He wants to help, and I think it helps him."

I collapsed an empty tissue box. "How so?"

"He misses James."

"We all do." I collected dirty glassware around the front room. "The yard looks gorgeous, but it's been eleven weeks. He can't cut my grass for the rest of his life."

"So said the woman who just returned to the land of the living." Kristen followed me into the kitchen. "I'll tell him you've hired a gardener."

"Perfect."

She sniffed the air. Scents of cinnamon and maple syrup hovered sweetly in the room. "Coffee cake?" she asked. I motioned toward the casserole dishes and platters crowding the kitchen table and her eyes bugged. "You've been busy. Are you planning to eat all this?"

I gave her a sheepish look. "I've sort of been feeding the neighborhood."

While my next-door neighbor and her husband appreciated the warm dishes to go with their dinners, and their three kids loved the treats I brought them, they did ask I stop feeding their family. I was spending too much money on them. Money I didn't have in the bank because I still couldn't convince myself to cash Thomas's check. Even though my credit card was almost maxed out from groceries, I would probably end up donating the results of the most recent cooking binge to Saint Anthony's soup kitchen, where Mom volunteered.

Kristen helped herself to a slice. "Oh wow, this isn't your mom's recipe." She moaned. "It's better."

"I added sour cream. It changes the texture. Makes the cake light and tender."

She shoveled the last bite and added another slice to her plate. "So what's with the cooking frenzy?"

"You know me. I have to keep busy. Keeps my mind off . . . things."

A soft smile touched her lips. "James wasn't the only artist in the house."

My mouth curved up at the corner. "Yeah, we were good like that."

I went to the sink and rinsed dishes. Kristen finished the coffee cake, then straightened several months' worth of mail on the countertop. A stack spilled and envelopes cascaded to the floor. She picked them up. "Whoa. What's this?"

I looked at what she held. Thomas's check. Buried and ignored with the other mail. "It's from Thomas."

"*What?* Why?"

"He was James's beneficiary. Thomas figured I was entitled to the money since James and I were about to get married."

"That was nice of him. God," Kristen flapped the check, "nice doesn't come close. This is huge! You can start your own restaurant with this kind of cash."

"Yeah, well, if that's what I decide to do."

She stared at the check. "It's dated on your wedding . . . um, sorry. The check's the same date as James's funeral."

I dried my hands and took the check from her. "That's when Thomas gave it to me, right before Lacy approached me."

"Who's Lacy? Is she that lady we saw you talking to in the parking lot?"

I nodded. "She's a psychic."

Laughter bubbled from Kristen. "A *what?*"

"A psychic counselor."

"Like a fortune-teller?"

"More like a psychic profiler, I think."

"No wonder Nadia took her card from you. I'd be concerned, too, if someone like that approached me. What did she tell you?"

"James is still alive."

Kristen's mouth fell open. The clock in the front room ticked. Then it ticked again. She sucked in a breath. "That's freaky. You don't believe her, do you?"

I twisted the engagement ring around my finger. I had asked myself *what if* on numerous occasions.

She narrowed her eyes. "Aimee?"

"No. I don't."

She sighed in relief. "Good. You had me worried there for a second." She peeked at her watch. "I have to go. Class starts in thirty minutes. Oh, I almost forgot." She dug into her purse. "This is for you."

Another business card. GRACE PETERSON, PHD, CLINICAL PSYCHOLOGIST. GRIEF COUNSELING.

"I'm glad you've finally come up for air, but I sense you're still holding something inside. Just in case you feel the urge, talk to a counselor. A *real* counselor." She flipped the card and tapped the handwriting on the back. "I've scheduled an appointment. Today at eleven. You can change the time or day. Cancel if you want. Up to you."

"Thanks," I said, unsure whether I would go. I tossed the card onto the kitchen table, right next to Lacy's.

"I'll call you after work." Kristen kissed my cheek and left.

By the time I'd cleaned, showered, and dressed in jeans, a light sweater, and flats, it was 10:58. Everything was spick-and-span, including me, but I was going to miss the appointment Kristen had scheduled. I wondered if I'd intentionally delayed leaving the house.

Beside Grace Peterson's card, Lacy's card with the buckled crease down the middle stared up at me. As I read the card over and over, I grew angrier. A hot spike of rage flared inside me. Why she had tracked me down at James's funeral to tell me he was alive boggled my mind. It was downright cruel. I thought of Thomas's check and wondered if she somehow knew about the money. Maybe she *was* trying to take advantage of me.

But there were two words on the card that grew bigger and bolder the longer I glared at them. MISSING PERSONS. They were printed right above her tagline HELPING YOU FIND THE ANSWERS YOU SEEK.

She'd better have answers, like why she had the gall to approach me. I picked up the card and grabbed my keys while at the same time despising the fact I was even considering meeting with her.

The address on Lacy's card was to a house in a residential district skirting the border of Los Gatos and Campbell. I eased to the curb in front of her one-story ranch. A portable sign was posted on the front lawn.

LACY'S PSYCHIC COUNSELING
TAROT CARDS PALM READINGS
WALK-INS WELCOME

The sign evoked a very different impression from Lacy, the psychic profiler. She was no better than a carny fortune-teller.

God, I was an idiot. Nadia had warned me not to be naive.

Through the passenger window, I saw Lacy watching me from her kitchen. The skin between my shoulder blades tingled and I turned away, directing my gaze outside the windshield.

Get out of the car, Aimee.

I sensed her eyes on me as I coaxed myself from the car. Or was that her speaking to me inside my head?

I shook off the feeling and got out of the car, shutting the door behind me.

"Hello, Aimee." Lacy stood on the sidewalk.

I jerked and stared. I hadn't seen her leave the house.

"Do you want to come inside?" She gave me an easy smile.

"I—" My mouth worked, but no words followed. Lacy watched me expectantly until I mumbled an apology and fumbled for the door handle behind me. I had an odd feeling she *did* know something about James. Something even I didn't know. And that scared me.

I slid into the driver's seat and thrust the key into the ignition.

Lacy knocked on the passenger window. I bounced in my seat. "Where are you going?" she asked.

"I'm sorry. Coming here was a mistake." I revved the engine and she jumped away from the car. I pressed the accelerator, using more force than intended. The car lurched forward and I sped away.

I took the long way home, side streets instead of freeways, all the while berating myself for being so stupid. *God, I'm an idiot.* By the time I arrived home, Lacy was sitting on my porch.

I hesitated at the picket fence bordering my front yard and she rose to her feet. "Don't worry. I'm not staying," she said, slowly approaching me. She held up my wallet. "I found this in the street."

I looked vacantly at the olive-green Gucci James had given me two years ago for my birthday. It looked out of place in her hand.

She smiled. It softened her face, making her appear younger than the late-forties age I assumed she was. "Everything's still inside," she told me when I took the wallet. "I only glanced at your driver's license to get the address. Nice picture."

I slipped the wallet inside my purse. "Your psychic talent didn't show you where I lived?"

She flinched at the bite in my tone. "No, sorry. It doesn't work that way. Though I can say the *real* reason you drove to my house wasn't to find out if I was a con artist. You came seeking answers about James. You had doubts when he went missing. You still have doubts."

My skin prickled and I looked away.

"You're angry with me."

"I think you should go." I felt uncomfortable around her.

She hesitated, opened and closed her mouth as though deciding to say something more. She didn't. Just nodded and went to her car. I watched her drive away, surprised to find myself wondering if I would see her again.

CHAPTER 5

My stomach growled. I heard James chuckle in the rumble of a far-off car engine. In the gentle breeze rustling my clothes, his voice tickled my ear. *Let's go to Joe's.*

Joe's was where we'd spent our Sunday mornings. It seemed like forever since James had been gone. I missed his laugh and the dark, silky timbre of his voice. I would never again hear him say *I love you*, and I was disinclined to do anything that reinforced James was gone forever, such as boxing his belongings, cancelling his magazine subscriptions, or sitting at our table at Joe's, alone. But for the first time in half a year, I felt the urge to go there, linger over a bowl of heirloom tomato soup and a citrus salad. The food was wonderful at the café, but Joe could never brew a decent pot of coffee. James often joked I should blend drinks to bring with us. We could pay Joe a mug fee like a wine corkage fee. Joe's bitter coffee had nothing on the elixir I brewed.

Rather than returning to an empty house with spoiling food, I walked six blocks to Joe's, hearing James beside me in the echo of my shoes on pavement. We had traversed this route many times and it was difficult to believe he wasn't walking alongside me now, our hands clasped. I curled my fingers, my palm cold and empty.

I arrived at Joe's and, pushing on the door handle, walked straight into the glass door. "Ow!" My hands flew to my face, eyes watering. My nose burned. I stomped in a circle, swearing as I rubbed the tender skin.

I pinched the bridge of my nose and jiggled the knob. It was locked. On a Friday?

Pressing my forehead to the glass, I peered inside. The café was dark and empty. The display cases bare. No muffins, meats, salads, or bottled drinks. In the corner of the far right window was a sign.

For Lease

I stared blankly for a long moment. Joe's Coffee House was closed. Gone forever.

I thought of the mornings James and I had walked here for breakfast. The familiar scents of roasting coffee, freshly baked scones, and potato frittatas were what had brought me here this morning. It was our place. It was *my* place.

I jerked back from the window. "This *can* be my place," I said to my reflection.

In that moment, I knew exactly what I wanted to do, what I had to do. Open my own restaurant, right here in Joe's old spot. It was what James would have wanted. I would do this for James.

Excitement buzzed through me like a jolt of caffeine. Before I changed my mind, I punched the lease agent's name and number into my phone and saved the contact file.

Anticipation bubbled inside me. I glanced around, my gaze settling on the storefronts two blocks up the road. Nadia might be on site at the art gallery. It was still under construction. I left Joe's and called Nadia.

~

"You go. Tell me what you think," Nadia encouraged.

"The gallery's not open to the public yet. I can't go inside."

"Of course you can. Wendy's hanging art for the grand opening."

"I'm not sure." I'd hoped Nadia would be there so I could share my idea about Joe's. My stomach growled again.

She made an impatient noise. "Tell her I sent you. She won't mind if you look around."

"All right. I'll peek inside." I paused at the corner. A car sped by and I jumped away from the curb.

"I need to prep for a conference call. I'll swing by your place this evening after work. I want to hear what you think of the color scheme and layout."

"OK."

"I'll see you tonight." She disconnected the call.

I almost walked past the gallery. Nadia had transformed the entire façade. Everything had been updated. Larger windows, tall side-by-side glass doors, overhead lights tucked under a wood-framed awning. Potted honeysuckle vines reached skyward on both sides of the storefront. An elegant font had been etched into the glass.

Wendy V. Yee Gallery
Where the Local Photographer Goes International

Photographs, not paintings.

Nadia had been working on a different type of gallery than I expected, and she'd created a beautiful space for Wendy to showcase her artists' photographic talent.

Propped on the wide window ledge was a breathtaking photo of a lavender-orange sky kissing aquamarine waters. The image was magical, simply titled *Belize Sunrise.* I felt myself falling into the picture, sitting on the sand and watching the morning light play on the tide. A salty, humid breeze teasing my skin. I wanted to go there.

According to the name under the title the photographer was Ian Collins. Considering how captivating the lighting was in *Belize Sunrise*, Ian was an extraordinary artist as far as I was concerned.

The gallery's double glass doors were propped open. Inside, the old floor had been replaced with wide-plank, blond-stained wood. The lighter color kept eyes off the floor and on the art. Whitewashed walls, still barren of artwork, were divided into three display areas separated by brick partitions. I could see the back wall, but the partitions divided the open space, lending the gallery a more intimate ambiance despite the open floor plan. James would have loved what Nadia had done.

My shoes echoed as I walked around. Voices carried from behind a partition. I heard hammering, followed by a thud and a grunt, and then a thick rope of cursing.

"Enough already, Ian. Let me call the contractor. He can do this for me."

"Get off the phone. He charges. I'm free."

"At the rate you're going, you'll spend more money on first aid. Save your thumbs. Bruce can handle this."

"This is the last hook." More hammering. *"Voilà, fini!"* the man with the hammer announced in a horrible French accent. A giggle bubbled from me and I clamped a hand over my mouth.

"Thanks, Ian, but don't quit your day job."

"I don't have a day job." Ian appeared from around the partition. He stopped abruptly when he saw me, his eyes meeting mine. I felt myself drawn to their amber depths. Light hair fell over his forehead, and I had an unexpected urge to run my fingers through the wave.

My face heated. Where had that thought come from?

The hard line of his jaw twitched and a smile tugged at the corner of his mouth. "Hey there."

I stared stupidly at him. His facial twitch lifted to a full-fledged grin. Oh wow.

"Ian?" called the woman. Light footfalls brought a woman into view. "Oh! I didn't know we had a visitor. Can I help you?"

I jerked in her direction. She was slender and petite, dressed entirely in black. Sleek ebony hair draped her shoulders. A hint of a smile touched her lips.

I shoved out my arm. "I'm Aimee Tierney. Nadia's friend."

She shook my hand. "Wendy Yee. This is Ian Collins," she tipped her head in his direction, "one of the photographers I work with."

"I saw the photo in the window. It's beautiful."

"Thanks," he said and grasped my hand. "Nice to meet you, Aimee."

"Sorry to have bothered you," I said to Wendy. "I only wanted to look at Nadia's design work."

"No bother. You're welcome anytime. Our opening celebration is next week if you're interested."

"You should come," Ian prompted.

My gaze bounced between them. "I don't know anything about photography."

"You only need to know how to enjoy yourself." He grinned. "Nadia will be here."

"I'll get you an invitation." Wendy went to the desk in the rear corner of the gallery.

I refused to look at Ian, but I felt his gaze on me.

Wendy returned and gave me a crisp, open-flapped envelope with a white cardstock tucked inside. "Next Thursday, eight o'clock."

"Thank you." I slipped the invitation into my shoulder bag.

Ian rubbed his stomach. "I'm starved. Let's go eat, Wendy."

"You go ahead. I have to finish up here." She waved him off.

"I'll bring something back for you."

"Thanks." She took the hammer from him and disappeared behind the partition.

Ian looked at me. "Lunch?"

I took an involuntary step back. He smirked. "If two women shoot me down in less than sixty seconds, I'll wonder if I've lost my touch." He crossed his arms and sniffed an armpit. "Or if I forgot to wear deodorant."

I snorted a laugh. "Thanks for the offer, but no."

"I'm not that bad of company. Let's grab a bite."

My stomach decided to exert its independence and remind me why I'd walked downtown. It growled loud and long.

Ian cocked a brow and motioned toward the door. "There's a firewood pizza spot on the corner. We can eat outside."

Rumble. "Pizza it is, then." I followed him through the doorway and thumbed at the photo in the window. "Do you travel often?"

"Every four to six months I'll take short excursions. Every few years, a longer trip. I have a photo expedition coming up," he said as we walked.

"It must be nice going to exotic places."

"It has its perks." He glanced at me. "Have you done much traveling?"

I shook my head. "Road trips. Nothing out of the country."

"If you could travel anywhere, where would you go?"

I blurted the first thing in my head. "The beach in your photo."

"It's a beautiful spot. You should go."

"I wish. Too expensive."

His eyes crinkled. "Yeah, money always seems to be the issue."

We stopped at a corner and waited for the light to change. "I haven't seen your work before. Do you show elsewhere?" I asked when we crossed the street.

"Aside from online? Only at Wendy's Laguna Beach gallery. She likes to promote local artists."

"You live in Southern California?"

"I used to. I grew up in Idaho before moving to SoCal. I've been in Los Gatos for only a few years. Took me that long to convince Wendy to open a gallery here. Lately, I've been on the road a lot."

"Always on the hunt for the next great shot?" When he nodded, I asked, "Do you shoot people?"

Ian held up two fingers pressed together. "I've never killed anyone. Scout's honor."

Color rose up my neck. "Oh, no, no, I . . . I meant pictures. Do you take pictures of people, like portraits?"

His expression darkened. "Landscapes are my niche."

We stepped aside to let a woman by pushing a stroller. "So, what do you do?" Ian asked.

"I'm a sous chef or restaurant manager, depending on the day." For the last couple of weeks, I hadn't been much of either. "Have you been to The Old Irish Goat?"

He shook his head. "I've heard of it."

"My parents owned the restaurant."

"Owned?"

My shoulders dropped a fraction. "Yeah, they sold it. As of next week, The Goat's under new ownership."

"I'm guessing you need a new job," he ventured.

"Looks that way."

Ian held open the door when we arrived at the restaurant. The hostess seated us on the side deck facing the street. She handed over menus and took our drink orders, water for Ian and iced tea for me.

When she left, Ian propped his elbows on the table, chin resting on clasped hands. "So, what's the story?"

I frowned.

He nodded at my face. "Your nose. What happened?"

My hand flew to cover my nose while I wrestled one-handed with my purse, searching for a mirror.

Ian chuckled. He touched my wrist. "It's not too bad. Just a bit red and swollen."

"Thanks a lot."

He laughed before his face softened. "Does it hurt?"

"A little. I'm trying to ignore it." But Ian staring at me wasn't helping. I wanted to crawl under the table and hide.

"Here, let me see." He eased my hand aside and gently prodded the tissue and cartilage. I hissed. "Tender?"

I nodded.

"Did your nose bleed?"

"No." I rapidly blinked my eyes. His touch was soothing. Unsettling, but in a good way.

"You might have some skin discoloration and soreness for a few days."

"A photographer and a doctor. You're a man of many talents."

"I wish, but no such luck. Just a photographer who's had his share of bumps and bruises."

"Whatever it takes to get the best shot?"

"Something like that." He leaned away. "You'll be back to your gorgeous self by the gallery's opening."

"I'm not beautiful now?" I couldn't help goading him. He smiled and a shiver of excitement coursed through me.

Our drinks arrived and we placed our orders, a personalized pizza for each of us.

"Do you know Joe's Coffee House?" I asked.

"The café on the corner? It's closed, isn't it?"

"I didn't know. I ran into the locked door."

Ian paused, his water glass halfway to his mouth. His lips twitched as though he was trying not to laugh. "If you were so desperate for a cup of coffee, I could have made you one."

I flashed a smile. "No one brews better coffee than me."

"Not even Joe?"

"Especially not Joe," I said, recalling his bitter java with the burned aftertaste.

"Sounds like a challenge. One of these days—you and me," he said pointing between us, "we'll see who brews the best pot."

"You make specialty coffees?" A smile spread wide across my face. I shook his hand, sealing the deal. "You're on."

"You should open a coffee shop in Joe's old place, especially if you can cook as well as you claim to blend coffees," he said with a crooked grin that made my insides dance upside down. "The stuff those chains serve is crap, pardon the French."

"Your French is horrible." I mimicked the *Voilà, fini!* I'd heard him say earlier.

"Tell you what"—he leaned closer—"I'll stop speaking French if you serve your coffee."

I folded the napkin on my lap and ducked my head to hide a smile. That was exactly what I'd been planning an hour ago.

Our pizza arrived and Ian ordered one to go for Wendy. Lunch flew by and when the waitress brought our check, I opened my wallet.

Ian dug out his from his back pocket. "I'll take care of this."

"This wasn't a date."

The corners of his eyes crinkled. He seemed amused. "If you say so, but you are a potential client. You're coming Thursday, right?"

"Yes, but—"

"You're going to want one of my photos. You'll need spare change for next week."

I gave him a direct look. "You're that confident I'll buy one?"

"A guy can dream." Ian tossed a credit card onto the table and I zipped up my wallet. The metal teeth snagged on something. I tugged out the offending paper and felt the color drain from my face. It was a business card from Casa del sol, a resort in Oaxaca, Mexico. No employee name or title. Just the resort address, phone number, and website. Lacy must have put it there.

"Are you OK?"

I looked up at Ian. "Yeah, I'm fine."

"Did I say something to offend you? If you really want to pay—"

I shook my head. "No, no, I'm good."

Ian lowered his gaze and watched me fidget with my wallet. His eyes dimmed and I felt his withdrawal. I wanted to explain my mood swing wasn't his fault, but then I would have to explain what bothered me. Telling him a psychic had slipped a mystery business card into my wallet sounded too strange. By the way, she thinks my deceased fiancé is anything but deceased.

Ian paid the check and we returned to the gallery, stopping outside the doors, which were now closed. I held out my hand. "Thanks for lunch."

His expression was guarded, but he smiled and took my hand. "You're welcome."

"It was nice meeting you." I turned to leave only to pause when he said my name.

"See you Thursday?" He smiled the warmth back.

I returned his grin and nodded. "See you Thursday."

CHAPTER 6

Nadia called and cancelled our evening. She had a new project under way and the client had asked to meet over dinner to discuss the plans before he flew out of town. "Wendy mentioned she invited you to the opening next Thursday. Are you going?"

"Probably." I thought of Ian. I wanted to see more of his photos.

"You can come with me. We'll be each other's date."

"As long as you don't kiss me good night."

She snorted. "Deal. So what do you think of Ian?"

"I loved—" the design scheme. Or that was what I'd planned to say until her question registered.

She laughed. "He's gorgeous, isn't he?"

"Your design scheme is gorgeous."

"Do you like him?"

"I like the work you did in the gallery."

"Aimee." She dragged out my name.

"OK. I like him. He seems really nice."

"Ask him out."

"What?" I'd never asked anyone out before. I'd never dated and James didn't count. He and I had always been a couple. "I can't. It's too soon."

"James died almost five months ago. You have your whole life in front of you."

"I'm not ready."

She sighed. "All right. Fine. I won't push. But one day you'll be ready. The human spirit is amazingly resilient, and the human body is surprisingly horny." She laughed and I rolled my eyes. "We'll go shopping next week. Pick up something hot for you."

"Sure," I said, more to placate than agree.

"I have to get ready. We'll chat later." Nadia said good-bye and disconnected.

Several hours later, I found myself staring at the business card Lacy tucked inside my wallet. I sat at the computer in the front bedroom we'd used for James's art studio. His supplies were still scattered throughout the room. An unfinished painting waited on the easel. I turned on the monitor and brought up the resort's website. Casa del sol. Tiled roofs sloped over hacienda-style arches that rose above Playa Zicatela. The hotel was located in the town of Puerto Escondido on the Emerald Coast of Oaxaca, Mexico.

I flicked the corner of the business card. It didn't make sense. James hadn't been anywhere near Puerto Escondido, which was almost a thousand miles from where he should have been according to the map app on my phone. He'd flown into Cancún with plans for dinner in Playa del Carmen after spending the day fishing off Cozumel. Thomas had gone to Cancún to retrieve James's body. Or so he told me.

Call Thomas, Aimee.

I felt more than heard the words in my head.

James?

Don't turn around, I told myself. He wouldn't be there.

As for Thomas, it had been over a month since his last visit. He'd stopped by to see how I was doing and ended up staying for dinner.

I called him.

"Hey, Aimee," he answered with a raspy voice.

I heard rustling through the phone line, then a steady, low hum in the background. It sounded as if he'd moved outside, or stood by an open window.

"Where are you?"

More rustling. He cleared his throat. "Overseas."

Europe? It would be dawn. He must be tired. "Sorry, did I wake you? I'll call later."

"No, I'm good." He groaned. I imagined him rubbing his forehead. "What's up?"

"Did you . . ." My voice trailed. Asking Thomas if he had retrieved James's body from Cancún and not someplace else like Oaxaca, Mexico, didn't seem like a logical, thought-out question. Neither did "are you sure you brought home the right body and not some other John Doe?"—which would have been my next question.

I had no proof other than a business card and the word of a psychic that James was not dead.

"Are you still there?" Thomas broke into my thoughts.

"I'm here. Sorry to disturb you. It's just—" I closed my eyes and breathed deeply.

"I miss him, too," he confessed after a moment.

"I know, thanks. I'll let you go. Good night, Thomas."

"Take care, Aimee."

I set the phone on my desk beside Thomas's check. I stared at it, thinking about the lease sign downtown.

Do it, Aimee.

I snagged the phone and called Dad. It was late. His voice mail answered. "Hi, Dad. Um . . ." I held the check. "I just called to say . . . well, I've figured out what I want to do. So, you don't have to worry about me. I'm going to be OK. No . . . I *am* OK. That's all. I love you. Mom, too. 'Bye."

I flipped the check over and my stomach followed. I was a culinary school graduate and could plan a five-course meal for hundreds of guests, but the thought of brewing coffee and baking muffins for one customer in my café was daunting. But at the same time, I felt liberated.

Aimee's Café.

James had suggested the name. He'd even sketched a logo the night before he left. If he intended to pursue his passion and open a gallery, he wanted me to do the same. Quit The Goat and start my own restaurant. Cook what I wanted, not what the type of restaurant dictated. Did I want to cook Irish pub food the rest of my life?

I spun the platinum engagement band around my finger. The diamond solitaire glittered in the monitor's glow. Even with James by my side, the idea was intimidating. But it was time to move forward. Nadia would say I was entering the next stage of grief. Onward and upward.

I endorsed the check, then I called the leasing agent and left a message. When I hung up, reality set in. My birthday was next week. I'd be twenty-seven and well on my way to becoming the proud, naive owner of a business with no plan, no employees, and no product.

Brenda Wakely met me in front of Joe's Coffee House at ten Monday morning. She was tall and lean, and wore a white silk blouse tucked into an electric-blue skirt with heels to match. Her bobbed white hair, dusted with silver streaks, curled around her ears.

She cleared her throat and introduced herself while unlocking the door. The alarm system counted down a warning. "Have a look around while I shut this off." She rushed down the hallway, past the restrooms to the back door.

Joe hadn't removed anything since he closed. Formica tables crowded the room. Vinyl chairs stacked against the back wall. Linoleum flooring, stained and peeling in heavy-traffic areas. The air was stale. A faint odor of burned coffee beans and bacon grease filled my lungs, stirring memories.

My gaze settled on the table in the corner. How many Sunday mornings had James and I sat by that window, watching passersby as we drank bitter coffee and ate omelets doused in Tabasco sauce?

Turning in a slow circle, I looked around the dining room. While the world had changed around Joe, nothing about Joe's had changed. Black-and-white pictures dating back fifty years decorated the rear wall. Plastic menus stacked by the cash register listed the same food selections he'd offered since I started eating here twenty years ago.

"What do you think?" Brenda asked.

"I loved Joe's. I miss this place."

"Me, too, but he had too much competition from those trendy spots. I do love their drive-throughs, so I can't complain."

I walked behind the service counter.

"The appliances need to be updated." She pointed toward the grease-stained commercial range through the kitchen service window. "Frankly, the entire place needs to be stripped and power washed." She held her hands away from the dingy countertops. "What did you say your business is?"

"A café." I pushed the keys on the antiquated cash register. The "2" key stuck. "Well, more a boutique coffee shop and gourmet eatery."

She smiled wryly. "Another coffee shop. A risky business, if you ask me." She tapped the leather-bound portfolio she held. "The owner wants the tenant to sign a long-term lease, fifteen to twenty years."

That was a long time. I inspected the cabinets. "Who owns the building?"

"Joseph Russo."

"Joe's the owner?" I should have known. Maybe I could call him directly, arrange a deal.

"Do you know him personally?"

"My parents owned The Old Irish Goat. They've known Joe for many years through the Chamber and other associations. Has anyone applied for the lease yet?"

"I have two other applicants. This space will go fast. Joe wants to make his decision by Thursday."

Three days to decide. I felt rushed, but I could miss out. Then what? I wanted my café downtown. The corner location was ideal, but more important, I felt a connection here to James.

I twisted the ring on my finger. "How much is the monthly lease?"

Brenda rattled off a number, more than I'd anticipated. One more reason to call Joe.

I should do more planning, and I shouldn't hurry into any decisions. But I didn't want to lose this location. I smiled at Brenda. "I want to apply."

"Wonderful." She opened her portfolio and handed me a few forms. We discussed the terms some more and while I completed the lease application and credit report, Brenda moved to the other side of the restaurant and sat down, tapping vigorously on her smartphone.

When I finished, she thanked me. "I'll run your credit report, and if your history checks out, I'll follow up with your references." She shook my hand. "I hope everything works out for you."

Brenda locked up behind us and waved good-bye. I returned home feeling giddy. Over the next few days, I researched, planned, applied for a business license, and put my finances back in order. For the first time in five months I had something to look forward to.

Nadia woke me late Thursday morning. I dragged myself to the front door. I'd been up late drafting business and marketing plans.

"My God, you're not shopping in that." She made a disgusted face at my rumpled shirt and PJ bottoms and pushed past me.

"Good morning to you, too." I yawned and closed the door. "What time is it?"

"Time for you to dress. We have less than two hours to find an outfit for tonight's opening party before my lunch meeting."

"I'll wear something I already have." I returned to the bedroom.

She followed me. "Like what?"

I shrugged.

She yanked open the closet doors and stilled. She blew out a breath as she glanced over James's side of the closet. His clothes were still there, undisturbed. She shut the doors. "Get dressed. You need something new. We're going to Santana Row."

"I have to shower."

"No time. Spray on perfume." She made a fluttery motion with her fingers around my head. "And brush your hair."

Twenty-five minutes later, dressed in jeans, T-shirt, and sneakers, my wild curls banded in a high ponytail, I stood beside Nadia as she flitted through a clothes rack. She roughly pushed hangers aside, giving each dress in my size a quick inspection. She pushed three into my arms and dragged me into the dressing area.

"I still don't understand why tonight's such a big deal." I toed off my sneakers.

"Hello! Ian will be there."

"Not interested."

"Uh-huh, sure."

"Nadia," I warned. I shimmied from my jeans and dragged my shirt over my head. A plain bra and boring panties stared back at me in the full-length mirror.

"Then forget about Ian. Do this for yourself. It's time to jump-start your social life. You need to date."

"I'm not dating," I said icily, and tugged the first dress off the hanger.

"Whatever. Hurry up, though. Time's running out."

I zipped up a dress, a cobalt sleeveless silk blend with a tailored bodice and straight knee-length skirt, and turned before the mirror. Would Ian think me too pretentious? The dress was gorgeous, but too showy for an art exhibit. Too over-the-top for Ian.

James would have loved this dress.

I unzipped the back and gave the dress a dirty look as it fell to the floor.

Why do I even care what either of them would think?

The next one was a black A-line with a full skirt, fitted bodice, and slim sleeves that capped my elbows. My black patent heels would be perfect with this dress. This dress would be perfect for tonight.

My phone rang. I spun away from my reflection and dug the distraction from my shoulder bag. "Hello?"

"Aimee? This is Brenda Wakely. Sorry for the delay."

"That's all right." I managed to sound casual even though my heart raced.

"I evaluated your application. You have plenty of funds in your bank accounts, but your credit has some issues. Your recent mortgage payments have been late and, unfortunately, your credit rating has taken a big hit."

I cringed. "Let me explain—"

"I was really hoping everything would check out for you, especially since you're a friend of Joe's. I can't recommend your application to him, and I now have three other qualified applicants."

I sank onto the chair in my dressing cubby. "Is there anything I can do?"

"Can you get a cosigner, someone with a better credit rating?"

I thought of my parents even though I wanted to do this on my own. Then I remembered their questionable credit history. They'd had trouble making payments to their suppliers. "I'm not sure. I would need more time."

"I'm afraid time is not something I have. The lease will probably go to another applicant this afternoon, tomorrow morning at the latest. Good luck finding a site. Have a lovely weekend."

Brenda hung up. I released a long sigh and stared at the ceiling.

Nadia banged on the door and I jolted. "Hello in there? Are you ready?"

"Give me a second." I slipped off the dress and pulled on my T-shirt.

"Did you pick one?"

I tossed the A-line over the door.

"Nice!" She cooed. "Love it."

I swore I heard her say that Ian would love it, too, as she left the dressing room.

CHAPTER 7

Nadia picked me up at eight for the gallery's opening. She was stunning in a sheath dress, the earthy color resembling dried lavender. Her auburn hair, parted on the side, skimmed her shoulders. Smokey liner framed emerald eyes and clear gloss highlighted her full lips.

She twirled an index finger and I turned around, the A-line skirt floating outward from my legs. I'd shaped my curls, twisting the loose waves high on my head, leaving a few tendrils to frame my face. I hadn't been this dressed up since James's funeral.

Nadia grinned. "Tell me if I'm wrong, but don't you feel good? You look amazing."

I twisted an errant corkscrew around my finger. "I'm nervous."

She pushed aside my hand and touched up my hair. "I have only one request."

"What's that?"

"Have fun."

I sighed. "I'll try."

She exhaled and raised her eyes toward the ceiling. "It helps to smile." She moved back and assessed me from head to closed-toe pump. "You look beautiful."

The corner of my mouth tugged upward.

"Much better," she exclaimed.

We parked two blocks from the gallery. The night air was crisp and I adjusted the wrap around my shoulders. Light spilled from the windows and faint notes of soft jazz drifted from the door. *Belize Sunrise* still took center stage in the front window. The $2,750 price tag was new.

My mouth fell open.

Nadia gave me a funny look. "What?"

I tapped the window above the price tag. "He must be damn good."

"He is. Wait until you see his other work." She held the door open for us. "You coming?"

Guests crowded the gallery floor. Waiters carefully navigated through Ian's fans, balancing trays laden with champagne flutes and canapés.

My gaze fixed on Ian in the corner of the main viewing room. He slipped his hands into the side pockets of his dark pants and bent his head toward the woman beside him. A burnished lock fell over his brow. I watched his hand slowly rise to sweep over his head while nodding along to whatever the woman shared with him. My stomach tumbled like his hair and I frowned at my reaction.

Nadia elbowed my ribs. "Don't forget to smile."

I pasted on a grin.

Wendy swept across the room. "Nadia, I've been looking for you."

"Hello, Wendy." She angled her head to receive Wendy's air kisses, then touched my shoulder. "You remember my friend Aimee?"

Wendy shook my hand. "So glad you decided to come. Please enjoy yourself, have a glass of champagne." She motioned toward a passing waiter before turning her attention back to Nadia. "A dear friend of mine loves what you've done for my gallery. He's a commercial property broker and wants to meet you."

"Do you mind?" Nadia asked me.

"Not at all. Go ahead."

Wendy directed me to the left side of the gallery. "Start over here to experience the full effect of the exhibit. I've arranged Ian's photos so the sun rises then sets as you circle the room. His photography is impressive. Be sure to see me if you want to purchase anything." She hooked her arm around Nadia and they wandered behind the first set of partitions.

I removed my wrap, folding the knit rectangle over my arm, and meandered through the gallery. Each image featured the sun rising or setting in an exotic, foreign locale. Ian had played with the light, and the colors reflected on a hillside, across a lake's surface, or through tall firs in a forest had a magical, surreal quality.

I paused before one image, an intense sun in a fiery descent over Middle Eastern sand dunes. The picture had been taken in Dubai, according to the tag on the wall. Three camels stood motionless on the crest of a dune, their shadows long fingers spreading outward across sands of vivid orange and gold.

"What do you think?"

A smile played on my lips. "You have an extraordinary talent for capturing sunlight." I lifted my eyes to Ian.

His gaze met mine. "I'm glad you're here."

"Me, too."

His forehead creased. "Can I ask you a personal question?"

I shifted the wrap to my other arm. "OK."

He pushed the wrap aside, exposing my left hand. He angled my ring finger so the overhead spotlights captured the brilliance of my engagement ring. "Why didn't you tell me you are married?"

"Because," I hesitated, licked my lips, "I'm not."

He tugged the wrap back in place. "Engaged?"

I shook my head.

"I'm sorry things didn't work out for you," he said evenly.

I pulled my hand from his and faced the photograph so he wouldn't see the tears filling my eyes. I didn't want his sympathy, but I could feel him study me as I admired his work. "When did you take this picture?"

He chuckled. "Two years ago."

I gave him a sidelong glance. "What's so funny?"

He dipped his head, hiding a smile.

"I bet you have a story for every picture."

He rubbed his jaw. "Yes, I do."

I waited for an explanation. He watched me with a secret smile. I folded my arms. "One of these days I'll get that story out of you."

His eyes crinkled. "I hope you do."

He glanced around the packed gallery. The noise had risen, more boisterous with the free-flowing champagne. I saw Wendy with a tablet, hurriedly tapping her index finger around the screen with what I assumed to be an order. Ian leaned close to my ear. "Anything I can tempt you to take home?"

You.

The thought stormed into my head and brought an image of Ian kissing me. My face heated and he quirked a brow. I blinked rapidly and cleared my throat. "You know which one I like."

The corner of his mouth lifted slightly. "*Belize Sunrise*."

"Sorry, but I don't have enough spare change."

"Happy birthday, Aimee!" Nadia announced beside me. I jerked in her direction.

Ian stepped back to widen our circle. Nadia offered me champagne. I groaned, taking the glass from her. She handed another to Ian.

"Today's your birthday?" he asked.

"Tomorrow, actually." I gave Nadia the evil eye. "I was hoping you'd forget."

She lifted a glass from a passing tray. "A toast to the birthday girl."

"Stop . . ."

"Let me have my fun," she griped.

"Happy birthday," Ian toasted.

"Thank you."

He kept his gaze focused on me over the rim of his champagne flute as he drank. Hiding a grin, Nadia hummed into her stemware, her eyes jumping from me to Ian.

Wendy approached. "Sorry to interrupt, but I need to steal the main attraction."

Ian set down his glass on a nearby high table. "Don't leave without saying good-bye," he said as Wendy whisked him away.

Nadia tracked their departure. "Damn, he looks good. Too bad he had eyes only for you. I mean, they were glued on you. I felt like the third wheel on my Townie."

"Your bike has only two wheels."

"As I was saying." She chin-pointed across the room. I glanced over and saw Ian surrounded by a small group of admirers looking at me. A hint of a smile appeared before he glanced away, his attention turning to the man beside him.

~

Toward the end of the evening, Nadia found me admiring *Belize Sunrise*. "Gorgeous," she murmured. "Hey, Mr. Property Broker and I are grabbing a bite to eat. Join us."

"So I can be the third wheel on your Townie? Not a chance."

She laughed. "It's not like that."

"Uh-huh. I'll walk home."

"Don't be silly. I'll drop you off."

"I'll walk with you." Ian's voice brushed over me.

Nadia grinned. "Even better."

"Do you mind?" he asked me.

"If it's not inconvenient."

He shook his head and tugged at his collar. "I need the fresh air."

"Then it's settled. I'm off." Nadia hugged me and shook Ian's hand. "Great show."

"Give me a minute. I need to let Wendy know I'm leaving," Ian said when Nadia left.

While waiting, I took a final, long glance at my favorite piece. Someone had turned the photograph away from the window to face the gallery interior. The price tag had been replaced with a new one, the word *sold* written in bold, black lettering.

Ian returned. "You look disappointed. Why so glum?"

I pointed at the tag. "I'm happy you made a sale, but I'd be lying if I told you I wasn't a little bummed."

He spied the tag. "Hmm, interesting," he murmured as he rested his palm against my lower back and ushered us outside. "Which way?"

"Eight blocks that way." I motioned to our left, then unfolded the wrap around my shoulders.

"Any plans for the big day tomorrow?" he asked as we walked.

I shook my head. "Staying home. Maybe dinner with some friends."

"I spent my twenty-ninth birthday hiding from crocodiles in the Everglades."

I laughed. "That's not my idea of a good time."

"I took some amazing pictures, though. Let's see." He scratched his chin. "On my thirtieth I spent the entire day on the back of a mule in the Andes of Peru."

"Let me guess, you spent the night sitting in a bucket of ice?"

He laughed. "No, but close. My ass was sore for a week."

We crossed the street and walked another block. "Any more birthdays I should know about? Or do they stop at thirty?"

"That's all for now." He directed us into a dimly lit alcove.

"What are we doing?"

"Celebrating your birthday." He held open the door and followed me inside. We were at La Petite Maison, a French restaurant. He held up two fingers for the hostess. "Two for coffee and dessert."

The hostess led us to a small table beside the lace-trimmed front window. Ian pushed in my chair for me, then whispered to the hostess before she handed us menus and left.

I glanced at the white-clothed tables and crystal lanterns delicately linked overhead. "For some reason, I don't picture you eating here often."

"Never been here." He turned in his chair and checked the space around us. He had a wicked grin when he looked back at me. "Not my first choice, but it's open." He glanced at his watch. "It's almost eleven."

The waiter arrived a few moments later with our coffees.

"This smells good." My eyes drifted low as I breathed in the warm, roasted aroma.

Ian sipped and shrugged. "It's OK."

"Not up to your standards? No wait." I held up my hand. "You can do better." I shook my head. "I don't know, Ian. All this talk and no action."

His eyes brightened. "Our bet's still on," he reminded.

"Actually . . ." I ran my hands across the table. "There've been some developments on my end."

He quirked a brow.

"The coffee shop idea has been," I paused for effect, "percolating."

"Nice!" He grinned. "Are you going to lease Joe's?"

"Maybe." I gnawed my lip. Ever since Brenda's call, I'd deliberated asking Thomas to cosign, or perhaps Nadia and Kristen should Thomas decline. If Joe had refused me, other leasers would, too.

"I wish you the best of luck, Aimee. Let me know when you're ready to find out who's the true brewmaster between us."

Does he honestly think he can brew better coffee than me? I thought, recalling our conversation at lunch earlier this week.

"Definitely," I agreed.

Our waitress returned with a red velvet cupcake. A single lit candle flamed in the center.

"What's this for?" I asked.

"Your birthday. Make a wish."

I smiled and closed my eyes, picturing my café with the logo painted on the sign above the door. Then I opened my eyes, and right before I blew out the candle, James popped into my mind along with the words the psychic had once told me. *He's still alive.*

I sputtered and coughed.

Ian pulled the candle from the cupcake. "Uh-oh, your age is showing."

A short time later, Ian walked home with me, and when we reached the porch I thanked him for the cupcake.

The porch light gave him a mysterious quality, highlighting the sharp angles of his face. A day's growth dusted his jaw. "I enjoyed tonight. And"—he flashed a smile—"I think I'm going to miss you." He ducked his chin as if caught off guard by the revelation.

"Really? Why?"

"I leave in a few days for a photo expedition."

The keys rattled in my hand. "How long will you be gone?" I asked softly.

"Ten days."

My mouth twitched. "That's a terribly long time."

"An eternity," he teased. He stepped closer to me. "I hope to see you when I get back."

"I'd like that. I had fun tonight."

"Me, too." He brushed his fingers across my cheek. "Maybe Joe's Coffee House will be on its way to becoming Aimee's when I return."

My cheek felt warm where he'd touched me. "Maybe."

His gaze lowered to my mouth, lingering for a brief moment. A small gasp escaped my lips. He chuckled softly. "Good night, Aimee."

"Good night, Ian."

I watched him jog across the street. As he rounded the corner toward downtown, I touched my lips. Ian had wanted to kiss me.

CHAPTER 8

James and I had been thick as thieves, closer than conjoined twins, since that first Saturday morning. After we iced his lip and he helped clean the mess Robbie and Frankie made of my lemonade stand, James spent the rest of the day with me, and almost every Saturday afterward. We were best friends who shared their dreams one moment and pelted each other with Nerf darts the next.

"We're getting married after college, and we're going to have three kids," he once announced while we played Nerf tag with Kristen and Nick in the open reserve behind James's house. Then he told me he wanted to be a famous artist while I stayed home and baked. And baked and baked and baked until my hips grew too wide and I couldn't fit through the doorway.

"Say what?" I had gasped and charged at him.

He dropped to the ground, hugged his belly, and laughed.

"You're going to be just as fat as me," I said. "If we're married, I'm going to make you eat everything I cook." I stood over him, aimed, and fired. Nailed him in the middle of the forehead. Then I ran, ducking behind a felled tree, and giggled. No matter how hard I tried, I couldn't picture James fat.

My favorite afternoons were rainy Saturdays. James came over after his football games and crashed, exhausted, on the couch. He skimmed through the comics while I read books, our heads resting on opposite ends. We didn't move until Mom's baked goodies lured us into the kitchen, our stomachs rumbling.

By James's twelfth birthday, I had known him for almost a year and had yet to be invited over to his house. No girls were allowed inside until he started high school. A stupid rule, James often complained with an eye roll, but one he obeyed. He'd seen the welt on his older brother's backside. Thomas had invited a classmate home to study for an exam. Their father, Edgar Donato, had arrived home early and didn't hesitate using his belt on Thomas after ordering the girl home. Girls and hobbies were distractions. Academics and athletics provided the foundation for the skills needed to carve their marks in the world. His parents had their sons' lives all planned out.

I'd selected the perfect present for James, something I knew he wanted but wouldn't think of asking for from his parents, and wrapped it carefully. The paper crinkled as I knocked on his front door. Today was his party. Only boys had been invited, but I wanted to give him my gift. I couldn't wait for him to see it.

A boy I hadn't met before opened the door. He was taller than James and older than Thomas, but his coloring was the same. Dark hair and eyes, an olive tint to his skin, hinting of the same Italian heritage. He must be Phil, their cousin. James had told me he visited frequently, usually when Phil's dad, James's uncle and Mrs. Donato's brother, traveled for business. Uncle Grant was constantly flying out of the country.

James was never happy when Phil came to town. He spent those days at my house, often leaving long after the streetlights came on. But Phil smiled down at me, and he seemed friendly.

"You're James's friend. Aimee, right?" he asked.

I nodded. "Is he home?"

"James! Door!" He yelled into the house and turned back. "Sorry you can't come to the party. James's dad has this dumbass 'no girls' rule. He really wanted to invite you."

My eyes rounded. "Mr. Donato?"

He laughed. "No, silly. James. I'm Phil, by the way."

"Hi!" I rolled up on the balls of my feet and back to my heels, anxious to see James.

Loud footfalls resounded in the hallway; then James squeezed between Phil and the door.

"Hey, Aimee!" he said right before Phil wrapped him in a headlock. Phil gave him a noogie.

"Happy birthday, little retard," Phil said in a Muppet voice. He sounded like Kermit the Frog and I giggled.

James squirmed from Phil's hold and shoved him. "You're the retard, retard."

Hurt briefly sharpened Phil's eyes. I wondered why the put-down bothered him when he'd just said the same thing to James, but then James spotted the present in my hands.

I grinned and showed him the wrapped package. "It's for you."

"Cool. Tell Mom I'll be right back," he said to Phil before leaping off the porch.

I started to follow, then turned around. "Nice to meet you."

"You, too." Phil grunted and shut the door.

"Hurry up!" James shouted. "I have only thirty-five minutes before the party starts."

He sprinted into the backyard and jumped over the waist-high gate separating his property from the open reserve.

"Your cousin seems nice," I said when he helped me over.

"He's not," James remarked, bolting into the woods before I could ask if Phil had ever been mean to him. Did he bully James? Maybe that was why James punched so well.

"Wait up!" I huffed, chasing after him. The gift's contents rattled, echoing off the oak tree canopy.

He slowed, jogging alongside me. "Let me carry it for you." He reached for the box.

I twisted away. "No! It's your present."

"What did you get me?" He leaped over a small log. "A football?"

"You already have one."

He jogged backward. "A Steve Young jersey?"

"Lame." I pushed by him and marched ahead.

"Let me see!"

"Nope. You have to wait." We had a spot, a circle of logs where we often met Kristen and Nick and plotted our next adventures.

James jumped in front of me and snagged the gift from my hands.

"Give it back!"

He raised the box high above his head.

"You can't open it yet."

"What if I want to? It's my present." His fingernail plucked at a piece of tape.

"Fine. Go ahead." I crossed my arms and pretended I didn't care.

"Really?" He gave me a skeptical look. He'd been teasing me.

But I couldn't wait any longer either. I'd been dying to see his reaction since I spotted the item at the art store. I moved closer. Dry leaves crackled under my shoes. "Yes, really."

He tore off the paper and stared at the wooden box in his hands. "What is it?"

"Open it."

He kneeled and set the box on the ground, flipping the brass latches. The lid creaked open. His eyes widened and mouth fell open. He ran his fingertips through the brush bristles and rolled a paint tube, burnt sienna, in his palm. "You got me art supplies?"

I tugged my sweater sleeves. Maybe I should have bought the 49ers hat Dad suggested.

"You said your parents wouldn't buy you paints, but that doesn't mean I can't give you any. Besides, how do you expect to be a famous painter if you don't have any paints?"

He grinned. "This is cool. Thanks."

My chest swelled and a smile bloomed on my face, the nerves gone. I hadn't been wrong about the gift.

He gave the box a quick inspection before upending the supplies. Brushes, paint tubes, and palette knives dropped onto a bed of pine needles. He converted the box to an easel and propped the canvas board that came with the set onto the ledge.

"What're you doing?" I asked when he squirted a glob of blue paint on the palette board.

"Painting a picture for you."

"Now?"

He didn't answer, his attention glued to a squawking blue jay protecting her nest from a squirrel clinging to the tree trunk. He painted the scene, his inexperienced brushstrokes already showing signs of promise. As I watched, I became as enraptured with his painting as him. In that moment, there wasn't anything that mattered but James's artwork until a voice off in the distance penetrated our world. My head snapped up in the direction it came.

"Your mom's calling for you."

James stilled. The brush tip hovered above the canvas. Color drained from his face. We'd forgotten the time.

He moved the wet canvas aside and we hurriedly collected supplies scattered about the ground, tossing them into the box. He closed the lid and flipped the latches.

"Hold out your arms." I did and he carefully balanced the canvas on my forearms. "Watch out, the paint's wet."

I repositioned my palms underneath to create a flatter surface.

"It's for you." He kissed my cheek, lips lingering on my skin.

I inhaled a short breath, surprised at the contact that felt just as nice as it was unexpected. It left a fluttery feeling in my belly.

He grinned. "Let's go."

I followed him back to his house. We walked as fast as we could without risk of damaging his first painting. Mrs. Donato waited for us on the back deck. Her eyes narrowed on James, taking in what I only now noticed. Paint splatters on his forearms and shirt. Dirt stains on his knees. Her gaze dropped to the wood box.

"What is that in your hand?"

James quickly glanced at me. He tried to hide the box behind his legs. "Paints," he admitted.

"Paints," she repeated and her lips thinned. "Paints are messy and childish. They're a distraction, a waste of time." She tugged his shirt where a blue thumbprint stained the collar. "I see you've already been wasting time. Best you understand now, James, that there's no room in your future for frivolous activities." She looked at me. "I'm guessing you gave him the paints?"

I nodded, too intimidated not to.

"It's a sweet gesture, dear, but he can't accept your gift. James, please return it or I'll be forced to make you toss it in the trash."

"But—"

"Are you arguing with me?"

His gaze dropped to his feet. "No, ma'am."

I grabbed the box from James. I didn't want his mom throwing it away.

Mrs. Donato moved to the door. "Come inside and clean up. Change your clothes. They're filthy. Hurry up!" she barked when James stalled, tossing me an apologetic look. "Your guests arrive in five minutes."

James practically ran into the house. My heart clenched over his disappointment. He really wanted the art supplies.

"Go home, Aimee. You can see James tomorrow."

"Yes, Mrs. Donato," I glumly replied. Tears burned and I swiped them away before they leaked.

Carefully walking to the side gate, I held the box and balanced what I thought could be James's one and only painting. His passion snuffed before any chance to glow. I tried working the gate latch, bumping the box around in my struggle. The lid popped open and dumped the contents.

I sank to the ground and started picking up brushes and paints. A pair of loafers stopped by my hands. Phil lowered to his knees. He tossed a palette knife into the box.

"Sorry about my mom."

I lifted my head. "Your mom?"

He dropped his chin to his chest. "I mean Claire. She's pretty much my mom because she's all I got."

"Don't you have a dad?"

He nodded. "I don't see him much. He works a lot. Anyway, in case you haven't noticed, Claire wants James and Thomas working at my dad's company when they grow up. James painting pictures isn't part of her plan."

I looked at the scattered supplies, money I'd wasted. I should have bought the hat. "What am I supposed to do with all this?"

Phil studied James's bird and squirrel chase. "He's pretty good. Maybe you can keep the stuff at your house and he can paint there. Claire and Edgar don't have to know." He zipped his lips and tossed aside an imaginary key. "I won't tell if you won't."

I liked his idea.

We shook hands and finished cleaning up. Phil handed me the box. "Hold it flat like this." He laid the painting on top of the box. "Now you won't drop it."

I slowly stood. "Thanks."

"I see why James likes you. You're sweet."

I ducked my head, blushing.

He opened the gate for me. "Maybe I'll see you tomorrow."

I liked Phil. He didn't come across as the bully James described. "Maybe," I agreed.

But I didn't see Phil the next day, or any other day for several years. James always came to my house, more frequently than before since I let him keep his art supplies in my room. As his skills improved and he acquired more supplies, my parents cleared a space for him in the sunroom next to the kitchen. Over the years, while I helped Mom craft new recipes for the restaurant, James painted, and his talent and our friendship flourished.

CHAPTER 9

The next day, I dressed in skinny jeans, a filmy blouse with thin straps, and heels for my birthday celebration. Kristen and Nadia were taking me to Chinese for dinner. Nadia hugged me hello when they arrived at my house. "I shouldn't have bailed on you last night."

"Mr. Commercial Property Broker didn't pass inspection?"

"He was a dud." She screwed up her face. "He made a pass at me."

I laughed. "That's not good?"

"Was he a lousy kisser?" Kristen asked. She'd moved into the main room and stood beside the dining table.

Nadia rolled her eyes. "No and no," she said to each of us. "He was good. Too good. He's married."

Kristen looked up. "Ouch."

"Wasn't he wearing a wedding band?" I spun my engagement ring.

Nadia scowled. "No."

Kristen studied the paper she held. "How did you find out?"

"I had breakfast this morning with Wendy. Gawd!" Nadia groaned. "I couldn't shut my trap about him so Wendy told me." She flopped into a leather chair and crossed her ankles on the ottoman. "He asked me to submit a proposal for a commercial site he owns in San Jose, near the arena."

"Before or after he made a pass?" Kristen asked. She put down the paper she held and picked up another piece covered with penciled notes.

"Before. I think I'll pass on him." She waved a hand. "I mean the offer."

"He's probably not the most trustworthy person. What's his name?" I asked out of curiosity.

"Mark Everson. Tall, blond, and gorgeous." She smacked her palms on the chair arms. "That sounds so freaking cliché, but it's true. He's older, midthirties. Wendy was surprised when I told her. She thinks he might be having issues with his wife."

I snorted. "You think?"

"I don't mean to be rude and change the subject, but are you opening a restaurant?" Kristen waved the paper she held. Stacked on the dining table were my research paperwork, business forms, and quotes from vendors I'd worked with at The Goat.

I walked to her side. "I'm planning to." At least I hoped so, assuming I found a cosigner for the lease. But I wanted to get my numbers in order before I approached Thomas. I'd get only one chance to pitch my idea.

"Omigosh!" Kristen squealed. "Are you serious? I love what I've read of your notes. Your ideas are fabulous."

Nadia stood and crossed the room. She pushed the papers around and picked up a list of menu selections. I'd been toying with recipe combinations, fusing diverse tastes to create exotic flavors. My coffee selection looked like a wine list at a restaurant. I'd have to trim the options, perhaps make several seasonal menus. Nadia flagged the paper. "You're really going through with this? From scratch?"

"Yes, I am."

She studied me. "Well, it's definitely better than lamb stew and red potatoes."

I took the lists from her and evened the stack, tapping the edges against the table. "If my parents had sold The Goat to me, I wouldn't have much leeway with new dishes. New World fusion wouldn't go over well at an Irish pub."

"Now you're talking." Kristen patted my shoulder. "I'm glad you're taking this step. You're moving on."

Nadia glanced around the room, her gaze landing on the framed pictures of James and me crowding the mantel. "Tell us how we can help. We can pack James's belongings if it's too difficult for you to do alone. There are some good charities where you can donate his clothes. We can help find one that has a good cause. I can also assist with the restaurant design, and I can recommend a good contractor."

I clasped the paper, wrinkling the edges. "Thanks for the offer, but I need to find a site first."

Her face lit up. "I can help with that, too, and I won't charge for my work."

I'd planned to ask for her assistance to design the space, possibly to cosign the lease if Thomas wouldn't, but I hadn't expected her work pro bono. Her offer was huge. "I'd love your help, but don't worry about James's things. I'll take care of them." Like later, such as when Lacy and that business card she'd slipped into my wallet no longer niggled the back of my mind.

"All righty!" Kristen piped up. "Looks like there's more to celebrate tonight than your birthday. Who's ready to get this party started?"

~

After dinner, we went to Blue Sky Lounge in downtown San Jose. Electronica music pulsed, vibrating the air. People swayed on the dance floor, limbs entwined with their partners. Nadia led us to a group of chairs circling a low table she'd reserved and ordered a carafe of sangria with a round of passion fruit champagne shots. While nursing her sangria, she made sure the shots kept coming for Kristen and me.

When we finished the first carafe, Kristen grabbed my wrists. "Come on, birthday girl. Dance with me." She dragged me onto the dance floor. Heated bodies plastered against us. Kristen hip-bumped me and I laughed.

She yelled in my ear. "You look happy."

"I *am* happy," I shouted back. I was reconstructing my life and myself, and I felt good.

Several song sets later, I waved my hand in front of my face. Sweat dripped between my breasts. "Water," I shouted over the music. We returned to our booth as the waitress arrived with a fresh sangria carafe and another round of shots, which Kristen and I quickly consumed. My head lulled. I rubbed my face, trying to wipe off the fuzziness.

"What did you think of Ian's show last night?"

I squinted at Nadia. "His photos are incredible."

"Ian's incredible."

A silly grin pillowed my cheeks.

"I knew it." Nadia snapped fingers in my direction.

My smile turned pensive. "He's leaving for a photo expedition."

"Will you see him when he gets back?" Kristen asked.

I shrugged. "Maybe." My brows bunched, my mouth forming a tight circle. Ian remarked he'd miss me, but he hadn't asked for my number. I hunched back in my chair. "I don't know how to contact him."

Nadia replenished my drink. "Wendy has his number. I'll get it for you."

A sudden lightness had me straightening in my seat. "Ian's fun. I had fun with him." I grinned stupidly from a combination of excitement and alcohol, and Nadia laughed.

"I can tell." She winked.

My gaze dropped to my drink and I watched the ice bob in the glass. They floated like tiny islands and it made me think of James's body floating in the water. The body Thomas had brought home and wouldn't let me see. The big, fat check Thomas had conveniently given me at the funeral. There were also the missing paintings. I narrowed my gaze on the melting ice. Something wasn't right.

I jerked up my head. Kristen and Nadia were discussing one of Nick's cases. He was a business litigation attorney and Kristen was relieved the case had been resolved. Nick could finally rest. They could plan the vacation they'd put off for eight months. I yawned and watched people on the dance floor. Or tried to. My eyes blurred and the floor listed to the left, or maybe I was the one leaning.

Couples undulated to a frenzied rhythm. Through the turbulent wave of swaying hips and limbs, one blonde woman stood in the center, her lavender-blue eyes locked on me. Lacy.

I blinked and she disappeared. I scooted to the edge of my seat and caught a glimpse of blonde hair and a green shirt. She was moving away. I scrambled from my chair and tipped Kristen's glass. Red liquid and ice spilled to the floor. She gasped and jumped out of the way. I murmured an apology and weaved around the chairs.

"Where are you going?" Nadia called out.

"Restroom," I shouted the excuse. I had to catch up with Lacy before I lost her.

I pushed through the dance floor, stepping on toes and shoving among humid bodies. Curses trailed me. Lacy remained elusive until I saw the ladies' room door open. She'd gone inside.

The door slammed behind me. Remixed music piped through the speakers. Two women, their faces heavily made up, hair tousled, and skin tattooed, primped before mirrors in the restroom's lounge. Another woman washed her hands. She gave me a cursory glance through the mirror and left.

I stood in the space between the sink counter and stalls. The restroom was practically empty, which was odd considering the line usually spilled out the door. Lacy wasn't here. I'd lost her. Spying the toilets, I scooted into a stall. When I finished, I washed my hands and glimpsed Lacy's reflection in the mirror. My skin pricked.

She kept her gaze plugged into mine. I couldn't look away or turn around. Her lips moved and words whispered in my head. *James is alive.*

I vigorously shook my head.

He still lives.

"Prove it."

He isn't dead. If he was, you'd know it. You'd feel it. Don't you still feel him?

I did. His voice in my head. His touch in the breeze. His laugh in the scattering of leaves on the ground. But that didn't prove anything.

In the mirror, Lacy remained motionless, unblinking. I weaved and grasped the counter to steady my balance. My palms were damp and moisture beaded on my upper lip. I shot a glance at the door, willing someone to walk inside. To tell me I wasn't having a crazy moment; that Lacy wasn't really here, locking me in a psychic trance. My feet wouldn't budge.

The primping women on the other side of the restroom put away their makeup and left without looking my way. The door closed behind them and a hush fell across the room as though all noise had been sucked out with them. For an instant, Lacy and I seemed separated from the rest of the world, hovering within the vacuum of space. No sound existed. Then suddenly, the noise returned, powering back into the restroom. Air vents hummed, music played, water flowed from the faucet in front of me. It also felt like something else had come inside when the women left, forcing its way into me as one thought.

James isn't the missing person. You are.

"I was sent to find you," Lacy said.

My head pitched back. The overhead spotlights pierced my pupils and I blinked repeatedly. Images flashed in my mind like slides clicking on their reel. James underwater, bullets zipping past. James struggling to stay afloat in the churning seawater. James collapsed on a beach, his face battered and bruised, and a woman hovering over him. Her raven hair draped his face. Espresso eyes burned with concern. Lips moved, asking his name. He didn't know.

James, I wanted to shout. *Your name is James.*

I felt lightheaded and dropped to the floor, my head connecting hard with the tile. Stars flashed overhead until they faded.

The last thought to cross my mind before I lost consciousness was that I drank way too much sangria.

~

"Wake up, Aimee."

My cheek stung and my head was on fire.

"Hello! Wakey, wakey." *Smack.*

Pinpricks sparked across my cheekbone.

"What happened to her?" came a voice I didn't recognize.

"Is she OK?" came another.

"Someone had one too many."

That was Nadia. I smiled.

"I think she's coming around," she said.

"It's her birthday," piped in Kristen.

Murmurs of understanding echoed around us. Feet shuffled away, the click of heels on tile. I heard doors slam and toilets flush. Reality returned.

Aw, crap. I was in the women's restroom. Passed out on the floor. *Eww.*

I blinked and squinted at the lights overhead and four sets of eyes staring back at me. I groaned. "What happened?"

"We were hoping you could tell us," Nadia said.

I shook my head, memories fuzzy.

"I wonder if there was MSG in our food," Kristen pondered.

We'd eaten Chinese. I was allergic to MSG. It made me lightheaded, but I'd never fainted.

"The menu said 'no MSG added,'" Nadia informed.

"Too much to drink." My head screamed. Whether from alcohol or when my skull tackled the tile, I didn't know. I raised my arms. "Help me up."

They pulled me upright, murmuring for me to move slowly and easily. The two strangers hovering backed away. I leaned against the counter and glanced around. The restroom was packed with a line crawling out the door. Like it should have been earlier. Lacy was gone. Had she ever been here?

My head throbbed. I pressed at the knot on the back and whined.

Nadia frowned. "Do you think you have a concussion?"

"I'll be fine," I bit out through clenched teeth. I didn't want to spend my birthday in a hospital. I wanted my bed. "Can you take me home?"

She handed me my purse. "I'm staying with you tonight, just in case."

We left the restroom and walked through the lounge. My skin rippled, ruffling the fine hairs on the back of my neck. I glanced over my shoulder. I didn't see anyone I knew, though I sensed Lacy nearby watching me.

CHAPTER 10

As she'd promised, Nadia stayed with me through the night, lying beside me in bed. She woke me every hour until I smacked her with a pillow at five a.m. and dragged myself from bed to sleep another restless four hours on the couch. We were walking zombies the next morning, her from lack of sleep and me from a hangover. She left early in the afternoon after I promised to call if I had any lingering headaches. She would force me to the clinic. I agreed to relax over the weekend, occupying my time with old movies and business plans. They kept my mind off the bizarre incident in the bathroom.

The sane part of me knew Lacy had been a hallucination fueled by a deep-seated desire for James to still be alive. Still, those images of him on the brink of death, almost drowning, haunted me. There had been too much blood on his face and sand plastered in the deep gashes across his cheek. I kept telling myself they were an illusion. They *had* to be an illusion. It pained me to think otherwise.

I shuffled through my notes on the dining room table and admired the café's logo. An outlined coffee mug under a heart-shaped swirl of steam with the words *Aimee's Café.* James's last piece of artwork. I pictured the café's color palette. Pumpkin, mahogany, and eggplant. Ian's

Belize Sunrise would be a perfect display on the café's wall. I wondered who'd purchased the image, and then I wondered about Ian. Where was he, and did I cross his mind? Would he take another picture like the one I loved?

I studied the sketch again and scratched the pencil through the word *café* so it simply read *Aimee's*. Ian had called my café Aimee's.

I tasted the word on my tongue. *Aimee's.*

"Let's grab a bite to eat at Aimee's," I said in a happy voice. "Aimee's has the best coffee."

I smiled. I liked the sound of it. Simple and memorable.

The doorbell rang and I jumped in my chair. I stole a glance out the front window on my way to the door. A taxicab was parked in front, and Ian waited on the porch. Seeing me in the window, he waved.

Heat inched up my chest and neck until my cheeks bloomed crimson. I swore, my hands fluttering to the wild mess piled on my head. Grimacing, I knew it looked like a bird's nest, about as neat and tidy as the rumpled pajamas I'd been wearing since I came home stinking drunk the night before.

I glanced longingly toward my room. No chance to change, and no chance to hide. Ian had already seen me. Thank God I'd been sensible enough to brush my teeth, and I'd done so only to wash out the vomit.

Opening the front door a crack, I popped out my head, squinting at the glare of the setting sun above the rooftops across the street.

"Fun night last night?"

I grunted. "What are you doing here?"

He shifted, rubbed the back of his neck, and motioned toward the cab. "I'm on my way to the airport. Red-eye flight to New Zealand, and I forgot . . ." He scratched his head.

I arched a brow.

"I forgot to, um . . ." He blew out a breath and yanked his phone from his back pocket. His mouth twitched in a shy smile. "Can I get your phone number?"

My pulse fluttered. The first thought through my head was that I'd save Nadia a phone call, and my own embarrassment. She wouldn't have to bug Wendy for Ian's number. I pushed the door wider and held out my hand for his phone. He'd already opened a new contact page, and now he watched me as I added my name and number. Then, before I lost the nerve, I also added my e-mail and street address.

His crooked smile grew into a full-fledged grin when I gave back the phone. He tapped a finger to the screen and held the phone to his ear. I heard my phone ring from where it rested on the dining room table.

Ian rested a finger against his lips. "Don't answer it," he whispered, then inhaled. "Hi, Aimee, it's Ian. I had a great time with you at my show, and an even better time afterward. I leave for New Zealand tonight but won't be gone long. May I call you when I get back?"

He looked at me then, brows raised in question. He nodded, inviting an answer from me, and I felt my chin dip in reply.

His eyes lit up. "Great. I'll see you then." He ended the call. "Now you have my number."

I laughed.

He tucked the phone away and placed a quick kiss on my cheek. I gasped softly, startled.

"See you in ten days." He bounded down the porch steps and to the taxi, waving before he sank into the backseat.

My hand lifted as the taxi sped off, a slight smile teasing my lips as I returned inside the house, breathless. The whirlwind that was Ian had left my head spinning, and not from a hangover. I lowered into the chair I had vacated, my smile broadening as I sorted through the paperwork.

By Monday morning, the headaches were gone and I'd pushed Lacy to the back of my mind. My week was booked meeting suppliers. I had appointments to inspect potential sites, even though my heart was still set on Joe's. And I still needed to call Thomas. Hopefully, asking him to cosign wouldn't be asking too much.

As I gathered my paperwork and keys, the doorbell rang again. Through the peephole I saw an older man with white hair and a thick stature. He wore a short-sleeved shirt and khaki pants. He pushed his hands into his side pockets as he looked across the front yard.

I opened the door and he smiled, exposing a row of tobacco-stained teeth. I recognized him instantly. "What are you doing here, Joe?"

"It's been a long time, Aimee." He held out his wide palm and affectionately clasped mine with his other when I shook his hand. "How have you been?"

"I've been . . . OK."

He nodded. "I hear you're opening a restaurant."

"Actually, it's a boutique coffee shop and gourmet eatery. But I need to find a space to lease." The fact that his leasing agent hadn't recommended me hung thick between us.

"May I come in?"

"Oh yes. Sorry." I stepped aside and opened the door wider.

Joe ambled over the threshold, his blocky frame a presence in the small room. I closed the door and watched him glance around, his gaze lingering in every corner. He looked at James's paintings on the walls, the framed pictures on the sideboard, and the engagement portrait over the mantel before his gaze settled on me. "Your parents told me what happened. I'm sorry."

I took a deep breath and nodded.

"James was a good kid. I liked him."

"Thank you."

He picked up a picture of James and me taken on the day he'd proposed, almost a year before. I was showing off my engagement ring. Joe frowned, and my breath caught in my throat. I wondered if he was noticing from the photo how the thickly applied makeup hid the cuts on my cheek and the bruise on my chin.

Joe returned the frame, adjusting the stand so the picture didn't topple. He shoved his hands back into his pockets and faced me. "My wife died five years ago."

"I remember." Joe had taken some time off. The service at the café had faltered, and he was unable to recapture the momentum he'd once had. He'd lost many customers. They found other restaurants and drive-through coffee shops preferable. They'd chosen convenience over nostalgia.

"It took a long time for me to feel any semblance of normal again." He shrugged his shoulders. "I still miss her."

My heart reached out to him. I knew exactly how he felt. Hollow and incomplete. Loss left an empty cavity in the chest.

I cleared my throat, blinking back tears. "Do you want some coffee?"

He exhaled. "Yes, please."

I indicated the couch. "Make yourself comfortable. I'll fix a new pot."

I swiftly retreated into the kitchen and, gripping the counter edge, took several deep breaths until the burning behind my eyes and in my throat that arose from the ache of loneliness diminished. I ground a mixture of beans, samples I'd received from suppliers I was considering. I set up the coffeemaker's brew cycle.

When I returned to the front room, Joe was flipping through one of James's old *Runner's World* magazines. He tossed the magazine on the table when he saw me. "My doc told me I need to exercise."

I handed him a mug. Steam wafted upward, a roasted hazelnut scent. "Walking is good."

"I walked here from downtown." He sipped the coffee. His eyes widened. "This is good." He drank again. "This is really, really good."

"Thank you. It's a custom blend," I said shyly.

He raised his cup in my direction. "Remember to put this on your menu. I'll order one every time I come."

I smiled. After years eating at Joe's Coffee House, he might now be my customer. "I'll remember."

He finished the coffee and set down the mug, rubbing his palms over his thighs as he settled farther into the couch. "I closed the coffeehouse because I couldn't compete. Those damn chains serving their shitty—" He cleared his throat behind a fist. "Er, sorry, they took my customers away. What makes you certain the same thing won't happen to you?"

"I'm not certain," I said honestly. "But I don't plan to compete with the chains."

He shook his head. "You'll go out of business within a few months."

"Hopefully not. It's my intention to offer something different, more like a coffee experience."

The corner of his mouth twitched. "A coffee experience?"

"For people who appreciate specialty coffees. Mine will be handcrafted and slow brewed, like the blend I made for you." I pointed at his empty cup.

He chuckled. "It's very good."

"Thanks." I grinned. "I still need to create a full menu, confirm suppliers, and more important," I ducked my head, looked at the hands clasped in my lap, "find a location."

"I know your parents, Aimee. I've known them for a long time. They're good people, and very good business people. I was surprised when they sold. I thought you'd inherit the restaurant or buy them out."

Me, too, but I wasn't about to confide my parents' financial issues. "Starting my own restaurant is better for me. It's something I need to do." It was what James had wanted me to do. But also, I had to prove to myself I could do this on my own.

"I know you applied to lease my building."

"Yes, but—"

He held up his hand. "My agent couldn't recommend you because of your credit issues. Yes, I'm aware of that, too. I also understand what you've been through this year. I understand why things fall apart, how bills aren't paid, and life stops. I've suffered, too. Listen," he set down his mug and leaned forward. "Now is when you pick up the pieces."

"That's what I've been doing, sir."

"I couldn't, and I lost more than my wife." He cleared his throat. "I'm accepting your application. My place is yours."

My mouth fell open. "What about my credit?"

"Bah, forget the credit." He slashed his hand in the air. "You messed up. I want someone I can trust. I know you and I know your parents. I wanted a fifteen-year lease, but I'll give you five. If you go out of business, then you won't be obligated for the remainder of the lease. If you want to renew our contract, we can renegotiate the terms, but I promise not to charge you more than the original lease, even if the market goes up."

He rubbed the side of his nose. I could only stare and nod as he continued. "It's customary to give a new tenant one to three months' free rent during build-out. I'll give you as long as you need, rent-free until the day you open, even if you take a year to remodel."

I blinked as my brain tried to compute what he'd offered. "Why are you doing this for me?"

He grinned. There was a gleam in his eye. "Let's just say you have people looking out for you."

My back straightened. "Did my parents put you up to this?"

"This has nothing to do with your parents. This is between you and me. I need a tenant and you need a site. So what do you think? Do we have a deal?"

This was crazy. The deal seemed unreal. I stared openly as Joe grinned back at me. His hand hovered between us, waiting.

I restrained myself from leaping into his arms. Instead I smiled and clasped his hand. "We definitely have a deal."

Joe stood and I followed him to the door. I felt like the luckiest person alive and I told him so.

"Good, you're going to need all the luck you can get. Everything at my place is falling apart. It's going to need a lot of work."

CHAPTER 11

"Oh my God, this place needs a lot of work." Nadia dragged her finger across the counter and held up the tip. It was covered in a thick layer of greasy dust. She made a squeamish face. "It's disgusting."

"It's charming. In a time-warped, *American Graffiti* way," Kristen said. She gave me a thumbs-up.

Dad stared at the high ceiling. Exposed wires hung where tiles were missing. Other tiles were cracked or water stained. "It has potential."

"See? Exactly!" I agreed.

Nadia retreated to the kitchen. "Are you considering a lease?"

"I've already signed one."

She stopped midstride. "What? When?"

"Last week." Joe and I had spent several days going back and forth over the terms, finally settling on an agreement Friday. I'd picked up the keys from him the following Tuesday. It was now Saturday, the first day I could get Nadia, Kristen, and Dad to meet me. Mom was at The Goat overseeing the pickup of furniture she and Dad were donating to Saint Anthony's. Dad would join her later. I glanced at my watch. Hopefully, Nadia and Kristen wouldn't linger long after Dad left.

"This place *is* a dive," Dad echoed Nadia. "But the square footage is exactly what you need. All this place needs is a little TLC."

"And a sledgehammer." Nadia moved back into the dining area. "Did you inspect the property before you signed the papers?"

"I looked around."

"You looked around?" Nadia swore. "Don't get me wrong. I'm thrilled for you. Your restaurant will be great, but they are a high risk for failure." She gave my dad an apologetic look and he waved off the comment before she looked back at me. "You can't make rash decisions." She pointed at the water stains on the wood paneling. "Did you ask how the leak happened?"

"No." I huffed impatiently. "Joe said the place would need a lot of work."

"Ya think? This place needs to be gutted, and who knows what's lurking behind those walls." Her gaze jumped from one spot to another, assessing details my amateur eyes didn't see. "You should have called. I would have done a walk-through so you'd have an idea of what you were getting yourself into. Remodels add up quickly and before you know, you're over budget. Or worse, out of cash. Did you look at other sites to compare?"

"Why? This place is rent-free."

Nadia blinked. *"What?"*

Dad whistled.

"Damn, girl," muttered Kristen, who'd been playing with the cash register. It dinged.

"For how long?" Nadia asked, suspicious.

"As long as the remodel takes. No payments until opening day."

Her mouth fell open.

"It's a pretty sweet deal. I like this place." It was full of memories. Dad's mouth curved upward. He knew this place was special to me. Outside the windows I saw the same view James and I had seen every time we dined—mothers pushing strollers, cars passing, the occasional bicyclist dodging traffic. It was pouring now, the season's first storm. I looked at my watch again.

Nadia launched her tablet and sat in the nearest chair. She tapped notes on a virtual keyboard. "Do you know what you want to do with this site?"

Kristen looked at me expectantly and sat in a chair beside Nadia. Dad shuffled closer.

I grinned. "I have tons of ideas, like baking amazing desserts to go with my custom coffees."

"What are you going to call your café?" Kristen asked.

"Aimee's," I announced, and pulled the logo sketch from my portfolio. I placed it on the table. All three leaned in to look.

"Slow-Brewed Coffees & Gourmet Eatery. I love it." Kristen patted my shoulder.

Nadia typed notes. "Off the top of my head, build-out won't be cheap. After construction, permits, insurance, furniture, employee wages, plus your own cost of living—"

"Relax. Don't worry," I interjected, and started rubbing Nadia's shoulders. "I'll spend wisely."

"Good. You can start with me. As promised, I won't charge you, and I'll get the best prices I can manage through my connections for all the other stuff."

"You have to let me pay you something."

She laughed. "I didn't say I was free, baby." A large grin curved across her face.

"I'm almost afraid to ask," I muttered.

She twisted in her seat and held out her hand. "I want a lifetime of free coffee, and your lemon scones, too."

I laughed outright, shaking her hand. "Deal. So, how long will the transformation take?"

She pursed her lips and hummed. "Consider yourself lucky if you can open in eight months."

I whistled. "That's a long time." I was anxious to break ground. Unconsciously, I looked at my watch again.

Kristen nudged me and nodded at my watch. "Going somewhere?"

I shook my head. "I'm expecting someone."

"Who?"

My face heated. "Ian."

He'd arrived home yesterday and had called this morning. I suggested we meet here, neutral territory. After two weeks of thinking long and hard, I still wasn't sure what I wanted from Ian. It was obvious he wanted more than friendship from me.

Kristen beamed, oblivious to my inner turmoil. "Ian's on his way over," she told my dad and Nadia. Dad's eyes narrowed on me.

Nadia stood, her smile covering half her face. "I guess that's our cue to leave."

~

I was measuring counter space when Ian arrived shortly after the others had left. He shook his jacket and hair. Water rained onto the floor. "Man, it's crazy out there." He blew out a breath and grinned. "Hi, Aims."

My pulse fluttered at the sight of him. He looked good. Really good. In a rugged, wet dog sort of way. I motioned for his jacket. "You're drenched. Let me take that."

"Thanks." He slipped it off. "I ran here from home."

"Where do you live?" I asked, hanging the jacket on the back of a chair.

"Seven blocks that way." He pointed in the opposite direction I walk home from the café. "We're neighbors."

I laughed. "If you consider a half mile neighbors. How was your trip?"

"Great! I got some amazing pictures." He set a wet paper bag on the table beside me, avoiding the papers I'd spread to show Nadia my ideas. Ian didn't want to get them wet. He gently nudged my shoulder. "I was right, by the way."

"About what?"

"I did miss you." My eyes widened and he chuckled, looking around. "So, you leased Joe's old place."

"Er, yeah . . . I did," I sputtered, still stuck on the *I did miss you* revelation.

"I can't wait to see what you do with it." He rapped his knuckles on the Formica counter. "Have you researched espresso machines yet?"

I'd barely had time to finish my business plans since Ian had left the country. Crossing my arms, I leaned a hip against the counter edge. "Not yet. Why?"

He mimicked my stance and rested his hand above his heart. "I'd be honored to recommend a brand or two."

My mouth quirked. "What makes you an expert?" I asked, genuinely interested despite the good-natured humor in his tone. Aside from photography and that he often traveled, I didn't know anything about him.

"I spent several months in Provence after I graduated college. Dated a barista and she taught me . . ." His voice trailed and face flushed. I arched a brow. The corner of his mouth twitched. "She taught me *a lot.*"

My eyes narrowed. "I bet she did."

Ian straightened. "Ah, now, don't be jealous," he chided and my face flamed brighter than his. "Come here, I brought you something."

Paper crinkled as he pulled a large bottle from the bag he'd brought. "What's that?" I asked.

"Cider."

"You brought juice."

He laughed. "Big-kid juice. Hard cider. I lived off this stuff on my trip." He patted his chest and jean pockets as though looking for something. He spied his jacket and dug into the side pockets. He retrieved two shot glasses.

"I've never had shots of cider before."

He rolled his eyes. "You sip the stuff. I grabbed these because they fit in my pockets." He popped the lid off the bottle with an opener he pulled from another pocket and poured the cider. "Normally, we drink this at room temperature. It's so damn cold outside it might be a little cool. Still good, though." He handed me a glass.

I sniffed the cider. Images of apple pie and tarts filled my head.

"Kia ora," Ian said, raising his glass between us.

"Kia what?"

"It's a Maori greeting. The Maori are the indigenous people of New Zealand. Loosely translated, it means 'good health.' I like to think it means 'cheers.'"

"Cheers," I repeated and sipped the cider. It had a dry fruitiness, delicious.

Ian sat in the chair from where his jacket hung and I lowered into the one across from him. He stretched his legs underneath the table and leaned back, tapping his shoes against my ankle. The slight contact ricocheted up my leg and straight to my core. He watched me intently. I shifted in my chair.

"Didn't your mother teach you not to stare?"

His eyes dulled momentarily before they flashed with interest. "If I didn't stare, I wouldn't be able to figure out why I find you more intriguing than before."

The tanned skin crinkled at the corners of his eyes. He meant to be lighthearted, but his quandary weighed heavily. I moistened my lips and rested my forearms on the table, cupping the little glass in my fingers. "Have you ever lost someone dear to you?" I asked seriously.

His expression darkened. "Yes, I have."

Despite my reluctance to tell anyone about my interactions with Lacy, I'd debated how much to tell Ian about James. I'd buried my fiancé and still mourned him. I missed him something fierce, and that longing only fueled the seeds of doubt Lacy had planted. Until those went away, it wouldn't be fair to let Ian assume I wanted anything more than his friendship.

"When we first met," I began, thinking carefully about what I was about to say. I didn't want Ian's pity, but I needed him to understand my frame of mind. "You asked if I was engaged. I was, for almost a year. My fiancé died last May. Actually, he went missing when he fell overboard while fishing in Mexico. His body was eventually recovered and I buried him on our wedding day. That was in July." I drank the rest of my cider in one gulp and wiped my mouth with the back of my hand. "Guess I am doing cider shots," I remarked wryly.

Ian gaped, his body frozen. After a moment, he shook his head as though shaking off the shock. "Shit, Aimee. I'm sorry." He grasped both my hands. His thumb brushed back and forth over my knuckles.

"I never saw his body. I never had a chance to say good-bye."

Ian murmured something incoherent. He tightened his grip. Had the table not been between us, I knew he would have pulled me against his chest and held me close within the protective band of his arms.

I studied our linked fingers. His hands were warm, strong; the movement of his thumb soothing. A deep ache for companionship burned within my chest, the heat spreading outward through my limbs. I lifted my gaze to his and saw something encouraging behind his eyes. My crazy, upended world shifted into place with a resounding click.

"I can tell you're going to be a good friend, Ian."

He made a noise in the back of his throat. "A friend, am I?"

Disappointment clouded his expression. "I'm sorry. It's just . . ." I extracted my hands and dropped them onto my lap. "I've never been with anyone else. It's always been James and me."

"James? Oh," his mouth circled. "Your fiancé." He propped his elbow on the table and rubbed his cheek, scratching at the stubble shadowing his jaw. "Are you nervous about being with someone else?" he asked quietly.

"No, not nervous."

Ian arched a brow.

"OK, maybe a little. I'm not ready for a serious relationship. Not yet." I had the café to think about. And James. His body had been underground less than a year—*if* there was a body underground, and that was the crux of it. The not knowing made it difficult to let go of what we once had together.

"My parents think I was too dependent on James," I admitted, more as an afterthought.

Ian snorted. He waved his arm to encompass the diner. "What you want to do to this place isn't the sign of a dependent woman. More like someone determined to make something of her life."

A tentative smile tugged at my lips.

He refilled my shot glass and raised his. "I'll make you a deal. I'll toast to us becoming great friends if you promise to tell me when you want something more with me."

My eyes rounded, then I tossed back my head, laughing at his deliberate word choice. When, not if.

"You're something else," I teased.

He shook his head. "Nah, just optimistic."

"All right." I lifted my glass. "You've got yourself a deal."

CHAPTER 12

The summer before I started high school, I had known James for six years and no longer wanted to be his friend. I itched for something more.

My thinking wasn't a sudden change of direction, more a subtle shift over the last school year, like a butterfly ever so slowly unfolding her wings upon emerging from a cocoon and taking flight. I started to notice things about him I hadn't before, like his scent. He didn't have that sweaty locker room smell the boys at my school had. His cologne meshed nicely with his own scent, making my insides cartwheel whenever he stood near and I breathed him in. *What a head rush!* It left me dizzy and confused, and on more than one occasion, I had to stop from plastering my nose into his chest. He would laugh and push me away.

But despite my potential embarrassment, I knew him better than anyone else. His endless pursuit to improve his artwork, his frustrations with his parents forcing him on a career path he didn't want, and his despondency over not sharing his work with anyone outside my family—else his family find out and they prevent him from seeing me—made for a heady combination in my head. I was falling in love with my best friend, and I desperately missed him.

Football practice had started and he had a menu of other activities keeping him busy. I hadn't seen him much that summer, but he did make a surprise visit one August afternoon. I was baking cookies for Kristen's birthday and had just removed the cookie sheet from the oven. When I straightened and turned around, I found James leaning against the kitchen threshold, watching me.

He was wearing slate pants and a white dress shirt unbuttoned at the collar, an outfit suitable for church on Sundays, not a hot, dry Thursday. And definitely not for football.

At sixteen, James didn't have the lean, gangly stature typical of guys his age. Years of football kept him in top shape. Unruly, sun-burnished strands tumbled on his dark head. He'd been running his hands through his hair. Something was on his mind.

"What are you doing here?" I asked, surprised to find him standing in my house. I shouldn't be. He had a key thanks to Dad, who'd grown weary answering the door every time James came over, which, before this summer, had been a lot. "Don't you have football practice?"

He shrugged. "I decided to take the afternoon off."

My brows lurched up. "And your parents are cool with that?"

He snorted, his forehead crinkling as he tilted his chin, giving me a wide-eyed look. His parents had no idea he was here.

"Dad's working late and Mom's at a charity function," he explained.

"So, you're playing hooky?" I set the cookie sheet on the granite counter.

He gave me a brilliant, face-splitting grin that made my heart clutch. My cheeks flushed. I ducked my head to hide the blush as I busied transferring cookies to the cooling rack.

"Are you here to paint?" I asked when I heard him approach.

"And to see you."

I couldn't stop the wide smile that spread across my face.

He leaned a hip against the counter and snatched a cookie. I grabbed his wrist. The cookie hovered an inch from his mouth. He cocked a brow. My eyes narrowed.

"Those are for Kristen. It's her birthday."

He popped the cookie into his mouth.

"James," I complained. My gaze dipped to his lips, and my thoughts changed to a new channel. How many girls had he kissed with those lips? Did he ever think about kissing me?

My face scorched. He smirked. I gave him an exasperated look and let go of his wrist, returning to my task. "No more," I warned. He would consume the entire batch, no thanks to his football appetite, if given the chance. "I don't have time to bake more."

"One more?" He pushed out his lower lip in a pout.

"Fine," I said, finding him irresistible. I shoved a cookie in his mouth. He grunted.

I nodded at his clothes. "Why are you dressed like that?"

"What's wrong with how I'm dressed?" He gave me an appalled look.

"Nothing!" I gasped. "You look nice . . . I mean, your clothes are nice, that's all," I sputtered. He had to be dressed up for a reason. "So, where are you going?"

"You mean, where have I been?" He lowered his face and took in his outfit as though he'd forgotten what he wore. His expression twisted. "It's Mom's latest scheme to prepare us for a life of board meetings and dinner parties," he groused.

I swiped my hands together, brushing off crumbs. "What's she got you and Thomas doing now?"

His lips twitched. "You look cute in that apron." He tugged the ruffled edge. "Where'd you get it?"

"You're avoiding the question." And distracting me. I pushed his hand away.

"So are you." He snagged my hand and wove our fingers together.

I inhaled sharply. Both our heads dropped to our clasped hands, then quickly rose. We locked gazes. Surprise brightened his brown eyes before a devilish smile spread across his jaw. He lifted our hands, arms bent at the elbow. His free arm looped my waist and tugged me against his chest.

I gasped at the sudden contact. I'd never been this close this way with him before. "What are you doing?"

"Showing you."

"Showing me what?" I squeaked, my voice shooting to the ceiling.

James chuckled. "I'm showing you what I've been up to. Follow my lead. Listen to my count," he murmured by my ear. He pushed into my chest, forcing me back. I stumbled and his hold tightened. He rested his chin on my head.

My entire body went rigid.

I felt him smile into my hair. "You're so tense. It's just me."

Just James. Holding me. I could feel the heat of his skin through my tank top and grimaced. That observation didn't help my naive, overactive imagination in the least, though I did notice his heart was pounding just as fast as mine.

We started moving and he began to count, a whisper in my ear. After a few stumbling missteps and several bruised toes, he moved us smoothly around the kitchen. We were dancing, and not the jump-up-and-down kind we did at the middle school socials but the fancy, grown-up kind.

"You're taking dance lessons."

He hummed in acknowledgment. I felt the vibration to my toes. "We're dancing the waltz."

I leaned back and looked up at him while trying to focus on the footwork. "What does waltzing have to do with meetings and parties?"

He gave me a disgruntled look. "Negotiations. Apparently, Mom wants Thomas and me sharp and quick no matter where we close a deal."

I imagined James in a business suit dancing with a beautiful woman in a silk blouse and pencil skirt. "You dance while you work?" I had no idea that was what people did when they got jobs.

He threw his head back and laughed. "No, you crazy girl. My crazy girl," he murmured into my hair and kissed my head, sending sparks of excitement through me. He'd called me his girl.

"Dad attends a lot of after-hours parties and has closed some big deals at them."

His parents' careers with Donato Enterprises were so different from my parents' work at the restaurant. I pictured their glamorous life. Long gowns and men in tuxedos sipping champagne from cut crystal while a twenty-piece orchestra played in the background.

James twirled us around the kitchen island, bringing me back to the smell of baked chocolate chip cookies and his closer-than-ever nearness. "You're very good at this." Like he was good at everything else he tried, from running precision plays on the football field to his self-taught painting techniques. His acrylic canvases were stunning.

"You make me look good," he complimented, adding, "and you're a fast learner." His breath ruffled my hair. We were dancing a hairbreadth from each other, prompting a thought to slip into my head as smoothly as he moved us in one-two-three-step circles.

"Do you dance this closely with the girls in your class?" I whispered.

James remained quiet for a long moment. I dipped my chin, feeling stupid and embarrassed for asking. But the thought of him holding other girls this way made me ill.

When did I become so jealous of who and where he spent his time?

Since he confided I was his best friend in the world. Since he held me while I cried after Roxanne Livingston stole my underwear in gym class and flung it like a slingshot to the ceiling, where it snagged on the fire sprinkler and was left for the entire school to see. James had wanted to beat the shit out of Roxanne, and I had wanted him for myself for longer than I cared to admit.

"No," James finally said. "Not like this. It's different with you."

My head snapped up.

His expression sobered. "I've wanted to dance with you since I first started lessons."

He had?

James slowed our tempo so we swayed side to side, and then we stopped moving altogether. "There's something else I've wanted to do."

"What's that?"

"Kiss you." And then he did.

My eyes rounded. I squeezed his upper arm. Our lips touched, once, twice, and again. His tongue traced the seam of my mouth and I gasped. He dipped inside. Then he was gone before I had a chance to wrap my head around the fact James was kissing me. My James!

I gawked at him.

He gave me a shy smile. "Hi."

I blinked. "Er . . . hi."

He cocked his head, his expression turning wary. "You OK?"

"Um . . . yeah. I think so."

"You think so?" He laughed, sounding nervous.

I touched my tongue to my lips. They throbbed. Everything throbbed. New, glorious, and spectacular sensations. I felt like the butterfly taking her first flight.

"Why did you kiss me?" I blurted.

"You don't know?" he asked, and I shook my head. He'd mentioned I was his best friend, but that was it. Just a friend.

"You're my best friend, Aimee," he said, echoing my thoughts. My shoulders sagged in disappointment and he curved a finger under my chin, tilting up my face. "Actually, you're more than that to me." His voice lowered, sounding shy. "I've told you before, you know me better than anyone. I've really grown to care about you."

My lips formed a small circle. "Oh," I breathed.

His face split into a grin that glowed brighter than the August sun. He bear-hugged me, lifting me off my feet. "God, I'm glad we're at the same school again. We'll get to see each other more."

"Like we don't see each other enough already?" I teased.

"We haven't seen each other enough this summer." He lowered me to my feet but didn't let go. "Hey, you can slip me notes again in between classes."

I turned crimson.

"I liked your notes. I've missed them."

I smiled shyly. "Then I'll be sure to write you more."

James released me and popped another cookie in his mouth.

"Hey! Stop eating Kristen's cookies."

"Stop making them taste so good." He grabbed my face, cupping my cheeks. I sucked in a breath, the move catching me off guard. He stared at me as if he were in awe. "God, your eyes are beautiful this close up. So blue. Like the Caribbean Sea. Can I kiss you again?"

"Yes, please," I breathed. This was all so new and I was hungry for more. The butterfly in my stomach flapped her wings, ready for another flight. James grinned, and I grinned back, and then we were both laughing and kissing.

"You sure you're OK to be here?" I asked after a few moments, thinking how upset his parents would be when they learned James ditched football practice.

"Don't worry about me. They'll never know. I'll get home before them." He kissed my nose to appease me.

The house phone rang and I jumped away from James. He laughed. "It's the phone, Aimee. Not your parents walking in on us."

"Ha, ha," I smarted, my cheeks turning brighter than an oven heat coil. I answered the phone, watching James roll up his sleeves and empty his pockets onto the counter—wallet, a receipt, change, and keys to the BMW 323ci his parents had bought for his sixteenth birthday. He wandered into the sunroom, where his art studio was set up in the corner.

I listened to Thomas on the other end of the line, looking for James. As Thomas spoke, my smile fell, and when he finished, I hung up the phone, noticing James had been watching me.

He frowned. "You OK?"

"You have to go. Your mom's on her way home. Phil's with her."

James swore. He didn't get along with his cousin. Once, he had caught Phil snooping through his desk. I knew James kept all the trinkets and cards I'd given him in the bottom drawer. He also kept the notes and letters I'd written him, too. Had Phil read them? James wasn't sure, but he did remark that a picture of us was missing. James and I were eating Popsicles, his arm casually draped across my shoulders. I was twelve and wearing my first bikini, which I'd cajoled Mom into buying on the condition Dad would never see me wearing it. The sight of his little girl in a scrap of material would be too much for him. So, when Kristen's mom gave me the picture for my scrapbook, I gave it to James. I didn't want Dad to find the photo, which didn't seem as big a deal now that I worried Phil had taken it.

James glanced around the kitchen, rubbing his forearms, thinking. "I should go."

"James, your dad—"

He rolled his eyes my way. "What about him?"

"He's home. And he's asking for you."

All the color drained from his face.

"James?"

"Gotta run. I'll call you later." He grabbed his keys off the counter and bolted for the door.

"James! Your wallet."

The front door slammed. I grabbed the wallet, which had his driver's license. He would need it on him if he planned driving anywhere besides the two blocks home.

I raced out the front door in time to catch his BMW turning the corner. I sprinted to his house, hoping to reach him before he went inside. I caught him on the walkway to his porch.

"James!" I huffed.

He whirled, eyes rounding as I came to a full stop on the sidewalk by his car. I bent over, hands on knees, and sucked in air. Lifting my head, I held out my arm. "Your wallet."

He blinked, his hands automatically going to his back pockets and finding them empty. He approached and took the wallet. "Thanks," he said, his gaze tracking a car behind me.

I looked over my shoulder to see Mrs. Donato pulling into the driveway. Phil sat in the front passenger seat, his eyes on me.

"Go home, Aimee," James ordered.

I turned back around. Edgar Donato stood on the porch, mouth pressed in a flat line. He held the door open, waiting for James.

James glanced over his shoulder. "Go home," he said again. There was an edge to his tone. "Please," he added when I didn't move.

My gaze jumped from him to Edgar and back.

His expression softened. He cupped my face, brushed his thumb along my cheekbone. "I'll be fine. Go home. I'll call you tonight."

"OK."

I watched him move into the house, pride keeping his shoulders back and spine straight. Edgar gave me a cursory glance and followed James into the house, yanking his leather belt from his pants.

I gasped, recalling James's story about Thomas's welts. *Oh, James!*

"Hey, Aimee."

I jolted, looking anxiously up at Phil, who stood one sidewalk line from me. He grinned. "Long time no see."

My anxiety, which I attributed more to James's predicament than Phil's unexpected appearance by my side, eased with his smile. He'd changed since we'd met five years ago. I found it extraordinary we hadn't seen each other since, considering how frequently he visited his aunt.

Phil's stature was still leaner and taller than either James or Thomas, and the tailored pants and shirt he wore added years to his nineteen. He looked refined and turgid. He was so much older than me, and so out of my league. I didn't understand the world the Donatos lived in, one with expensive clothes and cars, dinner parties and social functions. A lifestyle people like me saw only on TV. It was intimidating. Phil was intimidating.

I glanced at the house, twisting my fingers. "Will James be OK?"

Phil shrugged. "Edgar seemed angry. What did James do?"

"He bailed on football practice." As soon as the words left me, my stomach pitched. This wasn't any of Phil's business.

He chuckled. "So, the Golden Boy isn't so golden after all." He lifted his arm toward my house. "Walk you home?"

"Um . . . OK," I heard myself agree.

We walked at a slow pace, nothing near my leg-pumping sprint a few moments ago. My breathing was still erratic and sweat dripped from my hairline and down my neck. I tugged my shirt, fanning my chest. From the corner of my eye, I noticed Phil's gaze track my movements. I stopped messing with my shirt, suddenly self-conscious of the small breasts that finally had made an appearance this past year.

"You've grown since I last saw you," Phil remarked.

My cheeks, flushed and damp from running, scorched. I dipped my head and my eyes widened. I still wore the frilly apron from baking cookies. I yanked it off.

"You look cute. It suits you."

I crumpled the apron into a ball and crossed my arms, hiding the offending article and my breasts. "How long are you visiting?" I asked, steering the conversation from Phil's blatant inspection of me. I picked up my pace, wanting to get home.

"Not long. A few days."

"So, your dad's traveling again?"

His mouth quirked on one side. He was laughing at me. He didn't need a caregiver while his dad was away, not like when I'd first met him. He was a college student. Sheesh, what a stupid question.

Phil's expression turned serious, verging on worried. Was he thinking about James? I was worried, too. I couldn't get rid of the image of Mr. Donato removing his leather belt, anger reddening the cheeks that spilled over a too-tight shirt collar. He'd put on a good deal of weight the past couple of years.

"James will be OK, right?" I asked again, needing the reassurance. "Mr. Donato looked really intense."

"James will be fine. Edgar's stressed, that's all."

And he wanted to take it out on James? I gave Phil a panicked look.

He scratched his chin. "Look, Aimee, my dad's sick. Edgar's had to take charge at Donato Enterprises until I'm old enough to take over. I still have two years of college."

Two things struck me about his explanation. James hadn't been the person on his mind and his dad was dying. Boy, how selfish could I be? James's kiss and his impending punishment had me rattled.

"I'm sorry about your dad. That's nice he's giving you the company, though. You don't have to find a job or anything once you graduate."

"That's the idea. Dad told me a long time ago when I was a little kid he'd want me to take over one day." He stopped. We'd arrived at my house.

"Thanks for the walk," I said.

"Anytime."

I gave him a short wave, walking backward toward the porch.

"And thank you," he added, "about my dad. That means a lot. Hey!" he called when I reached the door. "Does James still paint at your house?"

My hand froze on the doorknob. How did he know James painted? Phil had given me the idea to keep James's supplies, but I'd never told him. James wouldn't have either. Outside of my parents, Kristen and Nick were the only two who knew about James's studio in our sunroom, and neither of them would have risked telling Thomas or Phil else James's parents find out.

Then I recalled my notes in James's desk. More than once I'd written to James, asking if he planned to come over after school and paint, slipping my questions to him as we passed in the hallway at middle school. Phil must have read the notes.

My heart sank into my stomach, and my expression must have given away the answer because Phil's face spilt into a large I-know-your-secret grin. I felt the blood rush to my toes.

Phil shook his head. "Don't worry. James's secret is safe with me. But I would love to see his work." He started walking toward me.

I swallowed. My hand twisted the knob and the front door cracked open. "I can't invite strangers into the house when my parents aren't home."

"But I'm not a stranger. In fact," he stopped at the porch step, "if things don't work out with James, I'd love to take you out."

I balked. Was he serious? Phil was so much older.

"I'm sorry, I can't have anyone inside. 'Bye, Phil." I slipped into the house. I wanted to put the door between us as quickly as possible.

"Think about it, Aimee. I've thought about you a lot over the years. It would be fun." He saluted, touching the tips of two fingers to his lips and waving them in my direction before he disappeared from my line of sight. The front door had closed.

I flipped the lock and turned around, sinking to the floor, my back against the door. I covered my face with my hands. *Eww!* Phil had asked me out. He knew about James's paintings and it was my fault. I never should have mentioned anything in the notes. Then again, James shouldn't have kept them. But that was James, and I couldn't blame him. He was sentimental. A gifted artist with a caring soul.

It would be another two years before I saw Phil again, and only sparingly thereafter, such as during the Sunday dinners Claire and Edgar hosted. Phil joined us every so often. Thankfully, he never asked about James's artwork again.

As for James, our kiss that day was only the beginning. With it, we'd crossed the bridge from friendship to a deeper relationship that grew more intimate with the passage of time. James never confessed his father punished him with the belt, though he did hiss and shift out of reach when my hand accidentally brushed over his lower back. He blamed it on a pulled muscle from football practice, so I didn't ask if that was really the cause of his pain. I didn't want to make him any more uncomfortable than he already felt. I could tell he was ashamed he'd disobeyed his father. He made a point to never miss another football practice for the rest of high school.

CHAPTER 13

JULY

One year after James's funeral, Aimee's was ready to open for business. Looking back, I never imagined coming this far or accomplishing so much. I never fathomed the life of a single, independent business owner would be my life. Then again, I'd never imagined a life without James.

But I had done it, and was surprisingly happy and pleased, despite the chaos of construction and doubts. Doubts about my abilities, and my doubts surrounding James's death. I kept those thoughts to myself. Bottled up and sealed tight. Other than a Mexican resort's business card, I still didn't have proof to fully convince myself James was alive. I just needed to figure out a way to start looking without my parents, Thomas, and friends thinking I was losing my mind, that I believed what a psychic told me despite witnessing James's burial. There were times I thought I was going crazy, like having hallucinations in a public bathroom.

The last nine months had gone by in a whirl of activity. My parents often visited to check on the progress at Aimee's. Ian frequently stopped by, too, taking breaks from editing photos. He would double-check the construction, claiming he wanted to make sure the subs weren't taking advantage of me. Cutting corners and skimping on quality work. I told him that was what I had Nadia for. No one messed with her. But I knew Ian used it as an excuse to spend time with me so I let him inspect the work. I liked having him around.

When July arrived, employees had been hired and trained, and supplies stocked on shelves. The pungent odors of paint and plaster dissipated, replaced with the robust, nutty scents of coffees and pastries. Everything was in place.

It was a late Saturday afternoon, the day before Aimee's soft launch where family and friends would test the menu and my staff could practice their training. So far, there hadn't been any major glitches to push out next week's grand opening. Well, until now. Gina, my shift manager and lead barista, quit. A friend had invited her to share a flat in London. She was leaving tomorrow morning.

Less than twenty-four hours before the soft launch and I had no experienced baristas. Ryan and Jilly had been trained by Gina.

I paced the length of the counter. Aimee's was a custom-order coffeehouse. I might be able to swing tomorrow without a lead barista, but before the official opening I needed someone who understood how to mix beans, syrups, and spices. I needed someone who understood the equipment and its quirks. What if something went wrong?

The bell over the door jingled and Ian walked inside. *Ian!*

Saved by the bell. Literally.

I rushed over. "I need your help."

He gripped my shoulders. "What's wrong? Are you hurt?" His eyes drifted over my length.

"Gina just quit," I explained, adding, "Tomorrow's the soft launch." As if he didn't already know.

A cocky grin stretched across his jaw. "You do need my help. Blending coffee, I presume?"

"Stop looking so smug." He crossed his arms and I huffed. "Yes, Ian. I need your help. Now is the time you can demonstrate your brilliance behind the coffee bar."

"Ye of little faith." He moved to the espresso machine as if he owned the place and I rolled my eyes. His gaze roamed over the rows of bean canisters, syrups, and coffee mugs.

Ian had spent a lot of time at my house since we met. We watched movies or just talked. I experimented with new recipes—stews, tarts, breads—and he taste tested. On one occasion, I found him flipping through my binder of blended drink recipes. I'd teased he didn't have to feign interest. The next day, he showed up with several coffee recipes of his own and I added them to my selection after I'd mocked his amateur palate. When I'd mixed them, they were damn good.

He gave me a challenging look over the machine. "Did you forget our deal?"

I grimaced, recalling our discussion on the first day we met. Judging by the recipes he added to my binder, there was an excellent chance Ian could brew better coffee.

Time for me to eat crow.

"No, I haven't forgotten." My eyes narrowed. He was so going to lose. "All right, you're on, but I want you to make this specialty blend." Leaning over the counter, I retrieved my binder and flipped to the Pangi Hazelnut Latte, named after a region in India where the hazelnut was produced. It was the most difficult recipe and called for a unique blend of imported beans and spices. Gina had a tough time replicating the drink. If the spices were slightly off, it wouldn't produce the same exquisite flavor.

Ian read the directions. He rubbed his hands together. "Watch and learn, sweetheart."

I snorted and propped a hip against the counter ledge. He moved about the station, selecting and grinding beans, then extracting the espresso. A dark, rich liquid dripped into the mug he had preheated. I breathed in the heady aroma and my anxiety eased.

Ian steamed milk and poured it into the espresso with a wiggle motion. He grinned and handed me the mug. On the surface was a heart shaped in cream. An exact replica of the heart-shaped steam above the coffee mug in Aimee's logo.

"You can do coffee art," I murmured. "I think I'm in love."

His eyes flashed. "Taste it."

I lifted the cup to my nose. Hazelnut, cinnamon, and something else. "You changed the recipe."

"Drink before you judge."

I did, and my insides turned to warm jelly. "Ginger . . . and?"

He looked at me expectantly.

"Cardamom."

He nodded.

"This is good." I took another sip. "Really, really good . . . oh my. This is sinful." I drank some more. "You're hired."

"Excellent. When do I start?"

I looked at him, trying to figure out if he was serious.

He folded the towel and moved around the counter. "You need a shift manager who knows what the hell he's doing and I need a job."

"What about your photography?"

"I still plan to travel and show my work. It's not about the money. I like to keep busy between trips. Why do you think I putz around here all day?"

"You're bored?" I asked, deflated. "I thought it was because you liked hanging out with me."

He ran a finger down my cheek. "Don't look so dejected. I do like hanging out with you. A lot."

My skin heated from my forehead to chest. He smiled. "I don't plan to take any extended trips for a while. For now, just short excursions, a few days here or there. I'll train the staff to step in when I'm gone. What do you say?" He held out his hand.

What do I say? His offer was lifesaving, and I'd get to see him every day. Not that I hadn't already seen him almost every day since we met. I clasped his hand. "We have a deal. Let me grab the employment paperwork. I'll be right back."

While Ian completed the forms, I finished hanging James's paintings, what I'd been doing before Gina's call. Where there had once been eight large boxes of canvases in my garage, I had only twelve paintings left to display, not counting the ones hanging on my walls at home. Thomas's warehouse manager had never located James's artwork. The police couldn't do much either. I'd filed a report months after I realized they were missing, and I wasn't entirely convinced they'd been stolen. No evidence of forced entry, no fingerprints when the police had dusted, and nothing else in the garage was gone.

Ian crossed the room and held the ladder. "I haven't seen these. They're amazing."

I climbed down after I'd hung the painting. "They were in the garage. I had more, but I can't find them."

"Did they disappear into thin air?" He spread his fingers wide and mouthed *poof.*

"Pretty much. I've looked for them. Filed a police report, too."

Ian studied me. "Sorry about that. He was very talented."

"Yes, he was." I motioned toward the adjoining wall. "It waits patiently for your masterpieces."

"Are you home tonight?" he asked, adding when I nodded, "I'll bring some over. You can pick the ones you want and I'll hang them first thing in the morning."

"Only if you promise not to speak French when you do."

Ian arrived a little before eight, right after I'd finished icing a lemon blueberry cake. He stood on the porch dressed in jeans and a black shirt. He gave me a lopsided grin. I opened the door wider and he lugged inside a large, flat canvas carrier. "I have more in the car. Where can I put this one?" I pointed at the dining table and he gently laid the bag on the surface, unzipping the carrier. "I have three here. Two you can display. I'll give you a percentage if they sell. The other photo is yours."

"Mine?" I moved to stand behind him.

He removed the largest frame from the carrier and faced me. *Belize Sunrise.* I gaped, my eyes flying to his. "For you," he offered.

"Ian . . . ?" My mouth worked. "I thought you sold it."

He shook his head. "I took it off the market for you. It's a gift." He'd been holding on to it for almost a year, waiting for the right moment to give it to me.

My stomach churned. I twisted James's ring before touching the wood frame finished to look like weathered boards from a pier. I thought of the price tag. "I can't take this."

He glanced at the walls covered with James's paintings. "If there's no room here, display it at the café."

"Oh, no, that's not why. It's too expensive." But my fingers itched to take the print from his hand.

He wiggled the frame. "You know you want it."

"Yeah, I do." And it meant a lot to Ian for me to have it. I couldn't deny him the satisfaction. "Thank you so much."

"You're welcome." He leaned the photo against a chair.

"I was thinking about this picture when I selected the café's color palette," I admitted. He seemed surprised and I touched his arm. "I love your work."

A dark intensity filled his eyes. His jaw tightened. "Thank you."

A strange desire rose in me and I yanked my gaze away. "Do you want a beer?" My voice sounded strained, high-pitched.

Ian took a breath, propped his hands on his hips. "Yeah."

I grabbed two bottles from the fridge and popped the tops, handing one to Ian. I watched his throat ripple with each gulp and I involuntarily swallowed. His nostrils flared. "What do I smell?" His eyes narrowed on the countertop. "Is that cake?"

"Lemon blueberry cake."

He gave me a devilish grin. "Need a taste tester?"

I scrunched my face. "Beer and cake?"

"Sure. Why not?" he said, searching the kitchen drawers. "Jackpot." He found the cake cutter. I retrieved two plates from the cabinet as he sliced into the cake. Fruit filling oozed from the center. "What's in here?"

"Blueberries. I made it with fresh berries, not the canned stuff."

He groaned, adding a slice to the plate nearest him.

"The cream cheese frosting is made with lemon curd, juice, and zest. Try some." Without thinking, I drew a finger through the frosting and held it to his mouth. Ian's eyes flared a split second before his lips closed around the tip. I felt his tongue lick away the frosting and electricity zinged to my core. My eyes widened. *Oh God.* That felt entirely too good.

I pulled my finger from his lip seal. A low pop resounded through the kitchen and Ian chuckled, a deep, sexy rumble. My cheeks flamed, but not nearly as hot as the current blazing deep inside me.

He watched me, assessing my reaction. Slowly, he took a bite of blueberry-soaked cake. Again, the ripple of his throat caught my attention and my own throat went dry. "You have a winner," he murmured, licking frosting from his lip.

Ian was standing entirely too close. I locked my knees to keep from falling against him. I often wondered what it would feel like wrapped in his embrace, his tongue flicking mine the way it had the frosting on my fingertip. I knew it would feel different from anything I'd felt with anyone before. He'd feel different from James. Maybe even better.

But Ian was a friend, and I'd made it clear from the beginning that was all he was to me despite my attraction toward him.

I blinked and turned away. "So, what else did you bring?"

He set down his plate and extracted two more framed photos from the case, leaning them against the back of the couch. *Misty Morning*, a photo of an aspen grove he told me he'd taken in the Sierra Nevada, and *Twilight Sands.* "The Dubai picture." I smiled deviously.

Ian looked at me warily. "What?"

"You promised me a story. What *is* it about this picture?"

He grimaced. "I hate camels."

"That's all?"

He crossed his arms. "They hate me, too. Well, that one did." He pointed at the last camel in line. Ian retrieved his beer and sank onto the couch, patting the cushion beside him. I sat down, tucking my legs underneath. He stretched his arm along the couch back. "Riding animals isn't my favorite."

"Ah, yes. The mules in Peru."

"That's right." He drank his beer. "It was a long ride trying to find the perfect dune for the shot. Every dune we passed before the one in the photo, that beast tossed me. The steeper the incline, the better for him because I would roll down, then have to climb back up. I was a walking sandbag by the end of the day. The stuff was in my hair, clothes, and"—he grinned around the mouth of his bottle—"you get the idea. My camera equipment didn't fare so well either."

"Oh dear."

"I'll say. It was an expensive trip. Won't be doing that again anytime soon."

"And the aspens?"

He put his half-full bottle on the table and faced me. "Another story for another day." His gaze dropped to my lips and my skin tightened. The room quieted except for the hum of the air conditioner, the occasional passing car outside, and our mingled breaths. The electricity

I'd felt between us earlier in the kitchen returned, charging the space between us. It acted like a magnet, pulling us toward each other. He slowly, almost cautiously, leaned toward me. My eyelids drifted close and lips parted.

"Don't," I whispered when his lips hovered above mine.

He stilled but didn't pull away.

"I really like you, Ian," I heard myself admit.

A low laugh rumbled in his throat. I could feel his smile in the subtle disturbance of the air between us.

"That's a good thing," he murmured.

"I'm really attracted to you, too." I moistened my lips. "But . . ."

"But?" he prompted when I hesitated.

Nerves danced up my back. I swallowed. When I didn't say anything, he leaned away. His brow pulled in and he slowly rubbed his bottom lip.

I set my beer beside Ian's and went over to the fireplace, standing underneath the engagement portrait. I needed the distance between us to say what I had to say.

"I want you to know that I . . ." My face heated with a deep blush. I swallowed. "I want you. I feel this thing happening between us."

His finger stilled on his lip. His eyes flared.

I shook my head, stopping him when he reached for me. "No, don't. Hear me out. I can't act on it. Actually, I won't. Not while . . ." I hesitated and inhaled deeply, collecting my courage. Ian had become just as good a friend as Nadia and Kristen with the potential to be so much more. I trusted him and found it very easy to talk with him about almost everything. Everything except my doubts about James's death.

Ian knew how long James and I had dated, and how difficult it was for me to suddenly find myself alone. Every dream and plan of ours had shattered in an instant like a windshield in a car accident. Unstoppable and explosive. As I picked up the pieces, Ian had laughed with me over some of the stories I shared about my years with James. On other occasions, he gave me the wide, solid expanse of his chest to cry on. If anyone deserved to know the truth about what plagued me, it was Ian.

"If you learned someone you'd lost was still alive, but you had no idea where they were, what would you do?"

The lines on his face deepened. He sharply inhaled, pausing before he answered. "I'd search every corner of the earth."

I pressed my lips flat and nodded tightly. Maybe that was what I needed to do, and I'd start with Puerto Escondido, Mexico.

Ian cocked his head, regarding me. "What's going on?"

"I have reason to believe James is still alive," I blurted.

Ian's eyebrows shot to the ceiling. He gave his head a slight shake. "What?"

"I think James is still alive," I whispered.

"How? Why?" he sputtered. "Didn't you bury him?"

I nodded. "But I never saw his body."

"That doesn't mean . . ." He stopped and rubbed his face with both hands. Leaning forward, he propped his elbows on his knees. "Why do you think he's . . ." He circled his hand in the air, unable to say the words.

"Why do I think he's alive?" I asked him, twisting my engagement ring. "It's a pretty far-fetched story."

"You don't think I'll believe you. That's why you haven't told me."

I nodded.

"Have you told anyone?"

I shook my head, spinning the ring faster.

We watched each other for a tense moment until he sighed deeply and reached an arm toward me. "Come here. Tell me everything."

I clasped his fingers and let him pull me down onto the couch. He didn't release my hand, resting our linked fingers on his thigh as we faced each other. He stretched his other arm across the couch back. Before I lost the nerve, I told him about the psychic at James's funeral, about how I'd driven to her house and dropped my wallet in the street in my rush to leave. And I told him how she'd slipped the business card to Casa del sol in my wallet when she returned it.

"You think James is living at that hotel?"

I lifted a shoulder. "I honestly don't know what to think." But I explained to him when I considered Lacy's warnings, the strange visions in the nightclub restroom, how James's paintings were missing, plus the fact I hadn't seen the body Thomas alleged he retrieved from Mexico, questions surfaced. While I wanted Ian to understand why he couldn't be anything more than a friend to me until I erased my doubts, part of me needed his reassurance those doubts were warranted.

Ian was quiet for several breaths and I shifted uneasily. "You think I'm crazy for believing that psychic."

"Do you believe her? Look, Aimee," he started before I could answer him, inching closer to me on the couch. Our knees pressed together. "I don't think it's too far-fetched to believe what a stranger tells you over those you trust, especially when you're vulnerable and grieving. That's being human. Here, I have a story to share." He settled farther back into the couch and tucked me closer into his side. "During my travels, I see some weird shit, stuff I have trouble believing to this day. There are things out there we can't explain. I still can't figure how the psychic my dad hired found me."

"Really? What happened?"

He played with the hair draping my shoulder. "My mother wasn't quite right up here." He tapped his index against my temple. "She'd disappear for long periods. Dad wasn't around much either. But once, when I was nine, back when we were living in Idaho, I was the one who disappeared. I'd been missing for five days before Dad found me. The police weren't getting anywhere so he'd hired a psychic to help. She told me magic showed her where I'd been hiding. I'll never forget what she looked like, blonde hair so long and fair it was almost white. She had the strangest colored eyes, too. I thought she was an angel."

"An angel," I repeated. Fair and ethereal like Lacy. My neck prickled.

"Humph." Ian shook his head and looked askance at me. The corner of his mouth lifted into a half smile. "I've never told anyone this before."

I was glad he had told me. It made me feel better about mine, less crazy.

He brushed the back of his hand along my cheek and his gaze stole to the engagement portrait. "You and James were together for a long time. I get how letting go of him must be hard for you. Just promise me you're not using the psychic as an excuse to keep yourself from falling in love again." His gaze bore into me. "Because I've already fallen for you."

CHAPTER 14

Ian was waiting at the café's entrance when I arrived at five the next morning. He arranged his pictures on the wall and I admired his work, pleased I'd been right. *Belize Sunrise* fit perfectly with the café's décor.

He climbed down the ladder. "Why are you grinning?"

"I knew your picture would look good here."

He tossed the hammer into the toolbox. "My pictures *always* look good," he retorted, and I play-slapped his shoulder.

When the staff arrived, I updated them about Gina, introducing Ian as her replacement. Aside from my chef, Mandy, who I'd worked with at The Goat, and my baristas, Ryan and Jilly, I had four waitresses and one waiter. Only two were working the soft launch, Emily and Faith. About ten minutes before opening I gathered everyone around. Today was a test-drive. Evaluate the workflow, sample the menu, and work out the kinks. Only friends and family had been invited and everything was on the house.

I was proud of the café's layout and décor, pleased with the menu Mandy and I had created, and ecstatic about the expansive selection of brewed coffees. Then I saw my parents standing outside the windows and my throat clogged with nerves.

"Look at me," Ian whispered in my ear.

I turned around. His eyes warmed and he cupped my cheek. "Everything will be fine. You'll be fine."

I nodded rapidly.

He peeked at his watch and grinned. "It's time."

"All right." I nodded, lips pressed tight.

He unlocked the doors and I froze. "Wait!"

He cocked a brow and I wiped my palms against my thighs. James should have been here. He would have wanted to see this. Somehow, it didn't seem fair Ian was the one beside me. But I didn't want him anywhere else but where he was. Next to me. I latched on to his hand.

He squeezed my fingers. "It's OK. I'm with you every step of the way."

That was exactly what I needed to hear. I took a deep breath and opened the doors, welcoming family and friends. A gust of wind blasted my face, carrying James's voice.

You did it, Aimee.

The soft launch could not have run smoother. Ian was a genius behind the espresso bar, blending coffees as fast as they were ordered. Ryan and Jilly barely kept up with him, but they were learning. Ian poured custom samples for Emily and Faith to distribute, further adding to my already expansive menu. Mandy's zucchini fritters and Thai chicken panini with mixed greens were sensational.

I watched Emily serve my parents and my heart raced.

"Relax," Ian murmured from behind me.

I inhaled deeply. He smelled of sandalwood and soap, with a dash of cinnamon mixed in. "They've spent their lives in the restaurant industry."

"So have you." He massaged my shoulders. "Stop twisting your apron."

I let go of the material bunched in my fists. "What if they don't like the food? What if Emily spills water in their laps? What if—?"

"They're your parents. Go talk to them."

I inhaled deeply. "You're right." Without thinking, I rose to my toes and gave him a quick kiss on the lips. It seemed the natural thing to do but surprised us both. For a moment, we stared at each other, stunned. Ian recovered first. He touched his thumb to my bottom lip, then let his arm fall.

"Sorry." I twisted my ring.

"Don't be."

I looked over at my parents. Ian pushed me in their direction. "Go."

I dragged a spare chair from an empty table and glanced at Ian over my shoulder. He gave me a smile that made my stomach flip before turning back to the espresso machine. I sat down between Mom and Dad. "Well?" I asked on a deep breath. "What do you think?"

Dad's eyes were misty and mine immediately sheened. He broke into a smile. "I'm so proud of you."

"These fritters are delicious," Mom said after a mouthful. "Tell Mandy I said so."

"Really? You like it?" I leaned back in the chair. "Thank God. I've been so nervous."

Mom sliced into her fritter. "Thank *you* for hiring Mandy. After we laid everyone off, I was worried. Many of them had been with us for years. They were like family." She rubbed my arm. "Your café is lovely."

I rested my hand over hers. "It was a lot of work."

"You pulled it off beautifully." Her eyes softened. "The way you've bounced back after last year. Your father and I—" She broke off and rubbed her eyes, nodding at my father.

"We knew you could do it, kiddo," Dad finished for her.

Mom sipped her water. "Why's Ian behind the bar?"

"Gina quit yesterday."

She hummed, watching Ian. "How convenient."

Dad smacked my back. "One of the perks of business ownership. Get used to it. Gina won't be the last employee who quits without notice."

Ian must have felt the weight of our stares. He lifted his head and saluted.

Soon Nadia arrived with Mark, the commercial property broker she'd met at Ian's showing. The one who had a wife. I quirked a brow when I saw them together. "It's business," she confessed.

"On a Sunday?"

"He wants to open a restaurant and I'm showing him the work I did here."

I raised my hands in defense. "Whatever you say."

"We're not dating," she insisted. "He just separated from his wife."

I glanced at Mark, who was talking with Nick, but his eyes were on Nadia, his expression one of adoration. He was definitely interested in Nadia and I told her so. I wanted her to find some happiness, too.

Nadia watched Mark. A hint of a smile appeared when Mark shook Nick's hand.

"Dating Mark might not be such a bad idea," I encouraged. "After he's divorced, of course."

Kristen busied herself taking pictures. "I'll e-mail them to you. Use them for your website, or print for your community board. You do have a community board, right?" She glanced around.

"Guess I better get one." I scratched a quick note on the memo pad I carried in my apron. My to-do list before next week was growing.

A couple of hours later, I meandered through the dining area, stopping at each table to ask about the food and service. I found Thomas sitting alone at a small table in the corner. The same spot where James and I had sat at Joe's Coffee House. I sat across from him. There were shadows underneath his eyes as he stared at James's paintings. "He was talented. He'd be honored you share them."

"I wish I had more." These paintings weren't his best work.

"I wish I'd found them for you."

A question formed in my mind, and as it took shape, I was appalled that I hadn't thought to ask it before. "Thomas," I started cautiously, "your mother didn't take his paintings, did she?" Maybe she had wanted something of James's to remember him by, or worse, had the paintings destroyed. Phil could have stolen them. And what about Thomas? Had he taken them and been too embarrassed to admit he'd removed the boxes from my garage? I'd been distraught, practically bawling, when I first asked him to look for them.

"I doubt it. She was never interested in his artwork."

I released the breath I'd been holding. While I was relieved she most likely didn't have them in her possession, I was still disappointed. At least I would have known where they'd gone. "Do you mind asking her?"

He shook his head, sucked down his coffee. Black, no cream. Then he smiled, his expression melancholy. "You've accomplished a lot in one year."

I glanced around the café, taking in the noise. Pots clanging in the kitchen. Mandy hollering orders. Ian grinding beans. The hiss and steam of the espresso machine. Glancing at my hands, my fingers fluttered, removing imaginary dirt from under the nails. "I still feel him, in here," I pressed my hand flat above my breasts. "Which makes it difficult to believe he's dead. I still feel that way, even after a year. Do you think," I began, hesitant, peeking up at him from under my lashes. I took a deep breath and pushed out my question before I lost the nerve. "Do you think the body we buried could be someone else?"

Thomas jerked. His eyes narrowed for a brief second before the tension receded like the ocean before a tsunami. "No," he said almost too calmly. "It's James."

My question had upset him, which didn't offer me any reassurance. "I'm sorry. Forget I asked."

He shook his head. "I feel the same, Aimee."

I still pressed my lips flat and nodded.

He pushed his mug away. "Thanks for the coffee. It was good." Standing, he smoothed the creases in his pants. "I'm glad Joe reconsidered your application. I knew you'd do a great job with this place."

My eyes narrowed as I eased to my feet. How had he known Joe gave me a second chance? I hadn't told Thomas anything about Joe initially rejecting my application. He had reconsidered before I ever had the chance to call Thomas and ask him to cosign.

Thomas looked past my shoulder and his face hardened. I followed his gaze and saw nothing out of the ordinary, only people in line to order and the door closing behind someone who'd just left. His face had gone red when I turned back.

"You OK?"

"Fine," he bit out. "I thought I recognized someone." He pushed in his chair and walked out after a quick good-bye.

I cleared his table. Emily interceded on my way to the kitchen. "The woman at table eight asked me to give you this." She handed me a postcard and hurried off to serve another table.

Table eight was empty. Whoever had been there was gone. I looked at the postcard and my world tumbled. It was a promotion for an art gallery in Mexico, El estudio del pintor. On the front was a paintbrush graphic, the tip dipped in the familiar Caribbean blue paint James used for his signature, and underneath, an image of one of James's missing paintings. *What the—?*

A loud crash resounded in the kitchen. Heads popped up, looking in that direction. I slipped the card into my apron pocket and rushed to the kitchen. My hands shook violently as I crouched on the floor, assisting Mandy with the broken dishes. I dropped more pieces back on the floor than I dumped in the trash.

Mandy impatiently shooed me aside and I excused myself to the restroom. I collapsed against the locked door, my breaths heavy as shock settled over me. With shaking fingers, I slowly withdrew the postcard from my pocket and stared. Sweat bloomed along my hairline. How was this possible?

"Aimee!" Emily knocked on the door. "Are you in there?"

I jolted. "Yes. Give me a moment."

"Mandy needs you in the kitchen."

"Tell her I'll be right there," I called out.

I slipped the card back into the apron and tucked the enormity of what it meant to the back of my mind. For now. I had to focus on getting through this day.

~

On the seventy-five-inch plasma screen in the Donatos' library, the New York Mets pitcher wound up on the mound at San Francisco's AT&T Park. It was bottom of the ninth against the Giants with the bases loaded. The Mets were up by three. The pitcher launched the ball toward home plate. It sliced through the air at ninety-two miles an hour and connected dead-on with Barry Bonds's bat. *Crack!* The ball soared over the field and dropped into a fan's leather glove, two rows behind the wall in the bleacher section. Home run!

James and Thomas leaped from their seats. They whooped and hollered, smacking each other's palms in high tens.

"Game over!" Thomas clapped his hands. "Time to pay up."

Edgar Donato swore. He leaned sideways in his leather chair and tugged out his wallet. He removed two hundred-dollar bills. "Have I mentioned, Aimee, how disappointed I am neither of my sons has remained faithful to the Mets?"

"Yes, you have, sir. More than once." We shared a smile. The Donatos had moved to Los Gatos from New York. Both Thomas and James quickly switched their loyalty to the San Francisco 49ers and Giants.

Edgar gave each of his sons a bill, and Thomas and James exchanged a fist bump. James bent over, cradled my face in his hands, and gave me a loud, wet kiss on the lips. "I'm buying us dinner, babe, later this week."

"Sounds like a plan." I grinned against his mouth.

James straightened and stuffed the cash into his front pocket. "You'll have to meet me in Palo Alto. I have exams this week so I can't get back down here."

Edgar lit a cigar, and the tobacco flared bright orange as he stoked the flame with short inhales. "Tell me, Aimee," he said, exhaling a lungful of smoke, "have you given any more thought to your plans after high school?"

"Yes, sir, I have." I shifted on my end of the couch to face him in the chair beside me. Graduation was in six weeks. I was nervous, anxious, and excited. "You already know I'll be at De Anza College for the next two years so I can continue helping my parents at The Goat, but after that I plan to apply to the California Culinary Academy in San Francisco, finish my degree there."

"Good thinking on your part." Edgar nodded, hands fisted on his knees. The cigar smoke curled upward, creating a hazy screen between us. "You'll be ready to take over when your parents retire."

James rolled his eyes. It was the same story with Edgar. Parents had the responsibility to leave a legacy for their offspring, and the offspring had a responsibility to be ready to take on that legacy.

"I guess that's the idea," I acquiesced.

"I think she should open her own restaurant after she graduates." James took my empty glass and moved to the bar. Behind me, I heard the pop and fizz as he opened a can and poured me another Coke.

"I don't know." I shrugged. "Perhaps I will have my own place, someday. My parents need me first, though."

Thomas followed James to the bar and poured himself another whiskey. "If you open a restaurant, I'll eat there every day."

I laughed, looking at Thomas over my shoulder. "You'll get fat."

Thomas lifted the whiskey bottle in Edgar's direction, who nodded.

"I like your parents' food at The Goat," Edgar said.

I gawked at him. "You've eaten there?"

"Several times."

My parents never mentioned they'd seen James's parents there. I had the impression their pub was beneath the Donatos' tastes.

Claire entered the room and announced, "Marie will have dinner ready in a few moments."

"Good." Thomas glanced at his watch. "I have to get home and prepare a proposal for the Chahaya Teak account. I fly to Indonesia on Tuesday."

Thomas had recently graduated from Stanford University. At twenty-two, he was already managing several of Donato Enterprises' larger accounts.

Footfalls echoed down the hallway.

"Phil, darling! I didn't expect to see you," Claire exclaimed, her face lighting up. "Are you joining us for dinner?"

All heads turned to Phil, who'd entered the room. He hugged Claire, whispering in her ear. His eyes scanned the room until they landed on Mr. Donato.

"I need a word, Edgar," he said, moving out of Claire's embrace.

Edgar rose to his feet, tugging out the creases in his pants. "After dinner."

"You killed the Costas deal," Phil accused, ignoring Edgar's request. "Why?"

Edgar's face turned red. His eyes narrowed on Phil. "It's Sunday. I said, we'll discuss this later."

"No! We'll discuss it now," Phil exploded. I jumped in my seat. James stiffened, his spine elongating. Thomas narrowed his eyes.

Phil moved farther into the room, stopping behind the couch, where he towered above me. "You've ignored my calls all week."

His voice blasted in my ears. I leaped to my feet and scrambled to the bar. James and I exchanged wary glances.

"Costas was a lucrative deal. Donato would have made a huge profit."

"At what expense?" Edgar's tone matched Phil's. "They're manufacturing furniture from Brazil nut trees. All of our background checks and research confirms their wood isn't sourced from sustainable forests. It's illegally obtained."

"That's bullshit. Talk to them. I'll get their president on the line."

"Don't waste your time. Donato associates only with environmentally conscious furniture manufacturers. Costas is not one of them. End of discussion." Edgar roughly stubbed out his cigar in the ashtray and picked up the whiskey glass Thomas had refilled. He made his way to the door, leaving Phil standing in the middle of the room.

"Don't you walk out on me!" Phil bellowed when Edgar reached the threshold. "I'm not finished!"

I glanced at James, who stood rigidly beside me. I sensed there was more to this discussion than a cancelled account.

Phil jabbed a finger at Edgar. "You had no right to pull the plug without consulting with me first."

"As CEO, I had every right!"

"You made me look like an ass."

Edgar laughed. "You do that on your own. You want to change how people perceive you at Donato? You want me to consider you for the president position? Then stop your reckless practices. Stop the risky deals. That's when we'll talk. I'll not have you bring this company down when you screw up, or else—"

"Or else, what?" Phil sneered. "You'll give the company to Tommy-boy? He doesn't have the spine to be president. Our clients will walk all over him. Donato needs a leader who has the guts to make those risky deals if we want to take this company to the next level." He jabbed a finger at James. "And that sure isn't Jimbo either. He'd rather spend his time painting flowers and banging his bitch."

I gasped, mortified. James crushed the soda can he held. I'd never seen him look so upset.

Phil looked wildly around the room, his chest heaving, taking in our startled expressions. His gaze landed on James, who glowered at him. Phil's expression turned to one of incredulity. "They still don't know? All these years you've kept it from them?" He laughed, rough and deep. "Amazing. You're much better at keeping secrets than I thought. Bravo, Jimbo." He clapped, the movement exaggerated.

"Phil, don't—" I started.

"Which means"—his head whipped to me—"she still doesn't know about us." He jerked a finger from James to Thomas and then jabbed his own sternum.

"Shut. The fuck. Up," James warned.

"James, what is he talking about?" Claire asked. Her face had paled. "What does he mean that you're painting?"

"It means your son wants nothing to do with Donato Enterprises," Phil answered for James. "He wants to paint pretty pictures, and he's been painting ever since the day you ordered him to give back Aimee's gift." He folded his arms over his chest. "He's quite good, actually. At painting, that is. I have no idea how good he is at screwing his girlfriend."

I felt the blood rush to my feet, keeping me rooted to my spot. Why was he being so cruel and crude? And how the hell did he know James was talented? Had he seen the paintings? I shuffled through memories, wondering if he'd been inside my parents' house. I couldn't recall my parents ever mentioning Phil had stopped by.

But despite the shock of Phil's announcement, I saw through his callous words. He was angry and hurt and taking it out on us.

He looked at me with a mocking tilt to his head. "Perhaps you can enlighten us about your sex life?"

"Phil!" Claire exclaimed, appalled.

James lunged for him, but Thomas grabbed James around the waist and held him back. "He's not worth it. He's never been worth it."

"Get the fuck out of my house," Edgar demanded.

Phil whirled on him. "Donato should have been mine!" he yelled. Spittle rained from his mouth. "It was my birthright. Mine!" He stomped from the room, slamming the library doors behind him so hard they bounced back open.

"Phil!" Claire chased after him.

James was furious. He shoved Thomas off him. I felt horrible for James. His paintings rivaled the fine art decorating his parents' walls, and to have a talent he cherished exposed in such a raw manner cut him low and deep. James would never forgive Phil.

Edgar paced to the window. He slid his hands into his side pockets and stared beyond the backyard. "So, you're an artist?"

James pursed his lips, his face taut.

"His paintings are gallery worthy, Mr. Donato," I remarked when James didn't say anything. His head whipped in my direction, eyes blazed. "It's true, James," I whispered vehemently.

"Is that what you want to do with your life?" Edgar asked James. He sounded defeated.

"I don't know what the fuck I want." He stormed from the room.

"Maybe we should have let him paint," Edgar murmured to his reflection in the window. He shrugged a shoulder and looked at me. "Claire was never keen on the idea. She didn't want the boys to have hobbies that could inspire a career anywhere else but Donato. And I agreed to support her, whether the boys wanted to work there or not. Their great-grandfather started the company. Every son from each generation worked in the company. So would her boys." He turned back to the window. "Just another regret I have to live with."

Thomas approached me. He rubbed my upper arm. "You OK?"

I glanced from Thomas to the hallway beyond the library threshold and back to Thomas.

"Phil's a prick," Thomas said, going on to explain how Phil's been under a lot of pressure to perform. "We're both in the running for the president position my dad vacated after Uncle Grant—you know, Phil's dad—passed away. As you heard, Phil hasn't made the wisest business decisions lately."

I nodded, not really absorbing what Thomas was saying. "I should go check on James."

I excused myself from the room and searched for James, finding him in his car, the motor running. I slid into the front passenger seat. James shifted into gear as soon as my door closed. The tires peeled on the asphalt. I scrambled to put on the seatbelt.

James took the back roads, heading uphill toward Skyline Boulevard and our meadow, the special place we went to be alone with each other.

Anger emanated through James's rough gear shifting. He steered the car around hairpin turns, his speed increasing. I grabbed the door handle. "There's no point in going to the meadow to have sex if we crash before we even get there."

James downshifted. The corner of his mouth twitched into a half smile before he swore. He slammed a hand on the steering wheel. "How the fuck does he know?"

"Who, Phil? I think it was our notes."

"Our what?"

"The notes we'd passed each other at school. Remember that one time you caught him raiding your desk? I think he read them as you'd suspected." I told him again the story about Phil walking me home several years back.

James slid me a look. "You never told me this," he accused. He stopped at the Skyline intersection and glanced in the rearview mirror. A car pulled up behind us, headlights on high beams.

"Yes, I did. You grumbled about Phil being an idiot and said you didn't want to discuss him. You never like talking about him. Besides, you were more interested in getting your hands on me. Remember? That was right after our first kiss."

James cracked a smile. He gave me a heated look. "That I remember."

I blushed. "Anyway, Phil promised to keep your secret even though I never admitted you were painting in the first place."

"Obviously he can't keep his mouth shut." James turned onto Skyline Boulevard. "I'm going to beat the shit out of him when I see him next."

The car behind us followed, its high beams brightening the interior of James's car like a lighthouse torch. James swore, his gaze jumping to the rearview mirror. "Fucking idiot needs to fix his lights."

I glanced in the side mirror. The car tailed us, leaving barely a car's length between.

"What I can't figure out is how Phil knows you're really good."

"Has he seen my paintings?"

I shook my head. "He's never been inside my house. Not when I've been there. My parents never mentioned anything either. But then, they hadn't told me your dad's eaten at The Goat. Today was the first I heard that."

James sighed. "Well, now my parents know."

I reached over and rubbed his thigh. "You aren't fifteen anymore. They can't tell you to stop painting."

"I know. It's just . . ." He rubbed his forearm. "I didn't want them to find out this way."

This was new. "You were planning on telling them?"

He shrugged. "I imagined inviting them to a gallery showing and surprising them. It would be my show. Maybe they would buy a piece and hang it in their library. Hell, I'd give them one."

Oh, James. My heart went out to him. He wanted more than recognition for his work. He wanted his parents to accept his artwork as more than a passing hobby.

"It was a stupid idea."

"I think it's a great idea."

"Too late now," James grumbled. He drove past the turnout for our meadow.

I glanced over my shoulder. "You missed the road."

"I know." His gaze bounced from the road to the rearview mirror and back. He drove another few hundred yards, then quickly pulled off the road, letting the tailgater pass.

I gasped. "That looks like Phil's car."

James waited until the car disappeared around the bend before making a U-turn. He headed back to the turnoff for our meadow.

James turned onto the side road and cut the lights. "Just in case."

"Sheesh, he's furious about something if he's following us."

"I don't know who it was, but I'm not taking any chances. I don't want anyone to know we're here."

"What did he mean, earlier, about the three of you?" I asked in reference to him, Thomas, and Phil.

I sensed James tense beside me in the dark.

"That's OK. You don't have to tell me."

He cut the engine. "It's no big deal. Don't worry about it."

James was downplaying it. Fury radiated off him, and something else I couldn't define. He was obviously worried despite telling me not to do the same. I reasoned he'd tell me in his own good time.

He opened the door and the interior light flashed on. I blinked as my eyes adjusted. James grinned.

"Come on. My parents will be disappointed we bailed on dinner, but I have to get back to Stanford tonight and study." His smile turned wicked. "Let's go have some fun."

James grabbed blankets and his Jawbone speaker and iPod. I followed him from the car and over a low fence. We wandered through the trees until they opened up to show the starlit sky. Our favorite spot was on the ridge overlooking the Santa Cruz Mountains. There wasn't a cloud in the sky this cool spring night.

James fired up the iPod, OutKast's "The Way You Move."

My brows arched upward. "That's an interesting selection. You're feisty tonight, aren't you?"

He rolled his shoulders and grinned, slow and sexy. My stomach quickened.

"Come here, baby." He pulled me into his arms and leaned down to kiss me. Before his lips reached mine, his entire body tensed. He lifted his head, his gaze sharp beyond my shoulder.

Gooseflesh rose. "What?"

He narrowed his eyes, then shook his head before looking down at me. "Thought I heard something."

"An animal?" I peeked over my shoulder and saw only shadows, eerily frozen in the moonlight.

"Maybe," James said. He kissed my nose. "You look beautiful."

I grinned and stepped from his embrace, tugging my light sweater over my head. I let it fall to the ground. James chuckled until the sound of my skirt zipper cut through the night. His face sobered, his gaze trailing the skirt I let pool at my feet. I stepped out of my flats and over my skirt.

A gentle breeze scented with wet pine and wood smoke whispered against my flesh, puckering the skin. I fisted my hands. "Cold here."

"You're so beautiful."

James closed the distance between us, his mouth landing hard on mine. His hands circled my waist, fingers dipping under the elastic of my panties. He slipped them off, dropping to his knees and kissing my leg. I inhaled sharply, shivering from the damp air and his moist kisses.

He tossed aside the panties onto my discarded clothes and tugged me down. He unhooked my bra, kissing the exposed flesh, and stretched me out on the blanket, covering me with the other one to keep me warm. He stripped fast and crawled underneath, pulling me close.

"I love you," he whispered against my mouth and kissed me.

"I love you, too."

He moved above me and I heard foil tear. He shifted, adjusting, pushing inside, and then he was moving within me. I locked my arms around his neck and clamped my legs around his waist, matching the rhythm he set.

"Don't let go," he whispered in my ear. He thrust deeply, his movements frantic.

"Never."

CHAPTER 15

It had been fourteen months since James left for Mexico and one year since I'd buried him. In some ways, I had moved on with my life. In other ways, not so much. James's clothes still hung in our closet. His art supplies collected dust in the studio.

I sat at my desk, clicking through the images Kristen had e-mailed from this morning's opening. I searched each one, hoping to find the one woman I never expected to see again. There were pictures of family and friends, my neighbors, and staff. Snapshots of the baristas and Mandy in the kitchen. Ian behind the espresso machine. Ian with my parents. Ian with Nadia. Ian standing beside his framed pictures on the wall. I clicked through more pictures. Ian, again. Damn you, Kristen, for taking so many pictures of him. And damn you, Ian, for looking so good.

I clicked to the next picture and exhaled in a rush. There she was, sitting at table number eight in the corner where the walls displaying James's paintings and Ian's prints met. Lacy. She held the postcard she'd given to my waitress Emily and was looking straight into Kristen's camera, her eerie lavender-blue eyes bright and wide. She hadn't expected Kristen to take her picture.

Why had she left so quickly after dropping off the postcard? And why hadn't she given it directly to me? Had Kristen and her camera scared her off? Had something—or some*one*—else scared her off? Thomas? He'd seen someone leave the café, thought he knew someone. It changed his entire demeanor. He'd seemed upset. Maybe that someone he'd seen was Lacy.

I retrieved the art gallery postcard from my back pocket. The gallery, El estudio del pintor, was in Puerto Escondido, Mexico. The card was small, only three and one-half by five inches, and the thumbnail image of the acrylic painting even smaller. I studied the painting, rapping my knuckles against my teeth. I'd seen the painting years ago, in my parents' sunroom, propped on James's easel. *Impossible.* The postcard image was an exact replica of James's *Withering Oaks* acrylic, a painting of the trees in the reserve behind his parents' house.

I flipped the card over. The gallery was located in the same town as Casa del sol, the hotel on the card I'd found in my wallet almost a year ago. I yanked open the desk's middle drawer and dug through paper scraps until I found the business card I believed Lacy had tucked in my wallet.

Opening a new browser window, I brought up Casa del sol's website. Nothing had changed on the site since the last time I looked. Nothing appeared unusual about the resort hotel. Then I searched for El estudio del pintor. Nothing. No website or page link. I tried several other search engines. None of them located an "El estudio del pintor" art gallery in Puerto Escondido, Mexico, so I Googled the address. An image of a storefront popped up and I clicked on the link. In the picture, which was embedded in a real estate website, the building appeared old, paint cracking and stucco chipped. It had no signage. The listing was at least two years old and indicated the property had been sold. Whoever purchased the site had recently opened the studio, sometime within the last twenty-four months.

Why was Lacy leading me to Puerto Escondido? James had flown to Cancún. He had checked into his hotel in Playa del Carmen, and he had fished off the coast of Cozumel. Thomas told me he had retrieved James's body from the Mexican state of Quintana Roo. Not Oaxaca.

If this wasn't the case, why would James lie to me about his travel plans? Maybe Thomas was the one lying, which meant Lacy had been the only one telling the truth all along.

James was still alive.

My heart slammed in my chest. I called Kristen. "Can I come over?"

~

Kristen and Nick Garner lived in Saratoga, a ten-minute drive from my house. Dressed in terry shorts and a Hello Kitty shirt, Kristen answered the door. Her ponytail bounced high on her head as she led me through the house. "Nick's in the kitchen. Do you mind that I asked him to join us?"

I shook my head. "He knows Thomas better than either of us."

"That's what I figured. Aimee"—she stopped in the hallway and faced me—"I have my doubts. Everything you told me on the phone seems so . . ."

"Crazy, I know." I adjusted my purse strap. My fingers were shaking. "But I have to find out what's going on."

She rested her hand on my upper arm. "Is this why you haven't dated since James, um . . . disappeared?"

"It's always been in the back of my mind."

She gave me an abbreviated nod. "Let's see what Nick has to say."

Nick was standing at the butcher-block island pouring a brown ale into a frosted glass. He wore a T-shirt and workout shorts, and his hair was damp. Nick played soccer in the city's recreational department adult league. He looked as if he'd recently returned from a game.

He offered me a beer and I declined. "Congratulations on the opening today," he said.

"Thanks. What did you order?"

"The Mediterranean omelet." He patted his stomach. "My new favorite."

I grinned. Overflowing with goat cheese, brine-cured olives, and fresh fennel and dill, the omelet had been a popular selection. "I expect to see you back."

"Without a doubt." He drank his beer, then rubbed his hands together. "So, what have you got?"

I retrieved the gallery postcard and business card from my purse and aligned them on the island. "Lacy slipped the hotel's card in my wallet."

Nick arched a brow.

"Long story," I said and pointed at the gallery postcard. "She had my waitress Emily give this one to me."

Nick's head snapped up. "She was there this morning?"

"Apparently so."

"Aimee says I took a picture of her," Kristen explained.

Nick straightened, inching closer to his wife. "Did she say anything to you?"

She shook her head. "There were a lot of people there. I've never met her so I don't know who she was."

"I'll show you what she looks like." I launched my phone and scrolled through the camera roll to Lacy's photo.

"I remember her," Kristen said. "I think I spooked her when I took the picture. She bailed right after."

"Her name is Lacy Saunders, and I think she left because she saw Thomas. She's a psychic profiler specializing in unsolved mysteries and missing persons," I explained for Nick's benefit.

Nick studied the picture. "Kristen mentioned you first met this woman at James's funeral."

"I wouldn't exactly put it that way," I admitted.

"Lacy chased her down in the church parking lot," Kristen clarified. "She told Aimee that James was alive. Nadia thought she was a con artist, and I have to agree with her."

"I did, too, until I realized most of James's paintings were missing, and then I received this." I tapped the painting on the postcard. "I'm afraid Lacy has been telling the truth."

Nick rubbed his right shoulder. "Don't jump to conclusions. At least not yet," he advised. "What did the cops say when you reported the theft?"

I'd told Kristen I reported the missing paintings to the police when I initially discovered they were gone. She must have mentioned this to Nick, too. "There wasn't much they could do. There weren't any fingerprints in the garage other than mine and James's. No signs of forced entry so it's questionable whether the paintings were even stolen. The best I could do was file a report. If anything surfaces at auctions or on the black market, they can match the description."

"They can be anywhere by now," Kristen surmised.

"Mexico?" I suggested.

Nick shrugged. "Europe, Asia. The next town over. Your neighbor's living room." He tapped the painting image. "If this is James's, it's possible the gallery owner purchased the canvas from an unreliable source. I want to know more about the woman who gave you this. I'm not comfortable with either of you interacting with her. She's suspicious."

"I don't have much to add other than she lives in Campbell. There's a sign on her lawn promoting her psychic counseling services. It also advertises her—" I broke off, glancing between them.

"Advertises what?" Nick prompted.

"She reads palms and tarot cards."

He made an impatient sound before his gaze hardened. "You went to her house?"

"I didn't go inside," I rushed to defend myself. "She creeped me out."

"Probably best to stay away from her," he suggested.

"Aside from that one time, she's always approached me, not the other way around. She'd talked nonsense about James. Or, I thought it was nonsense."

Nick drank more of his beer. "Sounds like she's a nut job."

"Why is she being so secretive?" Kristen asked.

I nodded in agreement. "I wished she'd just come out and explain everything."

"Lots of reasons why she hasn't," Nick said. "Someone hired her to pass on information to you. Or, lure you to them. Whatever the reason, they want to keep their identity a secret, which is the least likely explanation."

"And the most?" I asked.

"She's a con artist. She gives you bait"—Nick waved the postcard—"gains your trust, and insinuates she has more information. Then she starts charging. Does she contact you often?"

I shook my head. "She's never asked for money."

"She doesn't have you in the position to do so. Ignore her and she may go away."

"What if she continues to bother Aimee?"

"Get a restraining order."

I chewed my lower lip. "What if"—I hedged, gently knocking my shoe against the cabinet—"she's telling the truth?"

Nick looked at me seriously. "I feel for you, Aimee, I really do. James's death was hard on all of us, especially Thomas. He loved his brother and was extremely protective. It wasn't easy growing up with their parents."

"I know." I nodded, thinking of all the sacrifices both James and Thomas had made over the years.

"Thomas inherited a mess of a company I'm not sure he wanted, and running the operation sucks the life out of him," Nick continued. "Truthfully, I was shocked to see him at your opening this morning. He barely has time to eat. He's a good, honest man who wouldn't stand aside if there were any questions about James's death. If there were, he'd be the first one flying to Mexico to uncover answers."

He exhaled, his face softening, and propped his forearms on the island. "I find it very hard to believe James is not dead. Why would he leave his family? Why would he leave you? I'm sorry, Aimee. James is dead."

My eyes burned and I blinked back tears. Nick asked the same questions I'd repeatedly asked myself. Though my opinion of Thomas wasn't as generous as his. Not anymore. As for Lacy, she was still a mystery. I collected the cards and slipped them into my purse.

Nick rested his hand over mine. "If it helps any, I have a PI who's done some work on my civil cases. His name's Ray Miles, and he's a bit . . ." Nick hedged. "Well, there's no way to say it but straight out. He's shady . . . but damn good. He's not cheap either. I'll text his contact info. Give him a call. He can run a background check on Lacy, look into the gallery, maybe find out the name of the artist on the painting and where it was purchased." Nick tapped his phone and a few seconds later mine pinged.

We chatted a few minutes more before I left. I had to be up early the next morning to prep for Aimee's official opening.

By late morning the next day, I slipped into the café's office and called Ray. We spoke briefly about my situation, how I wanted proof Lacy was who—and what—she claimed, if James had indeed traveled to Cancún, and where the gallery in Puerto Escondido had obtained his painting. Ray quoted me a price and Nick was right. His PI was damn expensive, and the spare change in my coffers was dwindling fast since the final payments for the contractor and subs were due. Since my issue wasn't time sensitive, merely a curiosity, Ray agreed to handle my case when I had the cash. Besides, he had other cases he was working on and wouldn't be able to help me for another eight or ten weeks. Enough time for me to put money aside.

I never saw Lacy again. It was as though she'd never appeared. In and out of my life before I could make sense of our paths intersecting. During the first month after Aimee's opening, Thomas stopped at the café for coffee several times a week until his visits dwindled and he stopped coming regularly. The times I did see him, he appeared more withdrawn, cheeks hollowed and body leaner. Donato Enterprises was taking its toll. Where Edgar Donato had gained weight, Thomas was positively gaunt.

By mid-October, right after my twenty-eighth birthday, I had more than enough funds to hire Ray. If anything, his findings would help me close this chapter of my life. I could fully move on, mind, body, and spirit. Ray confirmed he'd send a report within a couple of weeks, and then I could decide how to proceed.

When we had worked out the particulars, I sat on the chenille couch in the front room. To my surprise, it was Ian who broke into my thoughts. His unwavering support this past year and deepening friendship. The smile that stirred something deeper within my soul, and the warmth of his skin whenever he stood near. With Ray's help, I could finally give Ian what he wanted. Did I want the same from him?

Yes!

But what if Ray did find James?

I turned my gaze to the engagement portrait, James and me locked in an embrace beneath a painted sky, the setting sun a blazing backdrop of orange and red, and I started shaking. My fingers and knees trembled. Not from anticipation, but out of fear. If James were alive, it meant something bigger had been going on around me and I'd been too naive to see it.

CHAPTER 16

NOVEMBER

Ray finally sent word on a Tuesday in the second week of November. His e-mail had arrived in the early morning hours, long after I'd gone to bed. I had read it before leaving for Aimee's, and reread it seventeen more times since then.

It was because of that e-mail I wanted nothing to do with Alan Cassidy's attention, let alone the fact I just wasn't interested in dating him.

"Here you go, Alan, your usual: one low-fat, no-whip, triple-shot, vanilla latte with two pumps hazelnut. Anything else for you today?" I asked, sounding more irritated and impatient than I intended.

He still smiled. "You amaze me, Aimee." He reached inside the pocket of his tailored suit and extracted two tickets, fanning them in his fingers. "Tonight's Sharks game. Join me?"

I stole a glance at the tickets. This wasn't the first time he'd asked, and knowing Alan, they were premium seats. I shook my head. "Sorry, Alan. Thanks for asking, though."

His bright expression faded and the tickets disappeared as quickly, tucked inside his jacket. "One of these days I'll find somewhere to take you, and you won't be able to resist." He saluted me with his to-go cup and sauntered out the exit.

Ian grunted behind me, and I thought I heard him mutter, "Oh brother."

When I started another pot of house blend, I caught money changing hands between Ian and Emily. Ian folded a five and slid the cash into his back pocket. He grinned at me.

"What was that all about?" I snapped.

His eyes widened. Feeling guilty, I apologized.

"You cost me five bucks." Emily playfully punched my upper arm and scooted past. She grabbed a plastic bin and started cleaning tables after the morning rush.

I looked warily at Ian. He gave me his back, pulling a damp towel from his belt loop, and cleaned the espresso machine. He started whistling. I pursed my lips. There was a victory smile in his whistle. "Ian?" I prodded.

He jerked his chin toward the entrance. "Alan asks you out at least once a week. Emily's convinced you'll cave one of these days."

I crossed my arms. "How so?"

"You'll go out with the poor schmuck." He chuckled as though the idea seemed ludicrous.

"Alan's not a schmuck. He's a nice guy. He's—"

"High-maintenance?" Ian supplied. I scowled and he stared me down, eyes warm with mischief.

"Shut up," I grumbled. So what if Alan ordered girly coffee? That wasn't my problem. I ripped open a foil bag of coffee grounds and the aroma buoyed my spirits. I breathed deeply, eyes shuttering. Tendons taut from standing for five hours loosened.

"Could you be cracking already?"

My eyes snapped open, narrowing on Ian's smug face. The two-day growth peppering his jawline did nothing to hide how pleased he was with himself, or how appealing I found his smile. His shirtsleeves were rolled, leaving his forearms bare except for the dusting of golden hair matching the untamed waves on his head. He popped a shoulder. "Doesn't matter anymore. I already won the bet."

I scooped grounds into the filter. "You don't think I'll go out with him?"

"Not a chance." His eyes fell to my engagement ring. "You won't date. Me or anyone else."

I spun the ring with my thumb, hiding the diamond in my palm. "I will too." *Eventually.*

Ian crossed his arms. "Prove it. Go out with me."

My breath caught. In all the months I'd known him, this was the first time he asked me straight out.

"Ian, you know I can't." Not yet. Besides, I was still reeling from Ray's e-mail.

"You mean, you *won't*." He turned back to the espresso machine.

"He's right, you know," Nadia said behind me. She leaned against the display case filled with pastries and salads and finger-waved "hello." Kristen stood beside her. Both wore workout clothes, their cheeks windburned to a bright red from a morning run.

I brushed my hands together, dusting off loose grounds. "So you think I should date?"

Nadia angled her head toward Ian, who was assisting another customer. "He really cares about you."

I already knew that. Ian had been very honest about his feelings on more than one occasion. I was the holdup. "He's a friend *and* an employee."

"If you say so."

I grimaced. Even I knew the excuse was lame.

"Go away. You can't have any coffee today." I turned to the sink and flipped on the water. Dirty mugs needed to be washed.

"I'll have your usual for you in a moment, Nadia."

"Thanks, Ian." She pushed away from the counter.

Traitor, I mouthed to him and he chuckled.

Nadia snagged a newspaper from the community reading rack. She scanned the columns on the front page as she walked through the dining area.

Kristen scooted behind the counter and leaned against the sink ledge. "Nadia cares only about you. We all do." She watched me rinse an excessively dirty cup stained with stale coffee. An unusually bright pink lipstick print kissed the rim. I scrubbed the discoloration a tad harder, using the coarse side of my sponge.

"What's wrong? You seem agitated," she asked when I didn't say anything.

I blew an exasperated breath. "I received an e-mail from Ray this morning."

"The PI? What did he say?"

I shook loose water from the cup and it slipped from my hand, shattering in the sink. I swore and Ian whipped around. "You OK?"

"I'm fine," I barked.

He rubbed his forehead and watched me for a moment.

"I'm OK. Thanks," I reassured in a softer tone.

He waited a beat before turning back to blend a coffee.

"Sorry," I muttered to Kristen and cleaned the sink.

She helped me pick up ceramic fragments.

"Ray confirmed James did fly to Cancún." I kept my voice low and out of Ian's range of hearing. "James did check into his hotel in Playa del Carmen. The local news articles about a missing American man who'd fallen overboard, his reservations for the boat trip, his death certificate—they're all legit. Ray spoke to the owner of the tour company and everything coincided with what Thomas had told me."

A curl escaped my hairclip. I pushed the offending piece off my face. My lips quivered.

Kristen rubbed my back. "You've questioned James's death for almost two years. I'm glad Ray was able to help. Give you some closure."

"He couldn't find anything about Lacy either. No records. She's gone, too. Moved out. The house is owned by a Douglas Chin. It's a rental. Aside from the business card, postcard, and Lacy's picture, I had nothing else to give him.

"I'm such an idiot. I'm so upset . . . No, I'm—" I shook my head. "I'm disappointed . . . in myself. I got all worked up *hoping* his disappearance and funeral was a sham."

"What about the painting on the postcard?" Kristen asked.

"The gallery owner at El estudio del pintor is the artist. He says the painting is his and any resemblance to another painter's style is entirely coincidental. Unless I go to the gallery myself, I have to believe what Ray tells me because there's no way I can afford to send him down there."

"Now what are you going to do?"

What I should have done months ago. "Move on."

"Well, I think you're doing a fabulous job. You opened a restaurant and it's a success," she cheered and angled her head toward Ian. "And when you're ready to date, I know a great guy who's very interested."

I smirked. "Ha, ha."

Ian finished topping Kristen's mocha with whipped cream and handed her the cup.

I threw out an arm toward the dining area. "You can tell Nadia I'll bring her coffee in a moment. The pot's almost ready."

Kristen laughed. "She'll get it after all?"

I grabbed a mug from the overhead rack. "She'd come back here and pour her own cup if I didn't. Ignoring her is pointless."

It was late when I arrived home that night. I'd spent hours washing the café's floor, counter surfaces, and cabinets, hoping to scrub away my despondency. It didn't work. I was still depressed.

A box had been delivered at some point during the day. It rested on my doormat. I tucked it under my arm and went inside, dumping my purse and keys in their usual spot. Then I made my way into the kitchen and examined the package. There wasn't a return address, only my street information and postage of international origin. *Mexico.* The postage seal inked over the stamps read "Oaxaca, MX."

My heart leaped into my throat. I ripped opened the box. Bubble-wrapped inside was a painting. *Meadow Glade*, a smaller version of the acrylic on my wall behind the dining table. The canvas in my hands was the original. I'd convinced James to paint our meadow on a larger scale because I loved the colors, the way the tall blades of grass reflected the early morning light. In the lower right corner, painted in the custom Caribbean blue hue James had mixed to match my eyes, the color he always used for his signature, were his initials. *JCD*.

My hands started shaking. I flipped the canvas. A note was taped to the back, handwritten on a small piece of paper imprinted with a hotel logo. CASA DEL SOL.

Dear Aimee,

Here's your proof. The danger has finally passed and James is safe. I've been asked to seek you out. It's time he learned the truth. Come to Oaxaca.

Lacy

James was alive? Oh my God! James was alive.

I started shaking uncontrollably, almost losing my grip on the painting. Beads of sweat dotted my upper lip and brow. Bile twisted low in my belly.

What the fuck was going on?

> **There isn't any solid evidence James is still alive,**

Ray's e-mail had stated.

> **Don't waste your time and money. There isn't any reason for me to investigate further. I recommend calling off the search.**

The facts Ray uncovered matched James's documentation and records. James's death occurred exactly as Thomas had reported.

Then why the hell was James's painting in Mexico?

I swiped at the tears I realized were raining down my face and picked up the phone. I dialed the one person who would understand.

"Hello?" Her voice sounded heavy from sleep.

"Kristen. James *is* alive."

~

After I booked a hotel room in Puerto Escondido, I'd spent the rest of the night staring at the ceiling or pacing my room. I couldn't sleep. James was out there.

Nadia woke me at 4:06 the following morning, pounding on the front door. I stumbled bleary-eyed through the house on two hours' sleep.

"About time," Nadia huffed after I opened the door. She pushed past me. "Bet you didn't expect to see me at this godforsaken hour." She stopped in the middle of the room between the leather chairs. Dressed in bedazzled Juicy sweats and a wool scarf wrapped around her neck, she glared at me.

I shut the door. "Kristen told you."

"She called a couple hours ago. She's been up all night worried sick you'd do something stupid"—her eyes darted toward the packed roller bag I'd stashed by the front door—"such as fly off to Mexico by yourself."

I raised my chin. "You can't stop me."

"Oaxaca, Mexico? Not the safest place to travel."

"That's the same as saying the entire state of California is unsafe." I shook my head and walked into the kitchen. I might as well brew some coffee. There was no way I would fall back to sleep before my flight.

Nadia followed me. "Kristen's very concerned. She doesn't want you to go."

"So she sent you to change my mind."

"She knows you won't listen to her."

"I'm not listening to you either." I scooped grounds and set the pot to brew. "My flight leaves this afternoon. I don't care what either of you have to say. I'm going." I headed toward the bedroom.

"Good."

I stopped. "What?"

She advanced on me, her makeup-free eyes narrowing on mine. "I said 'good.' I want you to go."

"Why?"

She squared her shoulders. "You've been stuck in the mud since James died."

"I've not been stuck—"

"Look around you!" she exploded. I flinched like she'd struck me. It took a lot to get Nadia fired up and she was obviously upset with me. "James is everywhere. His clothes are still in your closet. His paintings decorate every fucking wall. You have got to move on."

"I've tried . . ."

"Not hard enough."

"The restaurant—"

She waved in dismissal. "OK, so you opened a restaurant. Good for you. Great progress on the outside. But in here"—she poked my sternum—"you're stuck. You're a textbook case when it comes to grief. You've plowed through every stage but one. People die, Aimee. There's nothing you can do but pick up the pieces and move on. Why can't you accept James is dead?"

"He's *not* dead," I vehemently objected.

She propped her fists on her hips and closed her eyes. Moisture glistened on her lashes. "Listen, I get why you're doing this. After my dad left my mom, I had a really, really hard time getting over it until I accepted the fact he was gone. He'd left us. So, I let him go. Completely. Cut him off." She slashed a hand between us. "But you know what the problem with that was?"

I slowly shook my head, hesitant, unsure where she was going with this.

"It was very easy for me to dump any guy who tried to get close to me. I didn't trust them. They'd leave me, too. Maybe not that day, or a month from then. But eventually. They'd tire of me and move on. So I'd move on before they got the chance to." Her breath hitched as she inhaled. "You know what sucks about that?"

"What?"

She folded her arms tightly in front of her chest. "I'm lonely. There. I admit it. I'm really lonely. And I know you are, too. You'll always be lonely until you can let James go."

I stared at the floor, blinking rapidly. I was lonely, but my situation wasn't the same as hers. "There have been more times than I can count when I've come close to boxing James's clothes, packing up his art supplies. They're covered in dust; it's been that long since I've touched them." I motioned toward the room James had used as a studio, the one I now used for my home office. "Every time I try to get rid of his stuff, something stops me. Whether a gut feeling he is alive, or hope he'll show up on my doorstep one day, I don't know. But that feeling is there, and I can't ignore it.

"So, you see? Our situations aren't the same. You knew your father was never coming back. As for James, there's a good chance he's out there, somewhere. And I have to find out. I have to know for sure."

"That's why I want you to go to Mexico." She jabbed a finger at me. "I want you to see how that psychic bitch has manipulated you. Maybe then, once you know she's been leading you on, lying to you about James, maybe then you'll let yourself mourn. And finally, *fucking* move on."

I stood motionless. There was the very real possibility Nadia was right. Lacy was manipulating me. "What if I find him?"

"Seriously?" She cocked a brow. I crossed my arms. Her expression sobered. "Assuming he's alive, have you ever wondered why he's stayed away?"

I nodded. *All the time.*

"What are your plans?"

I glanced beyond her shoulder and locked on to James's *Meadow Glade*, the painting of "our spot." The entire scene was done in shades of green, capturing our meadow on a crisp morning when winter had phased into spring. It was soft, warm, and inviting. Pristine, like the way I wanted to remember it. Not foul, the way we'd left it.

The day after James had proposed, I'd taken down the painting. He was furious and insisted it remain. We had to keep up pretenses that nothing had happened in our meadow, that Phil hadn't come as close as he did to destroying our dreams. For James, the painting still hung on the wall. I wondered if Lacy somehow knew this when she sent the smaller original. "I plan to tell James how much I love him. I miss him, and I want to bring him home."

"What if he doesn't want to come home?"

My gaze dropped to the floor.

She harshly inhaled. "You aren't planning to stay there? What about the café? You've worked so hard to get where you are. Are you going to just give it up?"

"No! I—" I didn't know what I would do. I loved my café and the new life I'd built, and I couldn't walk away. But I couldn't walk away from James either. Not yet. I had to find him, and I needed to know why he'd left.

"I have to go to Mexico."

Nadia watched me for a long moment. She huffed, put hands on hips, and shook her head before wrapping me in a hug. She rested her chin on my shoulder. "I know you have to go, but don't go alone. Wait here." She walked across the room and, opening the front door, motioned to someone out of view. Ian walked in, carrying a duffel bag and camera case. He dropped them on the floor next to my roller and cautiously looked at me.

Nadia closed the door and stood by Ian. "He's packed and ready to go, but he needs your flight and hotel info." I scowled, and she raised her hands in defense. "His idea. Not mine. He offered to travel with you."

I groaned. This arrangement was ludicrous.

Ian held up both hands. "Don't worry. Everything's been arranged at the café. Trish is filling in; she's there right now. Mandy will help, too."

Trish was my other shift manager, but I'd never left her in charge. Ian was supposed to be my go-to guy when I couldn't be at the restaurant. How was I supposed to leave Ian in charge if he was with me?

"Kristen and I will help open and close, as well as with anything else that comes up," Nadia volunteered. She chuckled, nervous. "Hopefully there won't be too many fires to put out."

I gnawed my lower lip. My eyes shifted between them as they stared back. Ian shoved his hands into his jean pockets and walked over. He whispered in my ear. "Let's go find him."

I frowned at the dejection in his voice. The longing for me I'd glimpsed from time to time in his expression was gone. I yearned to see it again. An emptiness spread from my chest and down my arms.

Going after James is a mistake.

The coffeemaker beeped and I jerked. Whatever I'd been thinking scattered away. I lowered my arms. "Well, then . . . I hope you remembered your passport."

Faster than a magician could pull cards from his sleeve, Ian whipped out his passport from his back pocket. "I never leave home without it."

PART TWO

The Emerald Coast
Puerto Escondido, Mexico

CHAPTER 17

After a nineteen-hour flight with two layovers, I checked into Casa del sol, a boutique beachfront resort overlooking Puerto Escondido's Playa Zicatela, and waited in the lobby for Ian's flight to arrive. It was late Thursday afternoon, two days before the Torneo Internacional de Surf, something I hadn't been aware of in my rush to book a reservation. The tournament was one of many events taking place during Fiestas de Noviembre, an entire month of festivities celebrating local culture and traditions.

The open-air lobby bustled with tourists and surfers, their boards propped against walls or left on the floor with other luggage. Suitcases rolled across adobe tiles. Boisterous laughter vibrated the salt-heavy air. Waves thundered beyond the arched doorways. The scent of ocean spray drifted into the lobby, clashing with the acrid body odor of travel-weary guests drenched in sunscreen. All of this faded into the background as I stood away from the crowd.

Nerves pinged like firecrackers. I'd felt uneasy the moment I stepped onto the plane in San Jose and was nauseous, my skin clammy by the time the cab pulled into the hotel's parking lot. While I wanted to find James, I feared I would find him. His death and funeral had been a sham. For months Thomas had lied to me and James had remained hidden. They'd let me and everyone else believe James had died.

After all this time, and all the lies, would I want to take him back?

I didn't have an answer.

Feeling dizzy, I leaned against a support column and continued waiting for Ian, who'd taken a separate flight since mine had been fully booked. According to his last text, he was in a cab on his way over.

A woman with chicory eyes and high cheekbones approached. Her midnight-brown hair fell in sleek waves over slender shoulders, skimming the edges of the hotel manager badge pinned on her lapel. Her name tag read IMELDA RODRIGUEZ, and she gave me a glass of water.

"*Hola, señorita.* Welcome to Casa del sol." She frowned. "Are you feeling all right?"

I graciously accepted the water and drank greedily. "Yes, I'm fine now. Thank you."

"The humidity is an evil spirit around here. It sneaks up on you. Best to stay hydrated." She smiled and gave me the once-over. "Are you here for the *torneo*?"

"The what?" I blinked. "Oh no. I don't surf. Never have. I live near the ocean but haven't been in a long time. Not since—" James died. I buried my face in the glass and finished drinking, resisting the temptation to flash James's picture. Lacy's mention of danger hovered along the edges of my mind.

Imelda took the empty glass from me. "What brings you to Puerto Escondido then?"

"Art."

"*Sí,* very nice," she agreed. Her English, crisp and articulate, dripped with Spanish flavor. "Oaxaca has a lot to offer. Our village has much fishing and surfing, but there are a few galleries."

"Can you tell me where this one is?" I dug into my bag for the postcard from Lacy and showed it to Imelda.

"This is a good one. It is very close. You can walk from here." She pointed toward the front lobby archway to the road beyond the hotel's property. "Let me show you. *Un momento.*" She raised a finger and I followed her to a pamphlet kiosk by the concierge desk. She opened a map of Puerto Escondido and pointed to a spot between Playa Marinero and Playa Zicatela. "We are here, and you want to go here. The gallery is on el Adoquin, a street the tourists enjoy."

She tapped the map again, a different location. "This is our city hall. There will be music there tonight if you are interested and dancing and a parade in a few days if you plan to stay until then. The festivities are fun."

I took the map, memorizing the route and surrounding roads before I folded the paper.

"Here is the studio's brochure." Imelda lifted a glossy postcard from the kiosk, larger than the one Lacy had sent me. "Carlos's work is exceptional."

J. Carlos Dominguez, El estudio del pintor's owner, wasn't pictured, but the card face featured several of the gallery's acrylic paintings. They weren't James's missing canvases, but the artistic style was similar.

"Does Carlos feature other artists in his gallery?" I asked.

"A local sculptor uses his floor space, but most is Carlos's art, acrylics and oils. Several of our artists have made quite a name for themselves within the Oaxacan art community. Is there someone you're looking for in particular?"

"An old friend."

Imelda's smile faltered.

Voices rose across the lobby, snagging her attention. Newly arrived guests expressed their unhappiness with the accommodations. They'd reserved a bungalow, not the junior suite.

Imelda turned back to me. "Good luck finding your friend and do enjoy your stay. Now, if you'll excuse me."

She walked away before I could thank her.

A text message buzzed through. Ian had arrived. I met him outside the lobby entrance. His clothes were wrinkled and jaw unshaven. The entire flight, with layovers and delays, had taken him more than twenty-two hours. He looked as though a truck had dragged him several blocks. He waved when he saw me, his weary face splitting into a large grin.

I smiled and waved back.

He paid the cab driver and slung a camera bag over his head and shoulder while grabbing his luggage at the same time.

"How was your flight?" he asked when he reached me.

"Long," I said, groaning.

"Tell me about it," he complained. He swung an arm toward the reservation desk. "Let me check in. Watch my bags." He dropped them at my feet.

Several minutes later, room card in hand, he returned to my side. "I need a beer."

I wrinkled my nose. "You need a shower. The café on the terrace overlooks the ocean. Go clean up. I'll meet you there."

He tugged his shirt to fan his chest. "Good idea."

Twenty minutes later, I was seated at a table with a view of the shore below. Large waves crashed into the white sand beach stretching on either side of the resort. Palms rustled along the café's perimeter. My iced tea arrived the same time as Ian. He scrunched his nose at my drink. "Really?" He held up two fingers for the waiter. *"Dos cervezas."*

"Sí, señor." The waiter tossed coasters on the table and left to place the order at the bar.

Ian had changed into linen shorts, a rumpled oxford shirt, and flip-flops. His hair curled around his ears, still damp from the shower. He sat across from me, dropping a camera case on the chair between us, and inhaled deeply. "God, I love Mexico."

I inhaled and only smelled Ian. The heat of arousal washed over me. Strong and pure. I took a startled glance away and fixed my gaze on the pool patio.

"You OK?"

"Yeah, I'm fine." I lifted the hair off my neck. It didn't do much to cool me down.

The waiter returned with our beers. I pushed mine aside and raised my tea glass when Ian lifted his bottle. He frowned. "I'm not toasting over tea."

"I don't want alcohol on my breath when I see James."

"*If* you see him." He took a long draw from his bottle and searched my face.

My expression turned wary as I accepted the obvious. Ian wanted me, as much as I wanted to find James. And I had to find him, or at the very least, find answers to the questions about his death. It was the only way I knew how to move on.

I showed Ian the new postcard. He cocked a brow. "Is this the studio?"

I nodded. "Don't these paintings look like James's?"

"Do you really think James has been in Mexico all this time painting?" He studied the card and shrugged. "The style seems close. Hard to tell. The pictures are too small."

I peered at the card. "I can tell."

He took another swig of beer. "All paintings look the same to me."

"Like all your photos look the same as every other photographer's?"

He returned his beer to the table and grimaced. "Point taken."

I pushed the card back to his side. "James once told me every painter has a distinct characteristic to their artistic style. Van Gogh painted in blots of color. Monet broke colors down to create the perception of light within the paint. Kinkade's painted lights look so authentic; his paintings seem to illuminate themselves. James had his own trait, too."

Ian leaned over the table. "So, what am I looking for?"

"Acrylics were James's preferred medium. They dry faster than oils. On a big project, he'd mix a large batch of paint to ensure color consistency. One of the colors he mixed was a bluish-green. He called it *Les bleus de mon bébé—*"

Ian snorted. "My baby's blues?"

I waved my hand dismissively. "The color matched my eyes."

Ian rolled his.

I ignored him. "James used it to sign his name on every painting. Like this artist did here." I tapped a blotch of Caribbean blue on one of the images.

Ian squinted, our foreheads almost touching as we inspected the postcard between us. He leaned away and sighed. "Are you sure you're not forcing yourself to see something? I can't tell."

"Here, look at one of James's paintings." I scrolled through my phone's camera roll, landing on a photo of the Napa Valley painting where James's signature contrasted with the painting's yellow mustard fields. I gave Ian the phone.

His face paled, and his gaze snapped to mine. "Where was this picture taken? Is this at the café?"

My cheeks flushed. "You haven't seen this painting. It's in my bedroom."

"This isn't a painting." He quickly flashed the screen. I caught a glimpse of blonde hair.

"Oh, sorry." I must have flipped the picture on accident. "Let me find the right one."

"Who's the woman?" He showed me the screen.

It was the picture Kristen had taken of Lacy at the café's soft opening. "She's the psychic counselor who told me about James. Her name is Lacy."

"You mean Laney. When was she at the café?"

"The soft opening. Kristen took her picture."

Ian cupped a hand over his mouth. He stared hard at the photo, eyes narrowing. "I can't believe I didn't see her."

"She didn't stay long." I looked at him, suspicious. "By the way, her name is Lacy Saunders."

He shook his head. "Laney. Elaine Saunders. She's the psychic profiler my dad had hired. I've been trying to locate her for years."

I gaped. "She's your angel. Why would she change her name?"

"Simple. She doesn't want to be found." He returned the phone. "Will you text me the picture?"

I nodded and tapped a few icons. "At least there's one thing we know about her."

"What's that?" he asked. His phone beeped with my incoming message.

"Lacy has been here. Her memo was on notepaper from this hotel. Someone here had to have seen her. Maybe the hotel has her address."

"Maybe," he said his tone distant. He lifted his face toward the ocean's horizon, lost in his thoughts.

The untouched beer bottle sweated beside the barely touched iced tea. What the heck. I snagged the bottle. "Let's toast."

He dragged his attention back to me. "To what?"

"To us, and that we both find what we're looking for."

Ian studied me, his expression leading me to believe he didn't want me to find what I was looking for. It would mean he'd lose any chance of having something more with me. I swallowed uneasily. He finished his beer and stood, tossing Mexican bills onto the table. "All right, then, let's go find your painter."

CHAPTER 18

The Adoquin, the pedestrian walkway section of Avenida Alfonso Pérez Gasga, ran parallel to Playa Principal. Bright, bold storefronts lined the street and festival banners flew overhead. They crisscrossed the stone-paved walkway. Street performers stood on corners and banged steel drums. We wove our way through tourists, my pace quickening with each step.

"What's the rush?" Ian asked. He snapped a picture of a turquoise building striped in long shadows cast by the setting sun.

"It's getting late." I jerked my head for Ian to follow and kept walking. The weekend's competition had attracted surfing fans from around the globe. South African accents mixed with Australian. Tourists congregated in the street. They ate, laughed, and danced. They were also in my way.

Ian snagged my arm and yanked me back. He steered us away from a tourist jam, pausing to snap pictures of two old men. They puffed cigars in the doorway of a smoke shop. Their bellies hung low, exposed below the hems of their sweat-stained shirts. They looked unappealing and probably smelled worse.

What did Ian find so fascinating about them, and why did he bother taking their picture? He would never show the photos at his exhibits.

Ian released my arm and eased his pace. "Take a breath. Look around, there's so much to see."

"I didn't come here to sightsee," I complained.

He masked his face with the camera and pressed a button. Blinding light flashed. I saw stars.

"Shit." He adjusted the camera settings. "I didn't mean to do that. Rookie move." He played back the picture and chuckled, positioning the preview screen for me to see. "Nice deer-in-the-headlights look. Suits you."

"Stop taking pictures," I snapped. The studio was a couple of blocks ahead, according to the map Imelda had shown me, and I wanted to get there.

"Why? The late-afternoon light is perfect."

I huffed impatiently and he draped the camera around his neck. "Chill, Aims. You're wound tighter than a roll of film." He rubbed my shoulder. "There's a good chance the studio's already closed."

He nodded toward the slipping sun. "It seems I've had a change of travel plans. My next exhibit has to feature Puerto Escondido, Mexico. I have a surfing competition to shoot this weekend. I also want to get a few pictures of local landmarks and culture."

"But you don't exhibit photos with people in them."

"I might not have a choice this time," he said, as though he found the idea unsettling.

Ian had planned to use his funds to travel to the rainforests of Costa Rica. Instead, he'd sacrificed his trip and followed me to Mexico.

Because he cares about me.

The thought knocked around my brain.

I rubbed my face and sighed into my hands. "I'm sorry."

"Don't be. But promise you'll enjoy the trip, even if you don't find James. I need to know my money has been well spent."

I nodded and lowered my arms. Ian was right. Just because James's paintings might be here, didn't mean the man was.

As Ian had suggested, I breathed deeply, inhaling cigar smoke and the scent of barbecued fish from the taco stand across the road. I made a mental note to add some Mexican flair to Aimee's spring menu and let my body move with the drums' tempo. A small smile curved my lips.

"That's better." Ian returned my grin and preserved the moment with a click of his camera. This time the flash didn't go off. "Let's get our bearings. Today's goal is finding the studio. Tomorrow you can approach Carlos after you've had a solid night's sleep. You won't be so—"

"Tightly wound?"

"Yeah." He dipped his head, looking at the camera in his hands. He tried to hide an amused grin.

I scowled. "You don't think I'll find him, do you?"

He looked up. "I didn't say that."

"You think this is all a big joke."

He held up his hands in defense. "Hey, wait a second. Don't jump to—"

"You don't want me to find him."

He sighed heavily, glancing down the street before turning back to me. "I don't know what I want. I—" He clamped his lips tight.

"You, what?"

He dug his fingers through his hair. I continued to glare at him and he shrugged a shoulder. "I want to see you happy. I want you to live in the moment and smile spontaneously. Your entire face lights up. It's beautiful."

I blinked. His words left me breathless.

"You have that deer-in-the-headlights expression again," he murmured and started walking in the studio's direction.

I stared dazedly after him. Several paces ahead he stopped and turned. "You coming?"

"Um . . . yeah."

Ian took pictures as we walked. I matched his steps, stopping when he did, and made a point to notice what was around me. He adjusted the camera settings and aimed the lens at an old building. I wondered what he found interesting about cracking adobe, so I asked him. In response, he snapped my picture.

"Stop!" I squealed and grabbed for the strap.

He twisted away, laughing. "I haven't stopped since the day I started. What makes you think I'll do so now?"

I fell into step beside him when he walked across the street, his gaze on some other object. "How did you start?" He'd told me once he had been interested in photography for as long as he could remember.

"My dad was a sports photographer. I borrowed his camera without asking. Took pictures of bugs in the backyard." He gave me a sheepish look. "Make that a lot of pictures. This was before digital cameras were commonplace, so when he'd developed the film, half the roll was of bugs. I'd been expecting the worst sort of punishment when he found out. Instead he gave me his camera."

"He gave you the camera?" I envisioned those expensive cameras I'd seen sports photographers use, the ones with the large lenses where a stand was required to hold the camera steady. "How old were you?"

"Eight. And yes, he gave me his camera. It gave him the excuse to buy a new one he'd had his eye on," Ian explained. Then he stopped. "We've arrived." He pointed at the sign painted on the building beside us.

I stared at my reflection in the El estudio del pintor front window. The studio was dark inside. As Ian had suspected, the gallery was closed. I blindly reached for his hand when my legs started shaking.

His gaze met mine in the window and he squeezed my hand. "All's good, Aims. I'm with you every step." He craned his neck to look around the gallery's corner. "I think the entrance is off the courtyard."

He tugged me along and flipped the latch on a wrought iron gate. Weathered hinges creaked from wear. Potted plants and tropical flowers filled the small courtyard. Bougainvillea scaled the walls, vines speckled with magenta papery flowers reached for the sun. Water trickled from a glazed, ceramic fountain, drowning the street noise.

Two other retailers shared the courtyard, an upscale pottery and ceramic atelier and a real estate agency, which had a door propped open. I tapped the studio's glass entrance above the sign hanging on the other side. "What does it say?"

"'Feeling inspired. Gone fishing, or painting, or running. Will be back soon, but probably later.'" Ian grunted. "I can relate to this guy."

I pressed my nose to the glass the way a kid does at a candy shop, cupping my hands around my eyes to cut out the glare. The studio wasn't half the size of Wendy's back home, but the art on display was breathtaking. "The paintings are beautiful." I sighed against the door, fogging the glass. Canvases of differing mediums—oils, acrylics, and watercolors—covered two walls. Oceanscapes, sunsets, and what I assumed to be local landmarks. There were a few portraits mingled among them. From my angle, I couldn't see what was on the wall alongside me, and the window looking onto the main avenue took up the entire front wall. Sculptures on stained-wood pedestals lorded over the gallery floor.

A small wooden table was tucked into the far corner, littered with paint tubes, brushes, and paper. A petite easel propped on top. It reminded me of the craft table I had in my childhood bedroom. Behind a cluttered desk, stacks of newspapers and books crept up the back wall.

"I wonder if Carlos will be back today," I said against the door, fogging the glass again. I wiped the surface with my forearm.

Ian glanced around the courtyard. "Hold on. Let me check." He disappeared into the real estate agency.

I turned my attention back to the gallery and studied the paintings. Despite the different mediums, the style was similar. They'd been done by the same artist. From my vantage point, I couldn't read the artist's signature on the canvases.

I stepped away from the door and rubbed the back of my neck, which was damp from a mixture of nerves and humidity. Through the real estate office window, I watched Ian converse with the agent on staff, but the courtyard fountain washed away their voices. I wanted to know when Carlos would return, and I wanted the name of the artist on those paintings. I especially wanted to check the hue of the blue signature pigment from the artwork featured in the gallery's pamphlet.

I returned to the front and studied the pieces in the display window. There was a sculptured seagull diving into a wave, a framed watercolor where the artist had signed his name in the same gray hues as the rising sun painted on the textured paper, and an acrylic with a blue signature. I studied the painting's brushstrokes. As much as I wanted to believe James had created the artwork, I wasn't sure. There were similarities, but also vast differences. Unlike the paintings at home where the technique had been controlled and understated, the brushstrokes on this canvas were erratic and carefree. *Liberated* was the word that came to mind, but the end result was a creation just as magnificent as those on my wall at home. Then there was the signature, the writing as erratic as the style. Either the blue pigment had too much green or the window tint skewed the color. I needed to get inside for a better look.

Ian came around the building, talking as he walked through the wrought iron gate. "The real estate agent said Carlos has a habit of closing early. He's training for a marathon. Celine, she's the agent, saw him leave wearing those really small running shorts." He held up his hands, fingers splayed, and squeezed the air as though squishing bread rolls.

My eyes widened and he cleared his throat. "She did that, not me. Just demonstrating."

I rolled my eyes.

"Celine doesn't expect he'll be back today so we'll try again tomorrow. Early, OK? The sign on the door says he opens 'around ten.'" He air quoted.

I pursed my lips and absently nodded. His face fell at my lack of enthusiasm. He tugged my right sleeve. "Come on, Aims, you should be happy. You're one step closer to solving The Case of the Missing Fiancé."

I gave him an exasperated look.

He thumbed toward the window. "I did find out, though, this is the gallery. Carlos's studio is the apartment upstairs. He teaches art classes up there."

I sensed Ian watching me, but I couldn't pull my attention from the acrylic painting in the window. Maybe if I stared hard enough, the signature color would change. Was the lighting wrong or was I forcing myself to see something that wasn't there?

Ian shuffled his feet. "What's wrong?"

I tapped the lower corner of the window. "The blues don't match. I had hoped . . ." My voice fell. Hoped what? I'd find James madly painting, thankful I'd found him, and whisk him home?

What an unrealistic pipe dream that was.

I sank onto the wood bench below the window.

Ian eased down beside me and wrapped his arm around my shoulder. "You'll get your answers tomorrow."

He glanced at his watch and nodded toward the market half a block away. "Let's get something to eat, and some beers. We'll take them to the beach and watch the sunset."

I found myself smiling. "More pictures?"

He grinned. "Absolutely."

"You go ahead and get the food. I'll wait here." I wasn't ready to leave. I sagged against the window and slid on my aviators.

Ian patted my leg. "Back in a few." He stood and departed, but halfway across the street he jogged backward. "Don't do anything stupid," he yelled.

I waved him off and watched passersby behind the security of my sunglasses. My phone buzzed with a new message, one of many waiting in a queue of unanswered texts and voice mails I'd received in the last twenty-four hours. I retrieved the phone from my shoulder bag. Another text from Kristen.

`Call me!`

I scanned through the incoming log. Most of the voice mails were from Kristen. I should listen to them. I should have listened to *her* and never come. Had I set myself up for the ultimate disappointment?

Scrolling through her text messages, I scanned the most recent ones.

`I can't believe you're flying to Mexico. Did you arrive OK?`

`Where are you staying?`

`What's Puerto Escondido like?`

`Have you found anything out yet?`

`Have you found HIM?`

There was a voice message from Mom. *Why Mexico, Aimee? James is dead. You're chasing ghosts. We're worried about you. Please come home.*

I called Kristen. She picked up on the second ring. "Oh. My. God! I can't *fucking* believe you took off. What the hell were you thinking?

Crap, your customers are looking at me funny. Hold on, let me go into your office."

I heard the rustle of her clothes as she entered the office and closed the door. "Hello to you, too," I said when she was back on the phone.

She took a deep breath. "I'm pissed off you didn't listen to Nadia. You put too much trust in Lacy. God, you don't know that woman. What if she's a murderess? You can be her next victim. Why did you go?"

"You know I had to. Besides, Nadia agreed."

"She *what*?" Kristen swore. "She was supposed to talk you out of it."

"She didn't tell you?"

"No! She left out that *minor* detail when she told me we had to help at the café." She paused and I imagined her pinching the bridge of her nose as she always did while thinking. "Jeez, are you all right?"

"I'm fine."

"Where are you now?"

"Sitting on a bench in front of El estudio del pintor."

"And—?"

"And nothing. The gallery's closed. We have to come back tomorrow morning. Ian's buying dinner and I'm waiting. How's the café?"

"Crowded! Busy, but that's good, right?"

"It's wonderful," I said, longing for the routine.

"Will you call me tomorrow? No, wait, I'll call you. Keep in touch, 'k? I'm worried about you."

We said our good-byes and I tucked the phone away. I watched people saunter by, stopping at the gallery window to peer inside. Others hurried onward, faces lowered as they ignored the festive energy around them.

Slow down. Take a look around you. There's so much to see, so much to soak in.

Ian was right. I'd been rushing to a finish line, and I'd failed to enjoy the run along the way. How much time had I wasted on James?

The postcard and painting didn't prove he was alive, so I'd tried looking for answers in places they probably didn't exist. Like the blue paint in the signature and the paintings that resembled James's style. Everything was slightly off.

Like the man running toward me. He looked similar to James as he slowed to a jog, and eventually a fast walk. He checked his sports watch. Sweat drenched his sleeveless workout shirt, molding the fabric to his chest. An iPod was strapped to his upper arm, the headphone wire coiling up his back to the buds in his ears.

I stood on unsteady legs as he approached.

"Hola," he mouthed, smiling as he passed.

I stared, mouth agape.

He stopped and yanked the bud from his right ear. *"¿Está usted bien?"*

I didn't say anything. Only stared.

His eyes perused my length. "American?" he asked, his accent thick. "Are you all right? You look like you've seen a ghost."

Chasing ghosts.

My heart pounded in my ears. The blood in my face pooled into my toes. I felt dizzy, swaying slightly.

He stepped closer, bending slightly to peer into my shaded eyes through his own wraparound sunglasses. "Can I help you with something?" His words were warm, exotic. They rolled off his tongue.

This was insane! He'd been right here. All this time. All along. For nineteen fucking months.

A storm of questions brewed inside me, but I could only speak his name. "James."

He stretched upright to his full height, exactly six foot one. A large, all-too-familiar grin spread across his face. "I see. I'm the ghost." He extended a palm glistening with perspiration. "I'm Carlos."

CHAPTER 19

I collapsed on the bench. "Why did you leave?" I cried. "Fuck, James, I buried you!"

An overwhelming urge to smack him and hug him fiercely warred inside me.

He stood a good three feet from me, turning his head as though searching for someone. He wiped sweat from his brow with the back of his hand and frowned at me.

"W—Why are you looking at me that way?" He stared as though he'd never seen me before.

Touch me.

I hiccupped.

Hold me.

I hiccupped again, my throat locking on to the oxygen. I inhaled, again and again. Short, jerky breaths that strained my lungs. I couldn't exhale.

Oh my God, I can't breathe!

I pounded my chest.

He lowered onto his calves. His lips moved but I couldn't make out the words. I clawed his shoulders. *Touch me, James!*

He did, grasping both wrists. His lips moved again.

What?

Calm down, he mouthed.

I focused on his lips, those beautiful lips.

"Please, señorita, calm down."

I felt a hand behind my head, forcing my face between my knees. Stars burst behind my eyelids. My lungs suddenly worked again. I sucked in the saltiness of the ocean air and his scent. God, his smell. My James.

His hand eased from my head. He lifted his shades and my breath hitched. James's eyes locked on to me. "That's it. Focus." He smiled. James's smile.

"James," I whispered. Happiness burst inside me. "I found you."

He shook his head, but kept the grin. "Focus on me. Listen to my voice. Breathe in." He inhaled, nostrils flaring, and I mimicked. "Good. Now breathe out, slowly." His thumb brushed the inside of my right wrist, directly over the ulnar vein. The butterfly touch turned my arm to jelly.

"Close your eyes and listen to my breathing," he instructed, and my lids slid down. The world went dark and the street sounds faded away. There was only the two of us, the way we used to be. The strong, wide hand holding mine felt like James's. His breathing sounded like James's, the steady, relaxed rhythm, the way it had been when he woke beside me in the morning.

But he didn't sound like James when he told me to open my eyes. His voice was smooth and rich, but the tone grated on my frazzled nerves. Underneath the thick accent, the sound was deeper, raspier. Aged. His dark brown hair was pulled back in a rubber band. A pinkish scar starting at his left brow slashed across his cheekbone. His frame was leaner, but his mannerisms seemed the same, such as the way he tilted his head to search my face.

I swallowed. "James?"

He smiled. "No, sorry."

My lip quivered. "It's me, James, Aimee. Don't you recognize me?"

"I wish I did. You're not someone who's easily forgettable." He chuckled.

I scowled and flipped up my sunglasses. "Dammit, James, look at me."

He did. A split second of confusion skirted across his eyes before disappearing. There was no recognition, only concern.

"James?" I whimpered.

"My name's Carlos. I believe you've confused me with someone else."

I gaped at the man kneeling before me and he blankly stared back. He felt nothing for me. He didn't know me.

A tear fell and Carlos gently pressed his thumb against the hollow of my cheek, wiping the moisture away. I found the touch repulsive. This man was a stranger.

He nodded toward the studio behind me. "This is my gallery. Do you need water or anything? A phone?"

I needed to get away. I had to regroup, think about what to do next.

Go home.

My heart sank.

"Is there someone you're with?"

"No," I automatically replied. Then I nodded, pointing toward the market. "My friend, Ian. He's shopping."

He stood and offered his hand. "Do you want me to walk with you to the market?"

"No, thank you." I stood without his assistance.

"Will you be all right?" His eyes danced over me.

I didn't give him an answer because I didn't have one. Feeling defeated, lost, and confused, I walked away from James. Or Carlos. Or whoever the hell he was.

Ian found me in the produce section. He blinked as though surprised to see me and not quite sure why I was there. I held a strawberry in each hand, rolling the fruit between my fingers. Ian's gaze jumped from my hands to my face. Worry clouded his gaze. "What's wrong, Aimee?"

My mouth screwed downward.

He shifted the food basket to his other hand. "What happened?"

My lower lip quivered and I lowered my hands. The fruit plummeted to the floor and I fell apart.

Ian dropped the food basket and caught me in his arms. I sobbed against his chest. I didn't want him to let go.

At Playa Marinero, lying atop a wool blanket Ian had purchased from a street vendor, we watched the sun set. The fiery orb tucked low on the horizon against a backdrop of orange and pink hues that painted the sky. Waves gently kissed the shore.

Ian devoured his fish tacos, mumbling how starved he was with every bite. In between tacos, he snatched up his camera and took pictures of the vivid scene playing before us. I picked at my salad, pushing around beans and avocados, my appetite long gone.

"These tacos are amazing. Aimee's needs something like this on the menu. It's the sauce, I think. The chipotle adds some kick," Ian said, his words muffled around a mouthful of fish and tortilla. He frowned when I closed the lid on my to-go container. "Aren't you eating?"

"Maybe later." I propped my chin on bent knees and flexed my feet in the sand. The granules, sun-warmed on the surface, were cooler several inches below. They tickled as they sifted over my toes. I tried to feel James's touch in the brush of sand, or hear his voice in the breeze.

For the first time since I'd buried him, I sensed nothing. I'd never felt so completely alone.

Ian chin-nodded toward the ocean. "The waves aren't too bad here. What do you think, one or two feet? Down the beach, over at Zicatela by our hotel where tomorrow's competition will be, I read the swells can reach thirty or forty feet." He shoved a third of his taco into his mouth and mumbled, "That's intense, man."

"Hmm." I closed my eyes, soaking in the day's final rays of heat because my heart felt cold.

I sensed his arm extend in front of me, shadowing my face. "Down the beach there, over at Playa Principal, see all those fishing boats? A woman at the market told me we can pick our fish right off the boats, watch the men clean them, and follow them to the restaurant where they'll cook our dinner. Talk about fresh. We should check it out before we go home."

Home. Without James.

Ian ate his last taco in silence while I replayed the evening's events in my head. When he was done, I heard him wipe his hands and put the food container aside. I then sensed him studying me. "Are you sure it was James?" he asked for the umpteenth time.

"Yes." *No.* I shrugged and murmured against my knees, "I don't know. Carlos looked like him. Well . . . sort of. His face is scarred." I drew a finger along my temple and across my cheekbone.

Ian aimed the camera lens at the radiant sliver visible where the black ocean met the darkening sky. He pressed the button. "If he is James, he would have recognized you. There should have been a reaction from him."

"You would think so," I said in a flat tone. "Maybe he has amnesia."

"Then he would have been more curious about you. He'd wonder if you were someone from his past."

"He acted like he had no memory loss at all. It was like he was a completely different person."

Ian stilled. His gaze sliced into me.

I leaned away. "What?"

He shook his head. "Nothing."

He turned back to the horizon and held the camera against his face, but he didn't take any pictures. He seemed lost in his thoughts, miles from the sandy shores of Puerto Escondido.

CHAPTER 20

El estudio del pintor didn't open for another two hours, but I had spent the past twenty minutes studying Carlos as I would his paintings. I stood across the street, watching him through the gallery's large front window. He rearranged frames on the wall. Every so often, he stopped to inspect the changes, clasping his hands behind his neck or absently rubbing his forearms. Just like James.

At one point, Carlos retreated to the back room so I leaned against a lamppost and waited for the gallery to open. Tourists milled toward the beach, carrying towels and smelling of sunscreen. I pretended to read a paperback novel.

Another twenty minutes went by with no further sign of Carlos. I'd reached the end of the 285 pages I'd scanned at lightning speed. My patience was also at an end. I tucked the book away and crossed over to the gallery.

The **Closed** sign Ian had translated yesterday still hung in the entrance window, but I went inside anyway. The bell above the door jingled and I held my breath, waiting for Carlos. He didn't show, so I walked around. Would I find James's stolen artwork?

I stopped before an acrylic on the opposite wall and studied the artist's initials, *JCD*. The painting's sunset reminded me of James's *Half Moon Bay* piece, but the signature wasn't exactly like James's. The angle of the initials too steep.

I finished circling the room, ending at the desk in back. Books stacked against the wall spanned many genres and years, from Stephen King to Shakespeare, Spanish-titled novels and art instruction manuals in English. *Runner's World*, *Outside*, and *Sport Fishing* magazines had been piled into three separate towers.

Scattered on the desk were order forms, several issues of the local newspaper, and a collection of dirty coffee mugs. A brochure listed Carlos's art workshops, ranging from beginning techniques to advanced brush work.

"Ya cerramos," came a voice behind me. *We're closed.*

I whirled and faced Carlos.

He froze in the doorway to the other room. A smile slowly appeared. *"Hola, señorita."* He came into the main room. "I was wondering if I'd see you again. Aimee, right?" he asked, switching to English.

I nodded and slipped the brochure into my back pocket.

Turpentine and wood oil permeated the air between us, drifting from the soiled cloth Carlos held as he worked dried paint from his fingers. He wore low-slung jeans and a screen-printed shirt from last year's surf *torneo*, and he was barefoot.

Barefoot, sun-kissed, and sexy.

Heat flared across my chest and neck, spreading faster than a wildfire.

I'd spent the past forty-five minutes spying, but hadn't prepared for the sight of him standing before me, from the waves on his head to the curve of his brows and the ridge of his nose. The bone had been broken once. The alignment wasn't quite right.

"Still thinking I'm your James?" he asked in a light tone.

I blinked. "I'm sorry. You look so much like him."

Carlos's eyes sparked. "He must be very good looking."

"He was. I mean, is."

His expression turned wary. "How are you feeling today?"

"Better, thank you." I regarded the gallery. "You're quite talented. Where did you study?"

"Mostly self-taught. Some time ago I took courses at an institute north of here."

"How long has your gallery been open?"

"A couple years." He rubbed hard at a stubborn spot of paint on his right palm.

Look at me! Remember me!

"How long are you in Puerto Escondido?" he asked.

"Several days."

"What brings you here?"

"Searching for a friend. We've lost touch."

He hooked the cloth in his belt loop. "Have you found this friend?"

That same question had churned in my head all night. I'd hardly slept. "No, I haven't. Not yet."

He offered a smile. "I hope you find him."

I hope he remembers me.

"Me, too."

Over Carlos's shoulder I glimpsed a painting that looked like one James hadn't finished. A woman blissfully poised at the ocean's edge. Carlos's scene was bright and colorful compared with the one at home. James's acrylic had been done in grays and browns, the woman awash in despair.

"Can I show you something?" I dug through my shoulder bag for my phone. I wanted to find a picture of James's painting and compare his artistic style to Carlos's. I flicked through the camera roll and landed on my engagement photo. My hand faltered, leaving the photo to stare back at me.

"What've you got?" Carlos peered over my shoulder.

What the hell. I showed him the screen. "This is James. Do you see how much you resemble him?"

Carlos frowned and cupped my hand to bring the phone closer to his face. He studied the screen and I studied him, waiting for a reaction. A frown, a raised brow, a slight dilation of his pupils. Anything to tell me he'd been caught hiding something.

He didn't reveal a thing.

Oh, James. What happened to you?

He looked up from the phone and gave me a sad smile. "James was important to you."

I nodded, my throat tight.

"There's a resemblance, isn't there? Our noses are different, though. I have a higher forehead, too." His eyes crinkled. "Or maybe that's my receding hairline."

I glanced from the photo to Carlos and back. He was right. His nose was thinner, despite the possible break. Looking past the nose, hairline, and scars, Carlos was his own man.

He jerked his head toward the other room. "I have to finish framing. I've got orders to fill. So, unless you want to look at some of my other work . . ." He trailed off and frowned. "Will I see you again?"

He'd better. I wanted to watch him work, the way I used to watch James, so I needed a reason to hang around.

His workshops! The idea popped into my head and I slid the brochure from my pocket. "I'd love to do one of your art classes."

The corner of his mouth twitched. "Really?"

"They sound exciting."

"Have you painted before?"

I bit my lower lip. "Does finger painting count?"

He laughed. "No, it doesn't. Besides, my workshops are weekdays. Tomorrow's Saturday, and you said yourself you're here only for a few days."

My shoulders slumped and my mind cranked. I wanted a reason to see him again, something believable and not lame. Something that didn't make me a crazy woman stalking her deceased fiancé's look-alike.

Carlos yanked the cloth from his back pocket and rolled the edges between his fingers. "Tell you what. Meet me here tomorrow at ten. We'll do the Basics Workshop if you promise to grab some lunch with me afterward. Sound good?"

I smiled. "Sounds wonderful." A warm glow expanded through me. By lunch tomorrow, I'd know if Carlos was James.

I scanned the shoulder-to-shoulder crowd in the hotel's beach café. Ian had said he would meet me, but I didn't see him. My phone vibrated with a new text message.

`Look behind you.`

I spun around. Ian waved from a table for two by the deck's edge.

"You walked right by me," he said when I sat in the seat across from him.

I scooted in my chair and glanced around. The beach below was packed, especially farther down the strip where sun worshippers watched brave souls on boards master the Mexican Pipeline. "I had no idea we'd arrive in the middle of this chaos."

"Me neither. Isn't this great?"

I nodded at the laptop on the table. "How the heck are you getting anything done?"

"I have an incredible ability to shut out noise. Check this out." He tapped a few keys and swung his laptop around so the monitor faced me. Displayed on the screen was an image of an enormous wave curling over a surfer narrowly escaping the diminishing water tube. Ian had edited the photo to pop with color. Sunlight sparkled in the water's vivid turquoise hues. "I've titled the picture *The Mexican Pipeline*, for obvious reasons."

"It's incredible. When did you take it?"

"This morning before the sun was too intense. You should have seen the water, Aims. Those waves are insane. I'm guessing fifteen or twenty feet. And the tubes are deep, making for some tough rides." Eyes wide with excitement, Ian talked with his hands. He demonstrated the motion of the waves and how they broke off the shore. He turned the laptop around and his fingers flew over the keyboard. "I've been tweaking photos, seeing which ones I'll use at my next showing."

I snagged a cold fry from his plate. He looked at me from over his screen. "What've you been up to? Don't tell me." He raised a hand, palm flat. "You found Carlos and got him to confess he's James."

"Ha. Ha. Not funny, but yes, I met with him." I popped another fry.

Ian pushed his plate toward me. "You should have told me. I wanted to go with you."

He had already left for the beach when I woke this morning. When he hadn't returned after I finished breakfast, I'd grown impatient and walked to the studio on my own.

"I was perfectly safe."

He scowled. "How can you be certain? You admitted last night you weren't sure Carlos was James. He could be a mass murderer for all you know."

I rolled my eyes. "Between you and Kristen I'll be dead by tomorrow morning."

"If you keep running off to meet with strangers . . ."

"Ian—"

He tossed up his hands. "I won't apologize for being cautious. Promise you'll be careful. At the very least, let me know when you leave . . . just in case."

I chewed a soggy fry. "Fine."

"Thank you." Ian sighed, relieved. "So, tell me what happened."

"I spent forty-five minutes playing Peeping Tom from across the street until I went inside and spoke with Carlos."

"And . . . ?"

"And nothing. I can't figure him out. Carlos is leaner and tanner. Even his hair is lighter than James's."

"Simple explanation. Sun and aging."

"True. His scent is familiar, and some of his hand gestures are the same. His face is different, thinner nose, narrower cheekbones." Almost as if he wore a mask. "Anyhow," I shrugged, "I have a few more days so I'm going to spend time getting to know him. I registered for an art workshop."

Ian snorted.

"What?"

"You. Painting." He chuckled, playing with his keyboard.

"Shut up," I grumbled and ate another fry. "If he is James, there has to be a reason why he doesn't recognize me, don't you think? He must have amnesia. What else can it be? My gut tells me—"

"You're hungry?" He flagged a waitress who stopped midstride beside our table and pointed in my direction.

"A hamburger, please. With lots of fries." I grinned at Ian.

"And to drink?" she asked, sounding harried as her pencil scratched over her memo pad.

"She'll have a beer," Ian suggested.

"I'll have a mai tai."

Ian hooted, smacking his hand on the table. "Make that two."

"Anything else for you?" the waitress asked him. Her eyes peeked at his laptop. She pointed her pencil tip at the screen. "Is that Lucy?"

Ian paused, his gaze snapping from me to our waitress, ANGELINA, according to her name tag. "Do you know her?" he asked, sitting straighter in his seat.

"She reminds me of Imelda Rodriguez's friend. Mrs. Rodriguez is the hotel manager," she clarified when Ian frowned.

"Lucy stayed here several weeks ago, and the woman in the picture looks like her. She visits a lot." There was a shout from the bar. Angelina glanced over her shoulder. "I'll be right back with your drinks."

"What was that all about?" I asked after she left.

Ian showed me the laptop screen. Displayed was the picture I'd texted him of Lacy. He'd edited the image, enhancing Lacy—Laney, Lucy, or whatever her given name was. Surfing photos weren't the only images Ian had been tweaking. He looked poignantly at me. "Don't stop listening to your gut."

My stomach growled, echoing Ian's sentiment.

CHAPTER 21

I went to the beach after lunch while Ian sought Imelda. He wanted information about Lacy and insisted on meeting Imelda alone. He wouldn't explain why he needed to locate Lacy—who he referred to as Laney—only that she could help him find something he'd lost. If Ian learned of Lacy's whereabouts, he promised to give me her contact information. I wanted to know where she got James's *Meadow Glade* and who had asked her to find me.

A young couple vacated their lounge chairs as I approached. Honeymooners. The woman's diamond ring gleamed in the sunlight. She smiled as she passed, wrapping her arm around the man's waist. I watched them walk away, mindful I'd been twirling my engagement ring around my finger. Soap and time had dulled the precious metal.

I tossed my beach bag and an extra towel on the spare lounge to save a spot for when Ian joined me later, and then adjusted the sun umbrella to expose my legs and shade my face. November was cold at home and the afternoon Mexican sun felt warm and inviting.

Crowds gathered at the tournament farther down the beach. The loudspeaker crackled with announcements every few moments and the

Red Hot Chili Peppers played in the background. Neither tuned out the waves violently slamming the shore. They roared like thunder.

A waiter moved into view, blocking the Pacific. I ordered a pitcher of ice water with two glasses and another mai tai. Settling into the chair, I read a book to pass the time. Ian's meeting should be done soon and I wouldn't see Carlos until the following morning.

The waiter returned with my water and cocktail, and arranged the drinks on the wooden table between the chairs. My cell phone pinged with an incoming text message as I signed the check to my room number.

"Gracias, señorita," he said when I returned the bill. He then trudged through the blistering sand to another hotel guest sunbathing nearby.

I sipped the mai tai and checked my phone. Another message from Kristen.

> `Don't forget to call me or I'm flying to Mexico! Booking ticket in 3, 2 . . .`

I called her back. She picked up on the first ring. "Thank God, you're still alive."

"Alive and kicking. Is my café still standing?"

"Of course. Why wouldn't—?" She huffed. "Everything's fine. I'm fine. Nadia's fine. So yeah, we're all good, including Alan."

Mr. Girly Coffee. I rubbed my brow. "What about him?"

"He came to the café this morning for his usual and was disappointed you weren't here. He's really interested in you."

"That's nice," I drawled. "Too bad I'm not interested in him."

"Could it be because you're interested in Ian? And, omigosh!" She gasped. "He's traveling with you. Imagine that."

"Kristen . . . ," I warned.

"He thinks the world of you and you've pretended not to notice—"

"I've noticed," I blurted in defense.

"You have? Then do something about it."

"I can't. James—"

Kristen groaned dramatically. "Look, Aimee, all weirdness aside, I'm sure Lacy is lying. Come home. Just because she sent James's painting from Mexico doesn't mean he's there."

"But he is. I found him."

"What?" she croaked.

"I mean, I think I did. It's Carlos, the gallery's owner, but he looks different."

"You're not making sense."

"Which is why I need more time. A few more days."

Kristen was quiet. I watched surfers chase an elusive swell, only to get back on their boards and try again.

"When are you coming home?" she asked.

"My flight leaves Monday morning." I wondered if James would be on the plane with me. Could we pick up our lives where we'd left off? Not a chance. I knew in my heart things would never be the same with James, and it made me almost as sad as I'd been when he died.

"Be safe," Kristen said.

I sighed. "I will."

"Oh!" she exclaimed before I disconnected the call. "I almost forgot. Thomas came into the café this morning. He asked about you. I told him you were in Puerto Escondido."

My body tensed. I lunged upright and swung my feet off the chaise, mentally smacking my forehead. I should have told them not to mention anything to Thomas. "Did you tell him why?"

"Only that you needed a vacation. He got all funny about it, too, asked me all sorts of questions. He wanted to know why you'd picked that spot and if you'd planned the vacation or the trip was a spur-of-the-moment kind of thing."

"Do you think he was simply curious?"

"He could have been, but you know Thomas. He's been so weird lately."

Ian walked up and smiled when he saw me on the phone. I motioned for him to sit and he tossed aside my towel, stretching out on the neighboring chaise.

"Ian's here. I should go," I said to Kristen, and when she asked, I promised to call before my flight.

The sun dipped lower on the horizon, the heat sweltering. I squinted at Ian. "Any luck with Imelda?"

He shook his head as he poured water into the spare cup. Condensation had collected on the outside of the pitcher and dripped onto the sand.

I wanted to ask about Lacy and what he'd lost. I wanted to support him the way he'd been helping me, and I wanted his trust. I would keep his deepest, most personal secrets close to my heart.

I wanted him.

Air whooshed from my lungs. Why was I feeling this way now? What the heck was wrong with me? James was the man I want. I was here for James.

"Imelda didn't have time to meet," Ian was saying, "so I have an appointment late tomorrow morning." He drank half the glass in two large gulps. "She asked about you, though."

My brows lifted. "Me?"

"She wants to know what you think of Carlos's gallery."

"How does she know you're here with me?" I twisted my hair into a messy bun. "Maybe she saw us together."

Ian shrugged. "Ask her. She offered to treat you to lunch tomorrow."

"I'm having lunch with Carlos."

He glowered. "Grab a drink with her afterward."

"What a strange request." I wiped the sweat off my forehead with a towel corner. "I barely spoke with her yesterday."

"She's the hotel manager. Maybe she's being a gracious host."

I stared pointedly at Ian. "You don't believe that, do you?"

"Not for an instant," he said without hesitation.

We studied each other. I sensed Ian had something to say, but he remained quiet. After a moment, I readjusted the umbrella and Ian launched his laptop. Research, he told me. I returned to my book.

Thirty minutes or so later, he complained about the sun, wiping the sweat off his neck. "Since the ocean's too damn dangerous, I'll be at the pool," he grumbled, standing to fold his towel. He gazed across the surf and pointed. "Look! Even the pros need a tow from the break area."

I shielded my eyes with my hand and watched Jet Skis, water rescue sleds in tow, jam over the swells farther offshore. They aimed for the boarders treading water waiting for a shuttle to shore.

Ian shut down his laptop and slipped it into his bag. He threw his towel over his shoulder. "Coming to the pool?"

"In a little bit."

After he left, I rubbed sunscreen on my legs. The waiter returned with a fresh water pitcher and I ordered another mai tai. I settled into the chaise and closed my eyes, leaving the book opened across my thigh.

"Aimee."

My eyes snapped open. I squinted against the intense sunlight and glanced at the silhouette standing at the end of my chair. Rough material brushed across my legs. "Your skin is burned."

Carlos.

He bent over, blocking the sun, and adjusted the spare towel he'd placed over me.

I sat upright and pulled my legs into the umbrella shade. Carlos turned around and called out in Spanish to three men standing by the water. He motioned for them to go ahead without him. They waved and continued walking along the beach toward town.

He nodded at my table. "Pedro makes great mai tais. How's yours?"

The drink I'd ordered sat on the table in a condensation puddle. I frowned. How long had I been asleep? Long enough to fry. My shins burned.

"Pedro's the bartender at Casa del sol," Carlos clarified, mistaking my confused silence. He pointed at the edge of my chaise. "May I?"

"Sure." I shifted when he sat, adjusting my balance against the dip in the chair to compensate for his weight. He smiled and leaned over, picking up my book in the sand. The paperback had fallen while I slept. He shook off the sand before marking my page and put the book on the table.

The crowd from earlier had dissipated, the competition done for the day. Carlos still wore last year's tournament shirt, but had replaced his jeans with board shorts. His forehead glistened from the sun's heat.

"Were you at the competition?" I asked.

"For a little bit. The competitors are good this year."

"Do you surf?"

"Not in the last two years." He pointed to his face near the scar angling around his left eye. "I was messed up pretty bad. My cheekbones and nose were reset. Medical care in this region is still last century. I took a while to recover." He gave me a lopsided grin.

My mouth fell open. Holy shit! He must have hit his head hard enough to lose his memories. Total blackout. The accident and facial surgery explained why his bone structure was different from James's, but not the memory loss. Wouldn't he have tried to figure out who he was? Why hadn't he returned home? He seemed completely unaware of his identity before the accident.

I was about to ask Carlos when Ian approached. He'd switched his laptop for a camera. Carlos stood when Ian stopped beside my chair. Ian's thigh brushed my upper arm. I had to catch myself from leaning into his nearness.

"I didn't mean to interrupt," he said.

"No problemo." Carlos thumbed in the direction his friends went. "I should go."

Ian extended his hand toward Carlos. "I'm Ian, by the way."

"Sí, Ian. El amigo." He gripped Ian's hand. "Carlos."

"Nice to meet you." Ian stole a glance at me before he said to Carlos, "I've seen the fliers for your gallery. Your paintings are good."

"Gracias."

"Is all the artwork yours?"

Carlos slipped his hands into side pockets. "Only the paintings. The sculptures were done by my friend, Joaquin."

Ian crossed his arms. "I'm curious as to why you sign your paintings *JCD*. What's the *J* stand for?"

"Ian—"

Carlos's mouth lifted in a half grin. "Honest question. My full name is Jaime Carlos Dominguez."

I sucked in a breath. *James Charles Donato.* My pulse thrummed loudly in my ears. The initials were too much of a coincidence for them not to mean anything.

Carlos smiled at me. "Tomorrow at ten?"

I nodded, stone-faced. He grinned and jogged after his friends.

"You OK?" Ian asked me, and then frowned. "Let's get out of the sun. You look pale."

I gave him a blank stare. "I'm fine." I stood to put on my swim cover and weaved.

Ian pushed on my shoulder. "Sit down. Drink some water." He filled my cup, looking worried. "Slowly," he said when I gulped the sun-warmed liquid.

While I waited for the dizziness to subside, Ian folded my towels and packed the beach bag. As we walked to the hotel, he wrapped an arm around me. "It's almost dinner time and you need food. Let's freshen up and eat. My treat."

He could have offered to fly me to the moon and I would have accepted. Between Carlos and the sun, my head was a hot mess. I leaned into him and he supported my weight as we walked back to the hotel.

CHAPTER 22

By the time Ian arrived at my room, I'd settled on a blue sundress I knew he liked.

My hands shook while fastening the tiny bodice buttons. I left the top two undone, then decided to unbutton one more. I checked my reflection one last time and marveled at how calm I looked despite my heart's rapid fluttering. While the afternoon sun had left me feeling lightheaded, I couldn't help thinking tonight's dinner felt like a date. My first-ever first date. James and I had already been too comfortable with each other when he'd taken me to a movie as boyfriend and girlfriend. We'd known each other for years and had been to plenty of movies together.

Ian knocked and I jolted, spinning to look at the door. Gripping the knob, I jerked the door open. It crashed into the wall.

"Whoa." Ian smacked his palm against the door to keep it from hitting my backside. He wore a fitted V-neck black shirt, flat-front khakis, and flip-flops. And he smelled remarkable. Shower fresh and beachy.

He smiled, his mouth pulling up on one side. It made him look too sexy for our dinner to be a casual night between friends.

The camera strap across his chest caught my attention. It was twisted. I straightened the strap with trembling fingers.

He pressed my palm against his chest. "Relax."

"I can't." The room started spinning. I stared at his chest and leaned into him.

"Look at me," he said in a raspy tone. Our gazes met. "Let's forget about the café and the next exhibit. Forget about Laney-Lacy and why we're here. Tonight it's just us, no one else. Can we do that?"

I nodded, unable to look away from him. There was something in his voice, the smooth cadence of his words. I thought about more than Ian kissing me, and wondered how he'd feel over me, naked. What did his skin feel like under his shirt? My fingers curled into the cotton.

God, I must have sunstroke to be thinking like this.

Ian twined his fingers around mine and pulled me into the hallway. "You look flushed. Let's get some food in you."

He'd made reservations at the resort's restaurant on the second-level beach terrace. It overlooked the pool deck. We ordered, and after the waitress left, fell silent. I watched him fidget with his utensils, nudging the forks on his napkin and checking the knife's sharpness. He was as nervous as I was, and I found that amazing. I knew he cared for me deeply, yet he still followed me across the globe as I chased another man.

I would search every corner of the earth.

Ian's words echoed in my head. He was either very stupid or very much in love. With me.

I glanced away.

"What are you thinking?" he asked quietly.

A flush crept across my cheeks. I cleared my throat. "I'm thinking about you. Us. Why you're here," I boldly admitted. "Why did you come with me?"

He watched me for what seemed like eons. "I lost someone very dear to me because I didn't go after her. I was angry and hurt, so I let her go. But once my anger faded, I realized it wasn't her fault she hurt me. She couldn't help who she was. By then it was too late. She was long gone and I had no idea where."

He turned his attention to the ocean, the breeze rustling his hair. It didn't occur to me to be jealous of this woman who held his heart. His pain seemed too deep and old. Instead, I itched to run my fingers through the waves on his head to soothe him. "Who was she?"

"My mother." He leaned toward me, covered my hand with his. "Because of her, I learned not to let go too easily of the people I want in my life. Friends, people I care about a lot." His thumb caressed my fingers. "I care about you, Aimee. More than you know."

I felt the full impact of his words. They raced up my arm from where he touched me, electrons charging my skin. "I'm glad you're here. And I'm glad you invited me to dinner. This is nice."

He tucked an errant curl behind my ear. "I'm willing to bet the food won't compare to yours, but I'm just happy to be here with you."

"Our dinner has yet to arrive and you're already bashing it."

He chuckled. "I eat out a lot because of my traveling. But these past months you've given me a cooked meal to take home every afternoon. Makes it hard to try something else when I already have the best." His expression darkened, a reflection of sadness in the candlelight's soft glow. "It'll be a shame if you don't return to the café. Your talent's too good to waste. It needs to be showcased."

"Like your photos?"

He nodded. "There's magic in your recipes. I think you accomplished what you set out to do. You've created a unique coffee experience, and your customers return because your food and drinks make them feel good. It's like how *Belize Sunrise* makes you want to go there. True artists elicit an emotional response through their work. You, Aims, are an artist."

I blushed and inclined my head. Ian's compliment made me itch to dance and sing. But his concern worried me. "I'm not going to abandon my café."

"What about Carlos?" he asked. "In all likelihood he's James. What if he doesn't want to leave Mexico? Will you stay with him?"

Ian didn't hide his fear. It was there in his expression, the tightness in his shoulders. He was afraid of losing me.

"I hope it doesn't come to that." But I knew eventually I would have to make a choice.

The waitress arrived with our food and after we ate and Ian paid the bill, he surveyed his camera, adjusting the lens and settings. I watched the moonlight ripple on the ocean, the clicks and beeps from Ian's camera background noise. A faint smile touched my lips. I would always associate those sounds with him. Tonight we agreed not to discuss the café or his photography, but we still talked shop, and it didn't bother me. I loved how passionate he was about his work. I loved—

Ian snapped a picture of me. Light flashed, scattering my thoughts.

I blinked. "Why did you do that?"

"You're beautiful." He studied the digital image. "You were admiring the ocean and I liked your expression. It was serene."

"Oh." I folded the napkin in my lap.

"I hadn't seen that look on you before and I wanted to capture it." He showed me the image. I caught a quick glimpse before he turned off the camera, leaving me with the impression I'd been looking at a stranger.

"How are your pictures turning out?" He hadn't taken many landscape shots, mostly local culture and activity. Pictures of people.

"Not as bad as I thought."

"That's because you're really good."

He shrugged a shoulder. "I haven't always liked my work."

Emotions played across his face. Unease settled in the fine lines above his cheekbones. I stroked his fingers with my thumb. "I think your work likes you. You find beauty where others don't see it. Or rather, they choose to ignore. You have a gift."

Ian grunted. He put the cap back on the lens. "A few people here agreed to be my subjects and let me exhibit their image. Do you mind if I show pictures I've taken of you?"

I leaned away. "Me?"

"I wouldn't sell them. I couldn't sell you," he said almost as an afterthought. He set his camera aside. "I'll have Wendy send you a release form when we get home." He pointed to my empty plate. "Are you done?"

I nodded.

"Good. Let's go see what kind of trouble we can get into." He grinned wickedly and I laughed.

We went to the lounge for a cocktail. A mariachi band performed on a small stage that opened to the pool patio. It glowed under a canopy of white twinkle lights.

Ian snagged my arm, dragging me onto the dance floor, and I squealed. "It's too late to tell me you don't like to dance," he said over the trumpets.

"I never said I don't like to dance," I yelled by his ear. "I love to dance. It's the music. It's so . . . so . . ."

"Peppy?"

"Polka-ish!"

He raised bent arms, clapping by his left shoulder before shifting to his right, his movements exaggerated. Giggling, I mimicked him, spinning in a circle, arms raised. My skirt flared around my thighs. He snapped a picture when I came around.

"Stop!" I chided and grabbed at the camera. He moved out of reach. I planted fists on my hips. "We had an agreement. Put that thing away."

"Wait here." He retreated to the bar where he conversed with the bartender, handing over the camera and cash. The bartender tucked the camera away and slipped the bills into his pocket.

The music slowed. Brass horns emitted seductive notes. Guitar strings plucked a rhythm that tempted a sway from my hips. Ian approached and our gazes met across the dance floor. My lips parted. The intensity and determination in his eyes kept me rooted to my spot. He closed the distance and gathered me in his arms. A shiver coursed through me, and something akin to hunger. I pressed closer.

His hands moved up my body, achingly slow, until he cupped my face. He brushed his thumb across my lips, and then he kissed me. It was hot and desperate and tender all at once.

We moved over the dance floor, our bodies in sync. The music grew louder, our lips bolder, tongues tangling. Then I remembered where we were and why I was here. "What are we doing?" I gasped into his mouth. "What are you doing to me?" I could hardly keep track of my thoughts.

"Kissing you," he murmured against my lips. "Loving you."

He kissed me as no other man had, and until this moment, I'd been kissed by only one other man who mattered. But that was long ago and I had a hard time remembering how those kisses felt.

My thoughts jumbled. I was confused about what Ian was doing to me. I was confused about how I felt toward him. And I was confused about him. I should be pushing him away. Instead, I held on.

His hands moved over my back, frantic. His lips were everywhere, my jaw, my chin, the length of my neck. His tongue traced my pulse point, making me hyperaware of every inch of skin. It was too much. I tore my mouth away. "Why are you doing this?" I panted. "Why now?"

His lips skimmed across my cheek. He nipped my ear. "I couldn't compete with a dead guy. You worshipped him."

"So I wouldn't forget him," I cried, desperate. I felt out of control.

Ian dug his fingers into my hair and seared his gaze with mine. "He's alive, Aimee. Flesh and blood. *That* I can compete with."

"This isn't a game, Ian. I'm not some sort of prize."

His eyes hardened. "You could never be a prize. You are so much more than that to me. You deserve so much more than what you allow yourself to feel."

I was feeling all right. I was ready to burst with the sensations Ian's gaze alone stirred within me, let alone the way he touched my skin, how his mouth worked my lips. What was going on with me?

Push him away. Focus on why you're here.

"You're my employee," I said lamely.

"Then I quit." His mouth descended hard on mine. He groaned. Or was that me?

I trailed my fingers down his chest as I felt myself falling, letting go. Of everything safe and familiar. *God, I'm here for James.* I shoved him, breaking our kiss.

His eyes, dark and stormy, bore into mine. He showed me everything.

"Ian . . ."

"I love you."

". . . don't."

"Love me, Aimee."

My world crumbled. "I can't." I burst into tears and ran from the lounge.

I found a darkened corner in the lobby and sank onto a wicker chair. My blood thrummed and heart raced. Ian hadn't cracked the barrier I'd erected around myself. He'd blasted the wall with dynamite. Blown it to bits. He had made me see *him*.

Movement across the lobby caught my attention. Ian headed toward the elevators, his expression grim. He was going up to his room and he'd forgotten his camera.

I jumped from the chair and returned to the bar, convincing the bartender to give me the camera. I returned to my corner in the lobby, unable to resist skimming through the digital photos. They were phenomenal, split seconds of life caught in brilliant color. Every image had a story to tell, including mine.

I stared at the picture Ian had taken at dinner and saw someone I didn't recognize. Actually, someone I hadn't seen in a very long time. Me. Pleasantly at ease. Unguarded. A woman in love.

Air rushed from my lungs. My stomach tightened. I shook my head in denial, but the truth stared back at me. When he snapped the picture, I'd been thinking about how much I loved Ian's passion for his work. About how much I loved him.

Oh, Ian.

I turned off the camera and rushed to his room, knocking loudly. He yanked open the door and my breath snagged. He glared at me, shirtless, with pajama bottoms slung low on his hips. I was done for.

"Can I come in?" I showed him the camera.

He nudged the door wider and kept it open after I'd entered. I lifted the strap over my head, but didn't give him the camera. Not yet.

"I looked at your pictures," I admitted.

Loud, raucous laughter drifted from the hall. Late-night partiers returning to their rooms. Ian let the door swing shut and crossed his arms, his neck muscles flexing. He wasn't happy.

I swallowed. "I'm sorry, but once I started I couldn't stop. I know you don't like to exhibit portraits. Something about it makes you uncomfortable. I get that. But your work is amazing. Beyond brilliant." I moistened my lips and dared a step closer. "They moved me."

He motioned for the camera.

I took another step closer. "You move me."

"Aims," he growled. "I can't do this. I can't start with you and have you push me away. I'd rather stay friends if you don't want me that way. Give me the camera."

I put it on the chair beside me. "I won't push you away."

Our gazes locked. His jaw tightened. It was the only warning I had. One second he was by the door, the next he was pressed fully against me. His fingers plunged through my hair and his mouth landed on mine. The storm I'd awakened in him earlier took over.

My hands skimmed up his chest and curved around his neck and head. I didn't want him to end the kiss. His hands raced over my shoulders and down my back. He unzipped my dress. The material floated to the floor and he followed, pulling down my panties. Then he stood in front of me and I couldn't stop touching him. The smooth plane of his chest, the shallow dip in his lower back. He was hard where I was soft, strong where I was weak. He was my friend, and I couldn't stop myself from falling for him.

He cupped my breasts, forcing a gasp from me, and pushed us toward the bed until I was sitting on the edge. He dropped to his knees and rested his hands on my thighs, spreading my legs. I was open to him, exposed, and his eyes caught mine. One last chance to stop. One last chance to tell him this wasn't what I wanted. He wasn't who I wanted.

But I wanted him. All of him.

I nodded. He groaned, the sound primal, and bent his head. I cried out at the touch of his tongue, the caress of his mouth. I clutched his head, holding him to me, and shattered. Then he was gone.

My eyes snapped open. Ian stood before me, shoving down his pants. There was no denying how much he wanted me.

He climbed on the mattress and dragged me up to the pillows, settling his weight over me. He reached to the side table, sliding open the drawer.

"Ian," I cried.

"I'm here, baby," he whispered in my ear.

I heard foil tear. He shifted, adjusting, and entered me fully. "I love you," he said, then he started to move. I latched on to him, barely keeping up with the sensations sliding over me, in me.

"Fall for me, Aimee. I'll catch you." He thrust harder, and I felt him touch my soul. "Let go, baby."

I did, falling hard over the edge, shuddering, and Ian was there to catch me.

I slowly opened my eyes and took in the room. Ian's room. I lay prone in his bed, listening to him breathe. I found the steady intake and release comforting, and I imagined waking beside him every morning. A soft smile danced on my lips.

It was early, only a whisper of light seeped through the partially opened balcony, and I was wide awake. I'd slept hard through the night, the best sleep I'd had in months. Ian had loved me well into the night, doing things to my body I'd never imagined possible, and things to my heart I'd never dreamed. Remembering, my entire body flushed under the sheet.

Then reality let itself in the room, and the euphoria of last night's lovemaking dissipated like water on a hot griddle. I'd betrayed my feelings for James. I'd betrayed myself.

Tears leaked from the corners of my eyes as I eased from the bed, careful not to shake the mattress. I didn't dare look at Ian. I didn't dare allow myself a peek at how gorgeous I imagined he was in the morning, sleep rumpled and sexy. Vulnerable.

I slipped into my clothes and picked up my sandals, and then left the room. But before the door closed, I stole a glance. He watched me with a bewildered expression and I felt my heart fragment in two. One part for James. The other, I left with Ian.

CHAPTER 23

I arrived at El estudio del pintor fifteen minutes before class because I was tired of wandering the beach. I'd left the hotel before Ian came looking for me. I'd hurt him, and I wasn't ready to deal with last night.

But everything reminded me of what we'd done. My skirt brushed against the places he'd touched, still sensitive from the night before. The salty air tasted of his skin, and the breeze caressing my neck felt like his kisses.

Ian had pushed me to heights I hadn't been bold enough to climb with anyone else. Then I'd let go like he asked and invited him inside my heart.

He didn't belong there, even though I knew I'd let him in long before Mexico. My heart was supposed to be reserved for James. He was the reason I was here.

A young woman greeted me upon entering the gallery. She raised espresso eyes and put aside the paperback novel she was reading. *"¡Hola! ¿Cómo está?"*

"Muy bien, gracias." I answered the question with an apologetic smile. "I'm sorry. I don't speak Spanish."

Her eyes widened. "You're the beautiful American woman Carlos told me about."

My brows lifted and I pointed at my chest. "Me?"

She giggled. "*Sí!* I probably shouldn't have said anything, but Carlos mentioned more than once you were coming this morning." She walked around the desk and shook my hand. "I'm Pia. I work the Saturday shift because he is never here on Saturdays." She emphasized "never" with the wave of her hands. "*Sí*, you must mean something to him."

Interesting.

"Why do you think so?" I switched my bag to the other shoulder. My fingers trembled. I was anxious and nervous to see Carlos.

"Saturdays are for painting and"—she wrinkled her nose—"running. He runs. A lot."

"Isn't he training for a marathon?"

"He told you?" she asked, incredulous, then assessed me from head to sandal-clad feet. "Carlos can't figure you out. You want art lessons and you don't like to paint. I think he can't figure you out because he can't get you out of his head." She tapped a finger against her temple. "How come?"

I gave her a blank look. "I don't understand what you mean?"

She narrowed her eyes. "Why do you want to paint? You like Carlos, don't you?"

"He's an excellent painter." And I did like him. No, I loved him.

I should have left Ian's camera at the bar, then I wouldn't have gone to his room. *God!* I still wore James's engagement ring.

"Carlos is an excellent painter," Pia was saying. "But never on Saturdays. *Sí,* he likes you. I'm so happy for him. He's been so sad after he lost—" She smacked her forehead and giggled. "*Ei, ei, ei* . . . I've said too much, as usual, but I like you so I'll keep quiet. Carlos is upstairs." She pointed out the door. "Go back to the courtyard and take the stairs through the door on the left."

"Thanks," I said. "It was nice meeting you."

"Have fun," she called as the door swung closed behind me.

I went through the doorway Pia directed and up the narrow stairwell. The stairs opened to a room ablaze in natural light. Skylights dotted the ceiling. Large windows overlooked the street below, the blue ocean a thin line above the rooftops. Artwork in differing mediums—pastels, oils, acrylics, ink, and charcoal—decorated the walls. Rows of easels filled the room, aligned classroom style with one easel in front. Carlos's spot.

I called his name. He didn't answer. Where was he?

I had no idea what to expect. I didn't enjoy painting, but I wanted time with him. I would study him and the way he painted. Was he left-handed, too? Did he organize his brushes by bristle width and texture? James had done that.

Along the southern wall were three doors, the first wide open, revealing a storage closet packed with pigment tubes, brushes, turpentine cans, and blank canvases. I tried the middle door and found it locked. Feeling like Goldilocks, looking for the "just right" room that held Carlos, I tested the third door. It swung open. The room was brighter than the main room and I squinted, my eyes adjusting.

An easel stood in the center of the room beside a table laden with paint tubes and soiled rags. Tin cans, mason jars, and mugs held brushes and palette knives. Stacks of canvases, some finished, others with scenes abandoned halfway through completion, leaned against the adjacent wall. The style was so reminiscent of James. I instantly knew they'd been painted by Carlos. This was his private studio.

I moved farther into the room and stopped short. A sudden coldness hit my core, burning the way your esophagus does when you swallow too many ice chips. Propped against the back wall, behind the table and out of view from the doorway, were James's missing paintings.

Holy shit!

How did they get here? When did they get here?

I jerked my head around the room. Aside from Carlos's more recent paintings beside me, all the others belonged to James. Everything except the woman painted on the canvas in the far corner of the room. She lured me with her Caribbean-blue eyes.

My eyes.

There had to be a dozen paintings of this woman, hidden from view unless you came fully into the room. I doubted Carlos invited any visitors into his studio. He didn't want people to see these paintings.

I studied the woman closely on the first canvas. The almond-shaped eyes and contoured brows resembled me, but the blue hue of the irises was slightly off. I flipped to the next canvas. She had been painted from a different angle as though Carlos gazed down at her. The hair and eye shades still resembled me.

I picked through the canvases like folders in a filing cabinet. The model's coloring moved further from my shades deeper into the stack, the dates on the paintings getting older. Each painting was different from the next in the way Carlos might have visualized the woman but couldn't achieve the perfect match of color on canvas. They were flawed replicas of me. Like the signature paint he used wasn't a perfect match of James's blue.

Why had Carlos been painting me if he didn't remember me? Why did he deny he was James?

Sweat broke across my body. Wispy tendrils of hair clung to the back of my neck. My thoughts chaotic, my gaze jumped around the room, landing on the canvas clamped to the easel. It was another version of me. This one had eyes identical to the color and shape of mine.

Because Carlos had seen my eyes!

I thought I'd imagined his confusion the other day when I lifted my sunglasses, pleading he remember me.

On the table was a plastic container of custom-mixed paint. I unscrewed the lid and a sob escaped me. Carlos had finally done it. James's Caribbean blue.

Oh, James! I found you.

I noticed random things around the room. Paint tubes squeezed in the middle like tubes of toothpaste. Clean brushes ordered by bristle width and texture. Tools and supplies positioned on the left side of the easel because he was left-handed. Just like James.

Water ran in the next room, the one with the locked door. A handle unlatched, the floor creaked, and Carlos appeared in the doorway. He hesitated and blinked.

I pointed at the canvas on the easel. "Do you mind explaining this?"

He clenched his jaw and his eyes narrowed on the paint jug I held. His studio was probably off-limits to students and my presence had taken him off guard. But the unlocked door had invited me inside, giving me a peek at the image haunting him from a life he didn't remember, or had chosen to forget.

My arms stiffened around the paint jug. What if James hadn't wanted to marry me? What if he'd chosen art over me? What if his family's demands with the business had forced him to give everything up, including me? He'd stolen his own paintings, faked his death, and moved away. Started over.

On some level, I understood my thoughts didn't add up. They didn't make sense, except for one. James hadn't wanted me.

My eyes widened at the realization, then nineteen months of baggage cascaded down my cheeks in the shape of big, fat tears.

Carlos rubbed his face with both hands. His gaze skirted the room, finally resting on me. "What's wrong?"

"Nothing." I swore profusely. "Everything! I'm confused." I roughly wiped my cheeks against my shoulders. "I'm happy I found you and sad you left. *Fuck!*" I scowled at him. "What the hell are you doing here, James?"

He stiffened. "I'm not James."

"Then explain this." I jabbed a finger at my image on the easel. "And these." I pointed to James's canvases propped against the wall.

"Can you tell me why none of those scenes are places in Mexico? Did you know they're in California? Don't you find that odd?"

His eyes flared. "First of all, this is my studio. It's private. Second, these paintings are none of your damn business."

"They are when you're painting me!" I blasted.

"That's not you!" He fired back. "I didn't know you until two days ago. She's—" He swore, rounding the easel, and jerked a finger at the canvas. "I dream about that woman almost every night. It's the same damn dream, over and over, and . . ." His voice tapered and he looked away.

He was embarrassed, maybe ashamed. Perhaps he was infuriated with himself, remembering none of this was my business.

"I've never told anyone about her. Not even—" He stopped and shook his head.

"Have you wondered why you dream about her?" I asked.

"Constantly."

"Have you tried to find her?"

His nostrils flared. "She doesn't exist."

"She does exist!" I smacked my chest. "She's right here."

His eyes hardened. I sensed turbulence roiling under his hard exterior, anger at my entering his private domain, threaded with uncertainty. I latched on to that emotion and followed his gaze to where he stared fixedly at the painting on the easel. The woman bewildered him.

I held up the blue paint tube. "You first mixed this color at Stanford, an exact match to my eyes. You wanted something on each painting reminding you of me. I know, it's sappy, but we'd never been apart longer than a few days. It was hard for us being separated while you were at school. You used this color as your signature paint, as you've been doing on your paintings downstairs. This is the color you've been trying to mix." I jiggled the container, the thick goo sloshing inside. "The only reason you got this hue is because you, as Carlos, finally saw my eyes."

He looked at me as though seeing me for the first time. His gaze drifted over every inch of my body, rising to my face. He didn't say anything. I dropped the paint tube on the table.

Carlos swallowed. "What happened to him?"

I scratched my nail on the wood table and took a deep breath. "James went to Cancún on a business trip to take a client fishing. There was an accident on the boat and he went missing. His brother brought James's remains home after his body had been located. The memorial service was on our wedding day, seventeen months ago." I turned toward the window and stared at the ocean beyond the low rooftops.

"Why are you still looking if he's dead?" Carlos asked behind me. "Why here when he died on the other side of the country?"

"I had reason to believe you hadn't died, and I received . . . information . . . you'd be here."

I turned back to him. "I don't know exactly what happened to your face so you look different, and I don't know what happened to your memories so you forgot me, but I've found you. I've located the missing paintings and I've seen your paintings of me. You *are* James. I just don't know how to help you find yourself again. Don't you have any memories of us? Anything at all?"

He shook his head.

"Then will you come home with me? Maybe familiar surroundings will trigger your memories, help you get them back?"

He remained quiet, lips pressed tight. But I knew his mind was working overtime. Was he trying to remember? Searching for something familiar about me?

"Please say something," I begged.

He closed his eyes momentarily, erasing the uncertainty and questions I saw reflected in them. "I'm sorry for your loss, but I'm not James. I can't be. I have a life here, friends. Family. My sister Imelda—"

I gasped. "Imelda Rodriguez?"

"You know her?"

"I know who she is," I growled, stunned how the dots were connecting. What was going on?

Think, think, think. I rubbed my temples.

Carlos folded his arms across his chest and inhaled sharply. "I think you should leave."

"What? Why?"

"You need to leave. Now," he ordered.

I held my ground for the space of two heartbeats. He didn't budge, or change his mind, stubborn as he'd always been. When he didn't say anything further, I crossed the room and stopped in the doorway. "I don't know what Imelda has told you, but she's not your sister. You have a brother, and his name is Thomas. You also have a fiancée."

"You're wrong."

"In this case, I am absolutely right."

I ran from Carlos and to the beach. I had to clear my head. Sinking onto the sand, I turned my face into the wind, hoping the breeze would blow away the pain. The pain of rejection, the pain of betrayal, and the pain of everything that had been lost to us.

CHAPTER 24

A short time later, I returned to the resort and ordered a mai tai and two shots of tequila at the beach bar. I downed all three and collapsed on a lounge chair near the water where I waited for the numbness to set in. I'd fucked up with Carlos and royally screwed Ian. Carlos didn't want to see me again and there was no doubt in my mind Ian was crazy with worry, looking for me. Sleep sounded much better than dealing with the mess I'd created.

Rolling onto my stomach, I skimmed fingers along the sand, burrowing deeper to fist the coolness underneath. My knuckles kneaded the soft granules, the same rhythmic pattern I used when baking, and my alcohol-infused brain took me to Aimee's kitchen. I stood alongside Mandy, laughing, planning the day's menu as we pounded dough for the morning's baked goods. The beach's salt-infused air hinted of the sea salt we sprinkled on the pastries, the sand between my fingers as smooth as the silky texture of dough sliding underneath my palms. Like the dough Mom had first taught me to mix. And with the thought of Mom, my mind traveled back further. Back to Mom's kitchen, where the scent of freshly baked apple pie permeated the air and I sat on a stool beside a boy I once knew. He sprinkled sugar crystals over my head. Magic Memory Dust. He'd told me I would never forget him.

If only it were the same for him.

I wept, squeezing my fists tight, sand oozing between my fingers like dough. Soon, my whimpers subsided and the numbness took over, my body succumbing to sleep.

When I woke, sluggish and disoriented, I trudged up the steps to the hotel with the intention of grabbing a few more hours' sleep in my room. I couldn't think straight, and at the moment, avoiding my problems seemed like the best plan.

I cut through the pool area toward the main lobby.

"Aimee!"

I jolted. Ian marched across the patio. I walked faster. He jogged ahead and blocked my way. "You left."

I stared at his chest. "Last night never should have happened."

"Bullshit!" He roughly ran both hands through his hair and lowered his voice. "Look at me. Please."

I lifted my face. Rejection masked his, and I cried inside. I'd done that to him. I almost reached out, but stopped myself. "It was a mistake, Ian. I'm sorry. Forget it happened."

"It was the best night . . ." He swallowed and looked over my shoulder. His nostrils flared before he returned my gaze. The lines on his face deepened. "I will never forget."

Neither would I. But I had to finish what I started. I needed answers about James.

"Were you with him?"

"I can't do this right now, Ian." I motioned between us. "I'm here for James. It's always been about James."

"When will it be about Aimee?"

I ground my teeth. This *was* about me.

"Come over here. I have something to show you." He clasped my hand and led me to a table shadowed under an umbrella. His laptop was open. He pulled out a chair for me and sat in the one beside mine. He pushed away his laptop and angled his chair to face me.

"I found James's missing paintings," I blurted.

He sucked in a harsh breath.

"They were upstairs in Carlos's private studio." I picked at the peeling paint on the chair arm with my fingernail. "He doesn't remember me, and he acts like he's had no memory loss. I offered to help and he told me to leave. He also said Imelda is his sister. I don't understand what's going on with him."

Ian rubbed his palm back and forth across his chin. "What have I told you about my mother?"

I leaned away. "What does she have to do with James?" Ian gave me a fixed stare. I sagged deeper into my chair. "You haven't told me much. Only that your mom had some mental health issues."

"She had DID, dissociative identity disorder, what used to be known as multiple personalities. Mom had two. Sarah, her dominant identity, was my mother. Then there was Jackie." Ian ran his hands over his shorts, shifting in his seat. "She scared the shit out of me. In a way, Mom was very much like Jekyll and Hyde. I never knew who I'd find at home after school."

"Did Jackie hurt you?"

"Not physically, but she hated me, and she hated my father. Jackie didn't consider herself married, so she often left, days at a time during some spells. I'd have to fend for myself if Dad was out of town on business."

"Your mother must have felt terrible leaving you like that."

"She did, after I told her what she'd done, or showed her pictures."

I frowned. "She wouldn't remember?"

"Sarah had no memories of her time when Jackie was the dominant personality, and Jackie couldn't tell you a thing about Sarah. Total memory lapses, both ways. Simply put, Sarah and Jackie were two different people. They talked differently, too."

I reached for Ian's hand. "That must have been horrible for you."

He gave me a bittersweet smile. "My mom's the reason why I don't do portraits. She'd ask me to take pictures of her whenever Jackie showed up. She wanted to know how Jackie looked, the way she dressed and did her hair. What she'd do.

"My pictures always caught Jackie at her worse. Mom hated those pictures, and I hated the person I saw in them. You see a lot more detail in a blown-up picture on the wall than you do in a thumbnail-size clip. Including the shit people try to hide. It's in their eyes."

"What happened to her?"

"I don't know." He looked beyond my shoulder, his gaze internal. "The day Laney found me I'd been on my own for a week. Mom and I had been shopping. We were living in Idaho at the time. You can drive for miles and see nothing but fields. At a four-way stop in the middle of nowhere, Sarah left and there was Jackie. She looked at me in the rearview mirror and said two words: 'Get out.' She didn't need to say anything else. I got out of that car so fast, not thinking I didn't have a way home. All I cared about was getting away from her.

"Laney was at the diner where my dad and the police searching for me had met to study a map of the area. They were trying to figure out where they hadn't yet looked. Laney was there with her own family and offered to help my dad. The police laughed when she claimed she was a psychic, but Dad was open to all the help he could get. She led him directly to me. I was filthy and starving and had been hiding in a drainage ditch. I didn't want Jackie to find me. Mom came home two days after I did.

"Dad found a specialist, hoping to suppress Jackie. The doctor explained Mom had been severely abused as a child, which he believed was the cause of her DID. On an emotional level, she'd separated herself from the trauma. When I was born, Jackie arrived several months later. The shift between her identities became increasingly frequent over the years. The doctor told Dad raising a kid was too stressful. Mom needed to leave us if there was any hope for her. I haven't seen her since."

"That's why you're looking for Lacy . . . I mean, Laney," I said. "You want her to help you find your mom."

Ian nodded. "I miss her."

I squeezed his fingers. "I hope you find her."

"Someday." He removed his hand and tapped his fingers on the table. "Anyway, I was thinking about what you'd said the other day, how Carlos seems unaware there's a memory loss. It reminded me of my mother." He pulled his laptop toward him. "I don't think he has amnesia."

"You think he has . . . what did you call it? Dissociative identity—?"

"No, I—"

"Then what the hell's wrong with him?" I asked, growing impatient. "It has to be amnesia. He doesn't remember me."

"Or his real name, or anything about his former life. Friends, family, nothing. I bet Carlos knows absolutely nothing about James, right?"

"I don't think so."

Ian strummed his fingers. "I think he has dissociative fugue."

"Dissociative what? I don't—"

He raised a hand. "Hear me out. I can't prove that's what's wrong; it's only a guess. You'll want to consult with a doctor, or maybe ask Carlos, but fugue makes sense to me. The dissociation results from severe emotional trauma. Something happened to James when he came to Mexico. Whatever it was, his mind shut down and erased everything." Ian tapped his laptop. "It's sort of like what happens when a computer crashes and the hard drive dumps all the info."

"Then how am I supposed to help him?"

Ian's eyes softened. "I don't think you can."

I thought about my request of Carlos. "Familiar surroundings should work, right?"

"Recovery from fugue isn't guaranteed. Most of the time people regain their memories within hours of losing them. Sometimes days, and the memories return as suddenly as they disappeared." Ian snapped his fingers.

"But he's been this way for almost two years."

"There are cases where the disassociation has lasted years. There are also extreme cases where the symptoms last . . . well, indefinitely. I'm sorry, Aimee." He pushed the laptop toward me.

I watched the screen fade to black, hibernating. "He may never get his memories back?"

Ian pushed out a breath. "I think you should be prepared that James may be gone indefinitely."

I frantically shook my head.

"With DID, two or more personalities exist, but they swap places," he explained. "That's not the case with fugue. The preexisting identity is lost and a new one created. Unless someone tells the person what's wrong, the new identity has no idea it's a replacement. That could explain why James—I mean, Carlos—hasn't tried to recover his memories. He doesn't know he's James, and it's a good guess no one told him."

Ian gently rested his hand on my knee. "Aimee, it's likely James no longer exists. In a way, he is dead."

I pushed Ian's hand off. He flared his fingers before resting his hand to the table. Emotions warred within him. I could tell by the way he fisted his hand and took several deep breaths. He wanted to touch me, but kept his distance. I needed that distance to think.

I rubbed my forehead. "How can James be gone if there are hints of him inside Carlos?" I explained the signature paint, and the visions Carlos had. He'd been trying to paint me for months.

"I'm not an expert. I don't have those answers."

Ian's theory sounded too surreal and tragic. I wasn't ready to give up hope. "What if he does get his memories back?"

"Here's where things get tricky. If he does—and that's a very big if since he's been this way for so long—he'll be extremely confused, especially with the time gap."

"What time gap?"

"The one when James comes back. When he does, Carlos disappears, along with all of Carlos's memories."

I gasped. "He won't have any memory of his life in Mexico?"

"To him it'll be as though he left you yesterday. I don't know what else to say, but this is something you should look into, read about. I've left some websites open." He skimmed his fingers over the touch pad, waking the laptop. "And Aimee?"

I looked up from the monitor. Ian's expression was guarded as he glanced toward the hotel lobby. "Tread carefully. Fugue is the mind's way of protecting itself from something it can't process, or doing so is too painful. There's a reason James has been left here, away from family and friends. Someone doesn't want him to remember, but I think he's already asking questions."

"What do you mean?"

"My meeting with Imelda was cut short. Carlos is in there now."

Ian pushed from his chair and said good-bye.

I shot to my feet. "Where are you going?"

He thumbed over his shoulder. "The lobby. There might be a chance I can catch Imelda when Carlos is done."

I grabbed my bag. "I'm coming with you."

He stepped in front of me. "I don't think that's a good idea."

"Why not?"

He grasped my arms. I felt as though he was waylaying me. "I've dumped a lot of info on you. Take a moment to process."

"I want a moment with Imelda."

"Don't be rash. You're too upset right now."

"Bullshit! She violated him!"

His eyes widened, shocked by my outrage. I didn't give a shit. She'd stolen almost two years of James's life, our life together.

Ian tightened his grip. "You don't know if that's what she did."

"Neither do you!" I cried, trying to shrug him off.

"You're not being rational. Think, Aimee. I doubt Imelda's the only person who's screwed James over."

My lips pressed flat. "Thomas." He had to be involved, and I was willing to bet Aimee's he'd known the whereabouts of James and his paintings all this time.

Ian gave me a straight look. His line of thinking was on the same track as mine.

Adrenaline powered through me. My entire body quaked. I needed answers. "I need to talk with Imelda. Now."

"Don't risk the chance of scaring her off. Talk to her when you've calmed down." His fingers dug into my shoulders and a slew of emotions marred his face. I sensed his need to crush me against his chest and whisk me away. Far from the man who kept me from him.

He managed to keep his distance, elbows locked, but he felt miles from me. He was already letting go. "I know it's hard, but give Carlos his time with her," he said. "Until you showed up, he probably had no reason to suspect he'd been deceived. Use this time to understand what you're dealing with. Read the articles. Make a list of questions to ask Imelda. Figure out what you'll say to Thomas when you see him next."

I walked in a tight circle. He watched me cautiously. "Do you want some water? I'll get you a glass."

"No. No water." I reluctantly eyed his laptop. The sane part of me understood I should do as he suggested. Get a grip, read, then ask questions.

"All right, then. Well . . ." He ran blunt fingers roughly over his scalp. His sun-bronzed hair stood on end. "Come find me when you're ready. I'll walk with you to Imelda's office."

I watched Ian disappear into the lobby and had to stop myself from running after him. I had a sudden urge to drown in the compassion he freely offered, seeking refuge from the insanity of James's situation. I also wanted to storm after Imelda and demand she tell me what the hell she'd done to James.

But that wouldn't get me anywhere, as my actions this morning had proved. As Ian had requested, I wouldn't do anything rash. I'd already run off to Mexico before doing any research, which was exactly what I needed to do right now. I needed to understand everything before talking with Imelda and confronting Thomas. I especially wanted to be prepared before I approached Carlos, otherwise he would send me away again.

I sat in the chair and awakened Ian's laptop. My brows shot skyward. He had more browser windows open than I could count, stacked on top of one another like pancakes.

From what Ian had described, James's memory loss wasn't the result of a physical trauma. It was psychological, something so intolerable he couldn't cope. His mind had removed him from the situation by erasing everything. Then, like an empty hard drive, he took on new data in the form of a new identity.

Carlos.

Or to be more precise, Jaime Carlos Dominguez.

Someone had to have created the life for him. His initials weren't a coincidence. I thought of Imelda and what she could have told James while he'd been lost and confused, and his mind so empty he'd absorbed any information given. I thought of Thomas. Why would he do something so vile as staging his brother's death?

What happened to you, James?

I scanned the articles, digesting as fast as my eyes could feast on the words. I clicked links, opening more pages while saving others as favorites. I would have Ian e-mail the web addresses and read everything again later.

I also read what Ian had explained about fugue state, how James would have complete amnesia during the fugue period, forgetting all he knew as Carlos when his memories returned.

If they returned.

I read how some patients, going through years of fugue state, continuously worked to retrieve their original identities. They were aware they suffered from fugue. James wasn't.

Or he hadn't been until I showed up.

His real identity hadn't been disclosed to him. I surmised he was told he was a Mexican citizen, had a life in Puerto Escondido, and he'd been severely injured.

Like a surfing accident.

Why deceive him? And how did he end up hundreds of miles from where he should have been? His travel records confirmed his overnight stay in Playa del Carmen, just south of Cancún.

They had to have been falsified, that way his family and friends believed James died on a business trip, far from where he still lived. No one would find him.

A pop-up window opened, warning 10 percent battery life was left. Moments later, the screen went black. I slammed the laptop closed and went to the hotel lobby. Ian must still be with Imelda. I didn't see him. The front desk clerk gave me a map of the resort, circling the wing housing the management offices.

At the end of a corridor off the main lobby, I found him. He stood beside Imelda, who wept. Ian's lips moved, but I couldn't ascertain the words, not over Imelda's gut-wrenching sobs. Carlos stood off to the side, alone. Head bent and arm propped against the wall, he looked as though he tried to balance himself in a world that had been turned upside down.

I rushed over to him. His head snapped up and I stopped, unable to move past the rage rolling off him. It punched me in the gut. "James?"

"That's not my name," he snarled. He straightened and pushed by, knocking my shoulder.

I chased after him. "I'm sorry! Carlos, listen to me—"

Fingers grabbed my elbow, yanking me back. "Aimee, don't—"

I whirled and jerked my arm. "What're you doing, Ian? Let go of me!"

"Not now." He grabbed my other elbow. "Now's not a good time." He nodded toward Imelda hunched against the wall. "She told Carlos everything."

"Everything?" What the hell was *everything*? I glared at Imelda. "Tell me what you did to him." I tugged against Ian's grip. "Dammit, Ian. Back off." I stood on a precipice, ready to leap and wring her neck. My fingers clawed at the air. In the back of my mind, I understood I was losing grip on my sanity. James, Imelda, Thomas, Lacy . . . James's missing paintings, staged death . . . sleeping with Ian, opening my heart to him . . . it was all too much.

Ian held on, his blunt nails digging into the soft tissue under my arms. I screamed my frustration.

Imelda recoiled, facing the wall.

"Calm down," Ian yelled. He shushed, trying to pacify me.

"Fuck off! I didn't come all this way to sit back and wait for everyone to calm down," I shouted. "We are way past the point of being civil. She's had more than enough time to tell James, like nineteen fucking months! I want to know what the hell is going on." I yanked my arms, twisting. Ian started to drag me down the hallway, away from Imelda. "God dammit, Ian. Let! Go!"

"She's right."

Ian and I stopped struggling. In unison, we gawked at Imelda. His grip loosened and I slipped free, running hands over the reddened skin to assuage the sting.

Imelda eased away from the wall. "I should have told him months ago. I've hurt him; he's in horrible pain. He hates me." She glanced at Ian. His hand rested on my shoulder, ready to stall me. I still felt the itch to lunge for Imelda. She nodded at him. "It's all right. She needs to know. And . . ." Her eyes darted from Ian to me. "I've been expecting your arrival."

"What?" Ian and I said in unison.

Ian dropped his hand and I moved away. Imelda fixed sad eyes on me. "Come with me."

She brushed past, and I gave Ian his laptop, smacking the computer against his chest. Payback for the fingerprints he'd left on my arms. "The battery's dead," I grumbled, trailing after Imelda.

"Aimee," he said with quiet ferocity. I stopped but didn't turn. "I'll be at the beach café if you need me." I gave him an abbreviated nod without looking at him and walked away.

CHAPTER 25

Imelda led me to the beach. I followed through the mass of spectators, doing my best not to lose sight of her. Once past the surf competition area, I closed the distance, walking by her side. We continued along Playa Zicatela and I wondered if she planned to trek the entire way to La Punta, a rocky point at the other end of the beach, when she suddenly stopped and faced the ocean.

"This is where I found him."

I followed her gaze, beyond the surging waves. "Out there?"

"No. Here." She pointed to the sand by her feet, her exotic accent thick with emotion. "I came across him during my evening walk. He was drenched and wandering the beach. Dazed and disoriented, exhausted." She looked at me with an anguished expression. "There were cuts and scrapes over his entire body. His face was swollen and bloody like he had been in a fight. I do not think that is what happened."

"He hadn't been surfing, had he?"

She shook her head. "Zicatela's waves can break boards and backs. They are very powerful. You have to respect the ocean here." She pointed toward La Punta. "I believe the current pushed him against those rocks from wherever he swam."

A chill raced across my skin. In my mind's eye, I saw James tossed in the waves, repeatedly thrown against the rocks while he struggled to shore. Then I remembered the weird visions I'd had before passing out in the women's restroom, right after I'd seen Lacy. Had they been real?

"What happened to him?" I asked.

"No sé." Imelda's lips curved downward. "I do not know."

She glanced back at the resort. "The hotel's property had been in my late husband's family for many generations. He inherited the land after we married and started plans for the hotel. The resort was his dream, and became mine, too. We spent three years obtaining loans and building our savings for this hotel. It was so beautiful. *Magnífico.*" Her lips expanded into a shaky smile, then her eyes turned sad. "My husband had a heart attack six months after we opened. He died in my arms. I inherited everything—a hotel I did not know how to operate on my own and creditors breathing down my neck."

She folded her arms and rubbed her elbows. "Four months after he died, I had to make a decision: sell the hotel or walk. So I came here to think. I was ready to give up hope on our dreams. The hotel was all I had left of my late husband. That is when I came across Carlos."

"What did he say when you found him?"

"He did not know his name, where he was from, or how he arrived on the beach. Many months ago, he told me his first memory was seeing me.

"I took him to our clinic. His nose and cheek were broken. He needed extensive facial surgery. Our doctors did not have the skills. They did not know what to do with him. He had no memories."

"But he'd been reported missing," I said. "Someone would have figured out who he was."

Her eyes skirted downward. She circled fingers around her elbows with nervous energy. "He'd been reported missing off the coast of Cozumel so no one would connect the man in our clinic to the one who had gone missing nearly a thousand miles away. By the time he was reported missing, the clinic and I had already been paid off to keep silent."

"Who paid you off?" I asked despite having suspicions.

She moistened her lips. "Within hours after I admitted Carlos, an American arrived. He said he was a friend of Carlos, but I believed him a relation. They had the same eyes."

I started shaking even though I wasn't surprised. "Thomas."

"He made me an offer I could not refuse."

I crumpled onto the sand. Like Imelda, Thomas had paid me off so I'd go my merry way through life. "Cash the check," he'd told me on more than one occasion. "Open a restaurant," he'd urged. And I had. It kept me distracted from the truth he hid.

Imelda sat beside me. "This must be very painful for you. You were to be married, *sí*?"

"His funeral was on our wedding day."

"Ah, *lo siento*," she murmured. Her tone hinted of an apology.

I only stared at the sand.

"In the beginning, Thomas asked me to watch over Carlos," she continued. "I was to keep him safe and report anything suspicious."

I lifted my head. "Like what? He was on a business trip."

"His life was in danger. Someone had tried to kill him."

My heart beat furiously. Lacy had mentioned something about danger in her note, but the idea seemed preposterous. James had led such a normal life. "Who was after him?"

"I do not know. Part of my deal with Thomas was not to ask questions."

"Why would you accept such a deal from a stranger?" Her lips quivered and I gasped. "He paid off the hotel, didn't he? Was it worth it? My fiancé's life for your debt-free one?"

"I gave him a new one," she defended. "A better one."

"Is that what Thomas told you? Too bad you can't ask James what he thinks. He had a good life!" I shouted. "It was beautiful."

"Here, he is free. He does not have to keep secrets."

"What secrets? He had no secrets."

She gave me a flat look. "Are you absolutely certain?"

I looked across the ocean, my mind as chaotic as the fierce waves. Seeds of doubt sprouted in the pit of my stomach and grew thorny vines, twisting around my bones. No, I wasn't sure. Not anymore. If it was difficult for James to talk about Phil and the night of our engagement, then there had to be other things he didn't share.

"My friend Ian believes James has dissociative fugue," I said.

She raised her brows, impressed. "He is right. The doctors believe the memory loss is psychological. Thomas wanted to make sure Carlos did not remember anything about his previous life so we fabricated a new one. He brought in specialists. They reconstructed Carlos's face. Nobody would recognize him. Everyone was given a nice settlement to keep quiet. Money speaks louder than words here, especially American dollars.

"While I cared for Carlos at my home, Thomas built his life. He had his paperwork created, birth certificates, identification . . ." She gave me a quick look. "Carlos's old paintings from his life in America. Thomas made it appear Carlos had recently arrived in town to open his art gallery. He was my long-lost adopted brother. In the eyes of the world, Carlos was a Mexican citizen.

"Thomas believed the more substantial a life we created for Carlos, the less chance his memories returned. *Sí,* there were holes in our story, but since Carlos had only recently found me, his adopted sister, I did not have to answer his questions because I could not. We had only started getting to know each other again before his surfing accident." She spat the last two words as though detesting the lies she'd told.

I tried to wrap my head around the web of deceit. I couldn't imagine pretending to be someone I wasn't. "How could you lie for so long?"

She pressed her lips thin. "It was very hard in the beginning. I always thought Carlos would see right through me, but the checks from

Thomas kept coming." She stole another glance at me before staring at the sand under her toes. "They still come."

I rubbed my face. Oh my God. Thomas was still paying her.

"Did you ever try telling James the truth?"

She blushed and looked at her hands. I recognized the look.

"You fell in love with him!"

"Only as a sister does a brother! Please understand I had no one," she defended, pleading with open palms. "My husband died. My parents had died the year before, and I lost my adopted brother when he was a child. I was alone and finally had someone. That is why I gave him my brother's name. Carlos Dominguez. Carlos means 'free man.' I thought the name suited him. Thomas insisted the first name start with *J* because of the paintings. Jaime was my father's name."

"Why would Thomas want to hide James from his past? Why do all this?" Thomas had a lot of explaining to do. If I didn't murder him first.

"Do not be angry with him. He was only protecting his brother." Imelda stood, turning her back to the ocean. A gust of wind blew hair in her face. Strands lashed her bronze skin. She brushed them away, coiling the hair around her palm. "Take care of Carlos. He is very angry with me. He needs someone. I told him who you are, and that you are as much a victim as him."

I pictured the last time I'd seen him, how he looked at me in the corridor when I'd called him James. "I don't think he wants to see me either."

"Give him time. You are welcome to stay at the hotel for as long as you need at no expense. It is the least I can do to atone for my sins."

"You said you'd been expecting me," I reminded when she started walking away.

She stopped and faced me. "I am a Christian woman and I have greatly sinned. I fear for my soul, but I fear what Thomas will do more. He owns the note on my hotel and I do not want him to take it away from me, but I felt guilty deceiving Carlos so I asked Lucy to find someone Carlos once knew."

"Lucy?" I asked, frowning. Then I remembered. Lacy.

"I had hoped she could convince a friend or family member Carlos was alive and not trace it back to me. I did not want Thomas to find out." Her shoulders rounded and she angled her body away from me.

"Who is Lacy . . . I mean, Lucy?"

Her eyes brightened. She rested a flat hand across her breasts. "She is a frequent guest at Casa del sol who seems to visit when I need her most, sometimes before I am aware I could use her wisdom. She is my friend."

When she didn't say anything further, I blurted the questions stockpiling in my head. "Where is she from? How do I find her?" Ian would want to know. I wanted to know.

"She is . . . how do you say in English? An enigma? *Sí*, she is that." Imelda started walking backward toward La Punta. A watery smile curved on her espresso face, the kind that appears when you have a lifetime's worth of confessions and no hope to correct your misdeeds. "Lucy is a mysterious creature, is she not?" She turned and left me alone on the beach.

The return trip to the hotel seemed longer than the walk out. My feet dragged through the sand. I saw Ian watching me from his table on the deck, his expression pained. My heart twisted. Part of me wanted to go to him and leave behind the mess Thomas had created. But I couldn't leave James, not after what I'd learned. I averted my gaze, passing the café.

When I entered my room, the phone was ringing. I skirted around the bed and fumbled for the receiver on the nightstand. "Hello?"

"Finally! I've been calling all afternoon."

"Kristen?"

She snorted. "Who else would it be? Why haven't you answered your phone?"

I grabbed my cell. Four missed calls. "Sorry. I muted my phone."

Kristen laughed. "Painting went that well? Tell me, is Carlos—"

"James?" I finished for her. "Yes, he is. Thomas is responsible."

She drew in a sharp breath and swore. I tucked the phone on my shoulder and rubbed my arms. My flesh was goosepimply. I thought of the times Thomas had called, or ordered coffee at the café. How he'd asked about my day. Perfect, normal conversation, when all the while he'd been lying to everyone, including James. Bile knotted in my stomach.

"I'm speechless," Kristen said. "No wonder Thomas was being nosey."

"Imelda said—"

"Who's Imelda?" She made an impatient noise. "Start at the beginning. Tell me everything."

So I did.

"How does Ian feel about this?" she asked when I finished.

I chewed my thumbnail.

"What aren't you telling me?"

"I slept with him."

"Who?" She gasped. "Ian?" When I didn't reply fast enough for her, she laughed, low and wicked. "You're fucked."

"Tell me something I don't know," I said, working another nail.

"He's a great guy. He cares about you, and I'm willing to bet he loves you."

"He does," I admitted.

"He told you?" she asked, shocked. "Don't hurt him."

"Too late for that."

She made a sound of disappointment. "Do you want my advice?"

"Doesn't matter. You'll give it to me anyway."

"Seriously, Aimee, listen to me," she implored. "I know you've had your heart set on finding James, but Ian may be right. James's identity may never come back. You need to prepare for the worst."

"Am I supposed to give up on him? I just found him. I have to help him remember."

"Your flight leaves in two days. How do you expect to help him in forty-eight hours?" I chewed my lower lip and she swore at my silence. "You don't plan to stay there, do you? What about your café? Your family? Me!" she exclaimed. "We're all here."

"James is here." I tugged my hair, twisting the locks around my fingers. Now that I knew he'd been the victim of an elaborate scheme I couldn't leave him behind. I had to help. "Imelda has offered me a room for as long as I need."

"Aimee . . . ," Kristen pleaded. "Is this really what you want to do?"

"If you thought Nick had died only to learn he was alive and didn't remember a single minute of your life together, could you walk away from him?"

"Probably not," she said after a moment. "No, I couldn't."

"Do you see why I have to stay and try to help him?"

"I think I understand why you want to, but you can't force Carlos to be someone he's not. Don't do to him what James's parents had done his entire life. You and James belonged together, but you and Carlos are a whole different story. Figure out what you want before you approach him," she advised. "He may not give up his life in Mexico. So, while you're trying to convince him he's better off in California, you risk losing a man who loves you."

I was slowly accepting I had already lost Ian. I ached for him and James. But James needed me more.

I said good-bye to Kristen and hung up the phone. A knock sounded and I tensed. Ian. He wanted to talk, and it wasn't fair of me to avoid him any longer.

I went to answer the door, glancing through the peephole, and abruptly released the knob as though it singed my skin. Ian wasn't on the other side. It was Carlos.

CHAPTER 26

What is he doing here?

I took two steadying breaths, smoothed my skirt, and opened the door.

Carlos stood alone in the hallway. He lifted his head and the ceiling light caught the taut muscles along his jaw. He cleared his throat and stole a glance down the hallway. "I'm sorry. About earlier."

I felt the sting of tears. His pain radiated off him. He'd been betrayed in the worst way possible. "Oh, um . . . don't worry about it."

He rubbed his neck. His arm shook.

"Tell me how I can help you." I stepped into the hallway, the door clicking shut behind me. "Please, I want to help."

He fisted his hands in his pockets, which forced his shoulders to his ears. He still wore the faded jeans, fitted linen shirt, and flip-flops I'd seen him in this morning. I hadn't changed either from the blouse and skirt I'd put on after showering and leaving Ian.

I pushed that thought aside and schooled my face. "You can trust me." I inched closer.

A muscle thrummed in his cheek. He looked ready to explode.

"Trust me," I repeated. Ever so gently, I touched his wrist.

His eyes trailed my hand, lashes drifting lower. His jaw relaxed.

Maybe Imelda was right. Carlos understood we'd both been victimized. Thomas had played us like pawns on a chessboard and I feared the match was far from over. I had to win James back by convincing Carlos his life was with me.

He moved away, breaking contact. I dug my fingernails into my palm. He swallowed. "I was supposed to take you to lunch."

"Oh!" I straightened. "That's—"

"I want to take you to dinner."

"Ah, OK. Um . . ." I shifted, nervous. "Let me get my purse." I fumbled with the door handle. The room was locked. *Shit.*

"I'll get a keycard at the front desk," he offered.

"No!" I gasped. "No, that's all right. I'll get it later." I didn't want him to leave. What if he changed his mind about dinner? "I'll pay you back tonight."

The corner of his mouth lifted, but the smile lacked any warmth. "No bother. I'll take care of it."

He started to walk away, then turned and offered his hand. I wrapped my fingers within his larger ones and I wanted to cry. It seemed a lifetime since we'd walked like this, side by side.

Inside the elevator, Carlos pushed the button for the lobby. He leaned against the wall, arms crossed, and faced me. I scooted to the opposite corner and watched him. The air hummed between us, a charged mixture of words unspoken and questions unanswered. I clasped my hands, uncomfortable with his blatant inspection. Restrained fury oozed from him, rippling across my skin. Though his emotions weren't directed at me, I fidgeted, twisting fingers in my shirt hem when I'd rather wring Thomas's neck.

Keeping my voice light, I asked, "Where are we having dinner?"

"I'd planned for us to drive to the Riconada for lunch, but now"—he paused and rubbed his forearms—"someplace closer would be better."

Deep lines formed between his brows and he opened his mouth. No words followed. He looked at his feet, crossed at the ankles. "Um, well . . . I suppose we can dine on the beach at Playa Principal. We can walk there."

The bell chimed and the doors lumbered open. Carlos pushed away from the wall and I followed him through the lobby toward the beach. The late afternoon breeze had calmed and the sun sat low on the horizon, setting the sky ablaze in color. "It's gorgeous."

"My favorite time of the day," he remarked beside me. He walked the same as James, long strides full of laid-back purpose. When he talked, though, he was all Carlos. Richly accented English mingled with sporadic Spanish. He explained how the fishermen worked. They moored their boats offshore overnight, setting baited hooks over the side for the next morning's catch. Their wives would clean and prepare the fish for nearby restaurants and local markets right there on the beach, under the palms. He pointed at a line of palm trees, trunks bowed like arches over the sand.

He spoke animatedly about anything but us and what he'd learned this afternoon. He used his hands in fluid motions as he talked. Once again, I caught myself comparing him to James, which was difficult not to do. Everything about Carlos, the way he moved, or touched my arm to emphasize something he'd described, was all James. When he expressed how much he loved Puerto Escondido and couldn't fathom living elsewhere, I wondered if it was possible to be happy and sad at the same time.

"Did I say something to offend you?" he asked.

I turned in to the fading light and swiped at an escaped tear. "No, nothing you said. I just"—I swore—"this is all so—"

"Overwhelming?"

I laughed, a watery giggle. "Yeah, that's exactly it."

He grinned, and I found myself amazed over his self-control. Here he was, taking a woman to dinner who was once his fiancée who he had no memory of proposing to. What a mind screw. Didn't he have questions? Wasn't he upset? He'd been lied to and manipulated by those he trusted most for almost two years.

"I can't imagine what you're going through," I said.

"I'm trying not to," he admitted. "Not at this moment anyway."

The restaurant was a wood platform on the sand. Rope lights spiraled nearby palms with clear bulbs strung overhead. Market umbrellas shaded tables circling a space reserved for dancing. A Latin jazz quartet played off to the side.

Carlos must have been a regular patron because the hostess seated us immediately, bypassing a line of customers. She offered him a bright smile and led us to a table along the edge where we had a view of the sunset. Carlos pulled out a chair for me, then sat in the one beside mine. We faced the ocean, the water much tamer here than the wild waves at Playa Zicatela.

The hostess handed us our menus and excused herself. I glanced around. The restaurant was vibrant. Exotic and colorful voices meshed with lively music. I inhaled the warm evening air, a tropical blend of grilled seafood, mangoes, and ocean spray. The band's easy rhythm had me smiling. My shoulders swayed. "This place is wonderful. Beautiful, too."

"I thought you'd enjoy it," he replied, and then frowned.

I stopped moving. "What's wrong?"

He stared at me and my fingers fluttered to my hair, crimping the curls. "What are you thinking?" I asked when he didn't say anything.

He shifted, running hands over his thighs. "You've probably guessed I have many questions."

"Of course. Ask me anything. I want to help," I offered again. Anything to help us.

"Gracias." He turned his face to the ocean, where the sun resembled a neon orange slice melting on the horizon. "I'd planned to talk tonight, but now I don't want to. *¡Dios!*" He groaned, hooking his hands behind

his head the way James had done when he would work through his thoughts. My gaze shifted away. I had to stop comparing him to the man he used to be.

"This is fucking insane. Everything Imelda said—" He stopped, rubbing a finger against his brow. "Sorry."

I didn't know if he apologized for his language, or his assumption I wanted to spend the evening talking about us.

I did, but more so, I wanted just to be with him. Sitting beside him, watching the fading sunlight play along the sharp angles of his face. I could almost pretend life was simple. Normal. Just the two of us.

"What do you want then?" My fingers twitched with the urge to touch him, feel the warm tautness of his skin. But I couldn't. We were strangers. Instead, I traced the line of his jaw, the hard curve of his cheekbone with my eyes. The lines were new, the angles not quite the same, but he was still beautiful to me.

He pursed his lips in thought. "I just want to have dinner with you. Do you mind if we talk about this tomorrow? I need . . . um, time . . . to think."

"All right," I agreed. His questions could wait. We had a lifetime ahead of us.

The waitress arrived and we ordered our drinks and meal. While we ate, Carlos talked about his life in Puerto Escondido, his passion for painting, and how he retaught himself after his accident. He loved teaching young students. I told him everything about my life that had nothing to do with him, from my café to my parents and my friends. How my passion was baking, and how I'd created a niche for myself with custom coffees. He didn't ask what had brought me to his town and why I was there. I didn't ask what had happened to him and how he planned to recover. For all intents and purposes, we were on our first date. We shared stories, we smiled, and we laughed.

The band launched into a new song. The saxophone player belted a long note and the drummer banged his hands swiftly over the hide coverings. His body rocked with a beat that moved faster as the tempo built. Couples migrated to the floor and danced. I tapped my hands and feet, giggling at Carlos.

He watched me, swirling his cocktail. "You love to dance."

"Yes. How about you?"

He looked at the band and his lips pressed flat. "I don't dance."

Yes you do!

"Dance with me," I blurted.

His head swung around. "What?"

"Come on, dance with me." I stood and held out my hand in invitation.

He stared at my outstretched arm. My fingers started shaking when he didn't take my hand. His gaze crawled up my arm until it met with mine. "I said, I don't dance. Not anymore."

I remained still for a very long moment. He looked away, back toward the ocean. A tic throbbed in his jaw and fingers clutched the chair arms. I lowered my arm and dropped into the chair. Something shifted inside me and, for the first time, I saw him for the man he really was. Carlos.

The waitress brought our check and Carlos paid in cash, tossing bills onto the table. He stood, chair legs scraping hard on the floor boards. "I'll walk you back."

CHAPTER 27

We walked along Playa Marinero toward Casa del sol. Carlos tucked his thumbs into his front pockets and watched the water-hardened sand pass under his feet. His fingers absently scratched at his jeans, his brows furrowed.

I twisted a curl around my finger and slid him a sidelong glance. What had happened at the restaurant? We were having a good time. I thought we'd connected. Where James would have leaped from his chair and whirled us onto the dance floor, Carlos had balked. I debated asking him about it, but I'd promised to keep things light tonight.

Lost in his thoughts, Carlos hadn't said a word since we'd left the restaurant. He stopped abruptly and looked behind us.

"What's wrong?" I asked.

"I left my Jeep at the studio." He scratched his chin and glanced around. "I'll take you to the hotel first."

He started walking, pausing to quirk a brow when I didn't follow. I thumbed over my shoulder. "I'll go with you. You won't have to double back."

He hesitated. "You sure?"

"Of course. It's a nice evening." Besides, I didn't want to go to my room and spend the night alone where sleep would elude me once again. I had no idea what tomorrow would bring after Carlos had the answers to his questions. Would I stay with him in Mexico or fly home? Would Ian still want to be my friend? I'd pushed him away despite my promise not to.

Carlos's Jeep Wrangler was parked in an alley behind the gallery. He assisted me up, holding the door open as I settled in the passenger seat, and got in from his side. He drove back to Casa del sol, easing to a stop at the curb by the hotel's main entrance. A valet approached and Carlos waved him away. He kept the engine idling, hands clasped tightly to the steering wheel.

I didn't want to get out of the Jeep and Carlos hadn't asked me to leave. I peeked at him from under my lashes. "I heard there's a festival downtown."

He nodded, jiggling his knee.

"The weather's nice." I peered at the sky. The resort's glaring lights dulled the stars overhead. "I love warm nights like this."

He nodded again. "*Sí*, me, too."

Wondering where he'd go next if I didn't invite him to the festival, I asked, "Do you live nearby?"

He pointed south. "Less than two kilometers down Zicatela."

I studied his profile, the steady rise and fall of his chest. Suddenly, I didn't want to spend the night alone, or at a crowded festival listening to loud music. "I'd love to see your home," I said.

He looked at me, his gaze scrutinizing, and then shifted the Jeep into gear.

We drove along Calle del Morro, the avenue parallel to Playa Zicatela, past restaurants, surf shops, nightclubs, and hotels, to a neighborhood of beachfront properties. Carlos turned in to a driveway, stopping at a wrought iron fence. He pushed the remote hooked to his visor and the gate lumbered open. He eased through when enough space allowed passage, and stopped beside a narrow three-story house that was taller than wide. My mouth fell open. I ogled the top floor.

Carlos cut the engine. "The third level is a rooftop deck. The mountain and beach views are great from up there, especially on a clear day."

The ocean thundered beyond the palms edging his property. "You live on the beach." I groaned, envious.

His lips twitched into a wide, lazy grin. "Come, I'll show you," he said, hopping from the Jeep.

He led us past a small pool, across a low-clipped lawn sprinkled with sand, and through an opening in the adobe half wall separating his yard from the public beach. He turned and grabbed my hips. I sucked in a breath. He chuckled and lifted me onto the wall, sitting beside me. Our arms brushed.

I resisted the urge to lean into him and nodded toward the spectacular view. "OK, I'll admit it. I'm jealous."

"I can't imagine living anywhere else." He pushed out a lungful of air, cheeks puffing. "Well, that was before this afternoon. I don't know what to think anymore."

I gazed beyond the churning water to the starry sky, wishing the abyss between us wasn't bigger than the Pacific Ocean. At least I could see the horizon in front of me. I had no idea if one existed for James. Would he recover from the fugue? "Don't think," I pleaded. "Not yet."

"That's the problem." He sat upright. "I can't stop. It's damn confusing. I'm confused." He lifted my left hand and studied the engagement ring. "Imelda told me you are . . . uh, were . . . my fiancée."

"You gave me this ring when you proposed."

He looked at me skeptically. "Shouldn't I remember?"

"The fugue prevents you . . ."

"I should feel *something* for you." He was quiet for a moment, then rolled his lips inward. "Nope. I've got nothing."

My heart wilted. "I can help. Let me help you remember," I offered in a tone iced with panic. Didn't he want to remember me?

"It's not just the memory loss, Aimee. That guy you loved isn't me. He's gone."

"Shut up," I softly cried. "Don't say that. Please don't . . ." I clasped his hand. "What about the dreams? You've dreamed about me."

"I found an old painting of you in my studio. It could have triggered the dreams."

"I don't believe you." Anger spiked inside me. "After all you've learned today, how can you be so cold? Don't you feel anything?"

He laughed bitterly. "I feel, all right. I feel a shitload of anger for my brother . . . Thomas, right? And Imelda." He shook his head. "She told me she was my sister and I believed her. I fucking believed her. But with you"—he gave me an assessing glance—"I feel nothing but curiosity. I'm sorry."

I yanked my fist from his hands and staggered to my feet. I kept my back to him.

"My memories go back nineteen months. That's it. I save everything. Magazines, books. I frame every picture. If I lose my memories again, I'll have something from my past."

I thought of the gallery, remembering the magazine stacks and book piles. Unfinished paintings waiting for a signature or final touch-up. Signed paintings he never displayed. He had kept everything. Everything from Carlos. But I had everything belonging to James. "You do have a past, and I have pictures to show you. I have your clothes and more paintings. Your studio is still there in our home. We have a home."

"My home is here."

I wrapped my arms tightly around my midriff and stumbled away, stopping when he said my name. "I don't know if I want to remember the past."

I felt myself die a bit inside. "Can you at least try?"

"Why? I'd risk losing everything familiar to me. Everyone I love."

I squeezed my eyes shut. He understood the twisted logic behind his condition. "You're comparing nineteen months to twenty-nine years. What right do you have keeping James from me? You don't belong inside his body. You aren't him."

He flinched. "*Sí*, you are correct. I'm not him. Not anymore. Whatever you say won't convince me to leave everything behind. I won't go away with you. I don't know you."

I whirled on him. "You don't remember me. There's a difference."

He fisted his hands on his thighs. "I can't leave. I'm needed here."

"You can paint anywhere." I swept my arms in an all-encompassing gesture. "What's keeping you here? Surely not Imelda. She's not your sister. Your family's in California. I'm in California. What the hell is there for you here?"

He clenched his jaw and looked beyond my shoulders.

I looked behind me. "The ocean?" I asked in disbelief. When he didn't say anything, I blocked his view. "You might not feel anything for me, but I feel *everything* for you. You aren't the only one going through hell," I cried, hoarse. "The worst feeling in the world is never to be remembered by the one person I can't forget. The one man I haven't been able to let go." My voice cracked against a dry throat and I coughed—deep, racking barks. The fit ensued and I doubled over.

I felt an arm wrap around my back. "You need water. Let's go inside," he suggested and urged me forward.

I followed him through the kitchen slider and blinked against the glaring fluorescent lights he'd turned on. My breath hitched as I reined the coughs. Feeling disheveled with tear-stained cheeks, I asked, "Where's your bathroom?"

"Down the hall, on the left," he said over his shoulder. He retrieved glasses from the cabinet.

I went through the darkened hallway where Carlos directed and locked myself in the bathroom. I flipped on the light, turned on the faucet, and splashed handfuls of water on my face, taking extra care to wash the mascara spiderweb etched over my cheekbones. I blindly reached for a towel, dried my face, and then stared at my reflection. Bloodshot eyes embedded in a pallid complexion glared back at me.

How could Carlos believe nineteen months of his life were more important than the twenty-nine years James had? He was stealing James's life, robbing him of the years he could spend with me, and the one man affected the most had no say. James couldn't speak for himself. It was up to me to convince Carlos to give James's memories a chance.

I folded the towel, smoothing the creases, and placed it on the bathroom counter beside an illustrated children's book. I stilled and something twisted inside my chest. I spun around and saw a rack of picture books by the toilet and toys in the tub.

I whimpered, the towel and book dropping on the floor, and rushed from the bathroom. I stumbled into the brightly lit hallway. Framed pictures covered the wall like a checkerboard. Dozens filled the shelves in the front room. Photos of Carlos, Imelda, and people I didn't recognize, including a woman with brunette hair and russet skin. She looked happy, perfectly tucked into Carlos's side, his arm curved around her shoulders.

Most of the pictures were of two boys, one a small child and the other an infant. In one photo, Carlos cradled the newborn. In another, the older boy painted at a kid's art table. It was the table I'd seen at the gallery. There were dozens of photos of the boys together, and others with the older boy wrapped in the arms of his parents. Carlos, his facial scars red and angry, and the mystery woman, heavy with child.

I spun around, furling all ten fingers in my hair and tugged hard. My scalp burned, but the pain wasn't close to the ache piercing my gut. I snagged a frame, a school portrait. The boy didn't look anything like James had in his kindergarten picture. Who was this child, and why were there pictures of him everywhere?

"He's five, and he loves to fish," Carlos said from behind me. "He's my son."

"How? You've been gone less than two years."

I heard him shift. "He's adopted."

My hands shook. "The infant?" I croaked, barely above a whisper.

"He's mine."

The meaning of these children, everything, sank lower and deeper, settling in my soul.

I'm needed here.

"Where's their mother?"

"My wife. Her name's Raquel. She—" He broke off and cursed.

A tear slid down my nose. I impatiently brushed it away.

"She died birthing Marcus," he said after a moment. "It was . . . ah . . . sudden. An aneurysm. There was nothing the doctors could do."

I slowly turned to him. He stood in the middle of the room holding two water glasses, his face ravaged. I was sure I'd worn the same expression in the days following James's funeral. "You loved her," I said dully.

"Very much so."

I licked my parched lips. "Where are your sons now?"

"Staying with friends. They are good kids."

"I'm sure they are." I returned the frame to the shelf and paced the small room, twisting the engagement ring on my finger. My hands shook uncontrollably and the tremors spread, coursing through my limbs.

"I'm sorry," Carlos said in a rough, dry tone. He swallowed and blinked rapidly. His eyes shimmered with unshed tears. "I didn't think . . . I didn't know how . . ." He cleared his throat and set the glasses on the coffee table. "Seeing my children must be very strange for you."

"Who is she? How did you meet? When did you . . ." I pressed my lips together, hating the desperation in my voice.

"She was my physical therapist. I adopted Julian when we married. Marcus arrived shortly—" He stopped and rubbed the back of his neck. "Raquel and I weren't married for very long, but I—" He glanced away. When he turned back, he looked at me in earnest. "I can't dance with anyone else. It was her passion. It's too hard for me . . . *¡Dios!*" He groaned, distressed. "If I had once felt for you the way I feel for Raquel, then I do understand your hell. The loss is . . . unbearable."

Another whimper escaped my lips. I frantically twisted the ring, rubbing the skin underneath raw. Carlos's eyes dropped to my hands, narrowing on the band. "I took mine off months ago," he murmured.

"I can't." I wept, defeated.

He cautiously stepped closer. "Or won't?"

I rapidly shook my head. The room was getting smaller, the walls caving. Carlos moved closer. He gently rested his hand over mine, stilling my erratic motion. "I loved Raquel very much. It's been . . . difficult . . . with her gone, but I had to move on. I had no choice. Two rambunctious, beautiful *niños* needed me."

My lower lip quivered. "But you're here, James. You didn't die. You're still alive. I need you."

Carlos sadly shook his head. "He's gone. You have to let him go, Aimee."

Let go, baby. Just let go. Ian's words whispered through my mind.

Carlos led me to the couch, tugging my hands until I was perched on the seat edge. He pulled up a chair across from me and clasped my hands with his. "James was a lucky man to have a woman who loved him so passionately. Tell me about him. Tell me why you need him so much."

"What if you start to remember?"

His eyes filled with remorse. "There will be no start. You and I both know the change will be sudden. *If* it happens. I don't think it will."

I didn't believe Carlos. James was still with us, somewhere inside him. I studied our clasped hands, fingers entwined and warm skin touching. Was I strong enough to go home without him? Could I move on while he still lived far away and without me?

I sighed dejectedly. Then with grim resignation, I told Carlos our story.

CHAPTER 28

Since the day James had gone missing, I kept everything the same. His studio at home. The art on the wall. His clothes in our closet. Like Nadia had mentioned before I came to Mexico, pictures of James were everywhere.

And I'd held on to everything. Dreams of a future with him by my side. Hope he still lived and would come home soon. Memories of our life together, including one memory I'd sworn to never tell a living soul.

It had been a difficult promise, but I did it for James. When he was ready, we'd work through the trauma and heal together. Until that time came, he'd been reluctant to discuss the ordeal, or as I was starting to suspect, too afraid.

After the funeral, I wondered if the day would come I wouldn't have to suffer silently on my own. *You're still holding everything inside,* Kristen had told me months ago. If she only knew the secret I had buried.

I had wished for one last chance to tell James how I felt. How he had made me feel that day in the meadow. Alone and afraid. Now here he was—and in a way, wasn't—sitting before me and ready to listen.

Carlos held my hands, the contact reassuring as I told him how we'd met. It was odd reliving memories where James had played a role, and he couldn't remember a single moment. I explained how my family, not his, nurtured his talent. I shared the story of our first kiss and first dance. A smile curved my lips when I remembered James visiting from college. We'd made love under the stars in our meadow. Then I recalled how James asked me to marry him.

I stared at our clasped hands and slid my fingers from Carlos's grasp.

"There's more, isn't there?"

I nodded, tugging at the engagement ring.

"What happened to you?" he asked carefully.

Memories crept forth, slithering from the dark hole where I'd left them.

"We were at our meadow on the ridge, our special place," I said after a moment. "James had spread a blanket on the grass. We watched the sun set behind the hilltop, and he proposed."

"I'll paint the sunset for you, and many more, if you wear this," he said to me. An opened black velvet box rested in his palm, a square-cut diamond in a platinum setting tucked inside.

"Oh!" I cried. "It's beautiful."

I splayed my fingers and James kissed the space between the first and second knuckles. He slid on the ring. A perfect fit. We were a perfect fit.

"Marry me, Aimee Tierney. Be my wife."

"Yes!" My eyes misted. I threw my arms around him. "A thousand times yes!"

"Thank God." He laughed, and spun me around.

I squealed. "Did you have any doubt?" I teased, winded when he put me down, my body quivering as I slid down his length.

"None," he said and kissed me. "I have champagne in the car. Wait here."

I watched him jog toward his car and disappear into a thin tree grove. I heard the trunk pop and glass shatter. "Everything OK?" I called out.

"All's good," came a strained response. "Be right there."

I stood, angling the diamond at the sunlight. The gem sparkled. "It's perfect, James," I said when I heard footsteps behind me. I turned and bumped into Phil.

He smiled thinly. "Hello, Aimee."

I gasped and backed up a step. "What are you doing here?"

"Celebrating with you."

"I don't understand. Where's James?" I looked past Phil's shoulder.

"He's . . . busy." His hand shot out and clutched my jaw, his thumb pressing into my cheek. He held me in place.

Terror spread through me like spilled oil, slow and thick. "What are you doing?"

He didn't look quite right. His eyes glassed over and sweat sheened his forehead. He hauled me into his chest, fingers biting my flesh. Alcohol tainted his breath. "You're so beautiful."

"Phil, you're hurting me," I cried.

"I'm sorry." His mouth slammed down on mine. He tasted like gin.

Tears sprung in my eyes and fear clawed up my throat. I jerked from his grasp, stumbling backward. "James!" I screamed.

"Fuck James!" Phil's face turned purple with rage. He lunged for me, throwing me facedown on the ground, and I landed hard on my back. Air whooshed from my lungs.

"Your boyfriend and his fucking brother have taken everything from me. Everything," he bellowed in my ear. "Donato is my company. *Mine!*"

His hand curved around my skull, pushing my nose into the dirt. I couldn't scream. I couldn't breathe. My fingers clawed at the ground.

"I've already taken from Thomas. He's such a fucking idiot. He's got no clue what I've been doing with his precious merchandise." The sound of a zipper punctuated his words. He hooked his feet inside my ankles and spread my legs. "Now it's James's turn. Donato doesn't mean shit to him. But you! You mean fucking everything." His breath wind-tunneled in my ear. Saliva splattered my face. He yanked up my skirt and tugged aside my panties. The elastic bit into my skin. "He's taken from me, so I'm taking from him."

He pressed his fingers into me, a thick, dry invasion. It burned. My lungs burned. The rough ground dug into my cheek as I struggled for air. The pressure on my back, the sickening pressure invading me, and the viselike grip on my lungs was too much. My vision faded, blackening along the edges. Then all pressure vanished.

I sucked in air, short, rapid pulls. I lifted to my hands and knees, coughing. Spittle laced with dirt rained from my mouth.

"Aimee." James dropped to his knees in front of me. "Sweetheart." His voice ravaged. His hands ran over me, straightening my clothes, smoothing back hair from my sweat-drenched face. "I'm here."

Bile rose. I pushed aside his hands and crawled away. I heaved and spewed everything—everything but Phil's vile touch. I couldn't stop feeling his hands.

James came to my side, lifting me to my feet. His hands shook violently. "Come on, let's get out of here."

I glanced beyond James. Phil lay prone in the tall grass, unmoving. "Is he . . . ?"

"He's alive. Don't look." He gathered the blanket and hurried us to the car.

"You're going to just leave him there?"

"Yes, I am." He folded me into the front passenger seat, then slammed the door. He ran to his side, firing the ignition before the door closed. The car squealed away from the meadow and sped down the hill.

I started shaking, small vibrations increasing to a full-body quake.

"It's over, Aimee."

Dry grass and twigs clung to my skirt. Dirt marred my fingernails. I tried to clean them. "I'm dirty. I'm so dirty. We have to go home. Take me home." Nausea coiled in my belly.

"We can't . . . *fuck*!" He banged his hand on the steering wheel. "My parents are expecting us. They'll ask questions if we don't show, especially Mom. I want us to get to the house before Phil does."

I gagged. "He's going to be there?"

"He sure as hell better not be, but I'm not taking any chances. We'll make the visit with your parents quick. I promised your dad we'd come by after I proposed."

I looked in the visor mirror and whimpered. Leaves and grass clung to my hair. Scratches covered my right cheek and jaw. A bruise bloomed on my chin. My makeup was gone. I fumbled for my mascara and tried to apply the liquid coal. It smeared on my cheekbone.

James swerved to the side of the road and grabbed a towel from his gym bag. His hands shook as he poured water on the towel. "Look at me." He gently cleaned my face. "You can't tell anyone about Phil. Your parents, my family, our friends. No one can know what happened. Do you understand me?" He dabbed dirt from a raw scratch on my jaw. I jerked and he shushed. "There's shit going down at Donato, and Phil's involved." He grabbed my purse and dug out the concealer. He patted the powder on my cheek, blending the makeup into my skin. "I'll take care of Phil. He'll never hurt you again." He unscrewed the mascara tube. "Here, look up." I did, and with his steady painter hand, James applied the mascara. "It's my job to protect you. I'll always keep you safe. You hear me?"

I sucked in my lower lip and nodded.

"Look at me, sweetheart."

Our gazes locked and the intensity of his rage scared me. His eyes glass-hard, his face rigid steel. "I'll make sure Phil stays away. He won't touch you."

Blood trickled down James's temple and I whimpered. "You're hurt." I touched the knot on his head and he flinched.

"It's not bad. Only a cut."

I took the towel from him and poured more water. Dabbing gently at his face, I watched the dark liquid bleed pink on the white towel. "I love you."

"I know." James briefly closed his eyes. "God, I hate it has to be this way, but we have to go. Your parents are expecting us. If we're late, they'll ask questions."

"But I have questions," I whimpered. "Phil did this to hurt you. That's what he said. Why, James? What's going on between you?"

James shushed me. He cradled my face and pressed his forehead to mine. "I'll answer all your questions when I can. I'll tell you everything, I promise," he said, his throat thick with unshed tears. "Until then, you have to trust me to keep you safe. I know what I'm doing. Please, please trust me."

"OK," I conceded and forced Phil from my mind. To an unreachable corner of my soul.

We drove to my parents' house and plastered on smiles. We toasted with champagne, finishing a bottle among the four of us. The more I drank, the easier it was to forget what had happened in our meadow.

Then we walked to James's parents' house and did the same thing all over again. The house was quiet when we arrived.

"Is anyone home?" I asked James as we walked into the living room. Champagne chilled in a sterling silver bucket on the sideboard. At least we'd been expected.

Worry clouded James's face. He glanced around the room. His father had been ill. I folded my hand in his. "Let's go find your parents."

At that moment, Claire Donato rounded the corner with open arms. "Congratulations!" she sang, and hugged James.

Claire turned to me next. She clasped my hands. "Welcome to the family. We're thrilled to have another Donato."

I forced a smile, wincing at the pain in my jaw.

"You are planning to take our name?" she asked, mistaking my reaction. "God forbid you keep your surname, or worse, hyphenate your name with ours."

"Well, I . . ." My voice trailed. I looked at James.

He glowered and went to uncork the champagne. *Pop!* The noise ripped through the frigid air. I gasped and Claire jerked. She looked down her nose at James.

"I'd be honored to take the Donato name," I rushed to say. "I love James."

"Of course you do, dear."

James poured two flutes. "Where's Dad?"

"He's in his room. He's not feeling well tonight." Claire gave me an apologetic look. "His lungs have been temperamental today."

James spared his mother a glance as he poured another glass. "When's his next exam?"

"You know your father. He's more stubborn than you and Thomas put together."

James shook his head, refusing to be baited into an argument with his mother. He gave her a glass.

She shrugged a delicate shoulder. "If your father won't give up his cigars, he won't go back to the doctor. He'll put any visit off until the last possible moment. He's already cancelled two appointments his nurse scheduled for him."

James didn't look happy. He scowled and handed me a glass.

"When's the wedding?" Claire asked.

"We don't have a date yet. Perhaps next summer? July?" I gave James a questioning look.

"That will be lovely, you must use our church."

"We plan to." James wrapped his fingers around mine. He pulled me closer. "We also plan to have the reception at The Old Irish Goat."

Claire's face twisted. "Oh no. That won't do. That restaurant is too small."

"*That* restaurant belongs to Aimee's parents. They've generously agreed to host us."

"It'll be dreadfully crowded for all our guests. Where will you seat everyone?"

My fingers nervously twisted around the flute stem. "Actually, James and I want a small wedding. Close friends and family." Family that didn't include his cousin Phil. My stomach clenched.

The front door slammed. I stiffened, my eyes wild as James and I exchanged glances. A loud *whoop* came from the foyer. "Do I hear wedding bells?"

Thomas appeared in the doorway. A relieved sigh left me in a rush. James squeezed my fingers.

Thomas approached us. He hugged me, smacking a kiss on my cheek. "Congratulations. Welcome to the family, little sis." He gave my chin a mock chucking, brushing my concealed abrasions. I inhaled through my teeth. James knocked his brother's fist away. Thomas playfully shoved James's shoulder, and then drew him in for a manly hug. In the length of a heartbeat, James pushed him away, his patience with his family at an end.

"Aimee was just telling me about their wedding plans," Claire explained to Thomas, giving him a glass of champagne. "James, I think you should consider Phil for one of your groomsmen."

I felt the color drain from my face.

Thomas narrowed his eyes at me and James clenched his jaw. "I don't want him there."

"He's family, James."

"We'll discuss the wedding party later, Mom," he said thinly.

Thomas set his barely touched glass on the sideboard. "Well then, Aimee, I'll leave you to discuss the details with Mom." He crooked a finger at James. "Do you have a sec? We need to talk."

James's face tightened. "Yes, we do." He kissed my brow and asked if I'd be all right. When I nodded, he murmured he'd return in a moment, then we'd leave.

Claire put her glass next to Thomas's and skimmed manicured nails through my hair, straightening the thick waves. She pulled out a dry leaf and arched a brow. "I think you'll make a beautiful bride once we fix this hair. So unruly," she murmured, shaking her head. She tsked. "You wear entirely too much makeup."

~

Twenty exhausting minutes later, I extrapolated myself from Claire and her wedding planning with the excuse of needing the bathroom. Thankfully, the house phone rang and Claire took the call.

I went searching for James. His voice drifted into the hallway from the den. Light spilled underneath the double doors, as did Thomas's harsh murmur.

"I can't fire Phil. Grant's stipulations forbid it," he warned.

Through the partially opened doors, I saw James standing off to the side. Anger distorted his face. Thomas paced the room.

"I'll handle Phil," James replied.

"He's not your responsibility."

"Listen, I have a plan."

Their voices lowered. I held my breath, straining to hear. Only muffled tones reached me.

"You bring the DEA into this and we all go down," Thomas accused when James finished his explanation.

"Then let me deal with him. My plan will work."

"Bullshit!" Thomas exploded. "Your plan is crap. Phil's too unstable. You'll get yourself killed."

I gasped, slamming a hand over my mouth.

"Jesus Christ! Keep your voice down." James's eyes darted toward the den's entrance.

I drew away from the door. What was going on?

"Give me a year to terminate Phil's operations," Thomas implored. "Two tops to cut him off."

"No, we deal with Phil now. I'm done waiting," James snapped. "And I'm done turning my head like everyone else in this family when Phil exports merchandise purchased with dirty money. The illegal shit stops now, or I'm out."

Thomas rubbed his face. "I need time, James. You're not giving me any . . ."

A wide hand firmly latched on to my shoulder. I jolted, spinning around. Edgar Donato held me with his steel gaze. He pressed an index finger to his lips and smiled, almost jolly. "Come with me."

Between the champagne and what I'd heard, confusion clouded my head. My gaze darted between James and his father.

Enormously overweight, Edgar wobbled ahead with a cane, dragging an oxygen tank behind him. The wheels squeaked over marble tiles.

With one last glance through the door crack, I trailed after Edgar. I would ask James later what Thomas had meant. One thing was for sure, I wanted James out of the family business as much as he did.

Edgar led us into the library and went straight for the liquor cabinet. He uncorked a crystal decanter filled with an amber liquid. He poured two fingers into one glass and four into another.

"Should you be drinking?" I asked when he handed me the smaller of the two.

"My dear," he started, clearing a throat thick with mucous, "my health is way past the point of no return. Not much help I can do other than assisting it along the course it's taken." He raised the glass to his lips and chuckled. "Bottoms up!" He drank half the glass with the first gulp and added, "Welcome to the family."

I sniffed the liquor and took a hesitant sip. Edgar tapped the bottom of my glass, angling the crystal higher against my mouth. I gulped quickly. Whiskey burned a ditch in my throat and dug a hole in my belly. I gasped.

Edgar laughed, shoulders twitching. "You'll need more of that if you want to survive the family you're marrying into. Might as well start now."

With the whiskey topper on the champagne from earlier, my head felt light and fuzzy. My stomach twisted.

Edgar retreated to a wingback chair and settled down. He adjusted his cane and tank. A coughing fit consumed him, loud and rough, flooded in phlegm. His entire body quaked.

"Don't worry," he choked, spent. "You'll get used to it. The more you drink, the better it'll taste. One day"—he pointed at the scotch with his cane—"Johnnie Walker may be the only thing keeping you sane in this family."

My eyes fleetingly skipped to the door. I swallowed, feeling uneasy. In all the years I'd known James, I'd never been alone with his father. Before tonight, Edgar and I hardly spoke.

"Come, come. Sit." He patted the chair beside him.

I sat and braved another taste of the fire in my glass. Last one, I promised myself.

"I like you, Aimee. Always have. Your parents are good people, too."

My brows arched high.

"You're good for James. He needs you." He smiled and his eyes turned sad. "Thomas is so much like his mother. He has a relentless purpose that borders on ruthlessness. Thomas believes he can single-handedly take on the world. But James," Edgar nodded his head, "he reminds me of my younger brother. Spirited. A dreamer."

"I'd never get in the way of his dreams. I couldn't force him to be someone he wasn't . . ." I stopped, remembering who I was speaking to—the man who'd kept James from pursuing the life he'd wanted. I cleared my throat and stared into my glass.

"Advice I should have heeded decades ago. I am afraid . . ." His voice drifted, gaze wandering.

I frowned at his frankness. Perhaps it was a reaction to his medication. That would explain his unexpected openness. Then it struck me. The unfocused stare and the quiet acceptance of his condition. The ease of temperament that comes in the sunset years while reflecting on a life full of regrets.

Edgar Donato was lonely and very much alone in a world I was only beginning to realize James had kept away from me.

When he remained quiet, I asked him, "What are you afraid of, Mr. Donato?"

His head popped up. "Huh? Oh, nothing." Coughing into his fist, he cleared his throat. The fit ensued, the coughs harsher.

I went to the liquor cabinet and poured a glass of water for him. While he regained his composure, my eyes perused the room, drifting to the framed Donato family crest on the opposite wall. "I remember when James brought your crest to school for share day," I said, making conversation. "That was years ago. He told me all about the eagle."

"What eagle?" choked Edgar.

"The one up there. Your family's crest."

Edgar shifted, looking up. He barked in laughter. "That's not my family's crest. It's Claire's." Tossing back his glass, he finished his whiskey.

My mouth fell open.

"Aimee? You ready to go?"

I spun in my chair. James stood in the doorway.

CHAPTER 29

"Aimee, are you all right?"

I blinked at Carlos. He sat stiffly in his chair on the other side of the room, his face pale. I looked around, dazed. I must have been pacing while I spoke. My fingers were latched tightly on the engagement ring.

"Aimee . . . ?" he questioned in a firmer tone.

I took in everything around me: walls painted a burnt orange, mahogany wood flooring, bold furniture with decorative pillows—a woman's touch, toys stacked in one corner, cleaned up for the day, and numerous pictures portraying a once complete family that had lost their mother. Carlos was needed here more than I needed James.

I understood that now. Looking back at our relationship, while I had loved him something fierce, I also saw our faults. James was good at putting off the things that made him uncomfortable and I was too agreeable. His family should have been told about Phil.

As Carlos stared at me with an appalled expression, I realized marrying James might not have been the best thing for me. In the nineteen months since he'd left for Mexico, despite how difficult those months had been, I'd become a stronger, more confident person. And I didn't want to lose the life I'd created for myself.

A voice whispered in my head, one I hadn't heard in a while. *It's OK to let go, Aimee.*

My eyes widened. It never had been James speaking to me in the wind, touching me with a tear. It was me—the part that was brave enough to move forward. The part that knew I was capable to make it on my own.

Carlos crossed the room to me. I slid the ring from my finger for the first time since James had put it on. It had been a perfect fit, but perfection can be an illusion. I stared at my naked finger, the band of pale skin pink and tender. I lifted Carlos's hand and placed the ring in the center of his palm.

"What are you doing?" He fisted his hand around the ring.

"What I should have done a long time ago. I once promised James never to interfere with his dreams. In fact, I hated when he kowtowed to his parents. I wanted him to leave Donato Enterprises, open a gallery, and paint. He would have had a richer, more fulfilling life. He was going to do it, right before . . ." I swallowed and took a heady breath. "Right before he died." I lifted my gaze to Carlos and finally found James. "But look at you, you did do it. You're living the life you'd hoped to achieve. I won't take this from you. I won't force you to be someone you aren't. I'd never force you the way your parents had."

"Aimee . . ."

"No . . . no, this is good. You'd wanted your own family because the one you grew up with was so—"

"Dysfunctional?" Carlos supplied.

"To put it mildly." I gave him a smile of understanding. "Your boys need you."

And I was needed back home. I missed my café, the fresh brewed coffee and warm spices. The sugary scent of cakes and scones. The jingle of the door opening for a new customer or the return of someone familiar. I missed my chef Mandy, and Emily's scheming, always looking to make an extra buck with her bets. Most of all, I missed Ian. Aimee's wouldn't be what it was today without him. I wouldn't be where I was today without him, emotionally and physically, and every level between. I didn't want to lose him.

"*Dios*, Aimee . . . everything you told me." Carlos swore again, rubbing the back of his neck. "Will you be OK?" He frowned, unconvinced when I nodded. I'd spent hours sharing memories, some blacker than others. "Are you sure?"

I looked inward. With the darkness exorcised, I recognized the calm acceptance of my situation. It had been there for some time, patiently waiting for me to grasp hold. Nadia would be impressed. I was moving on.

"For once, I'm positive I will be OK. Better than OK."

It was 3:30 a.m. when Carlos dropped me off at Casa del sol. I stood alone on the walkway as he drove off, waiting until his taillights disappeared. I had no idea when I'd see him again. *If* I'd see him again. The finality of our relationship seemed more permanent at this moment than it had when I'd buried his body.

Imelda intercepted me as I dragged myself through the lobby. Her clothes were rumpled, hair disheveled. She looked exhausted. "Thomas is here," she warned.

My gaze snapped to hers. "Where?"

"The bar."

I looked through the wide entrance to the hotel's lounge. Underneath dimmed lights, the bartender methodically wiped the counter. The place was empty except for a lone man sitting at a table along the far wall. A single bottle and one glass kept him company.

The bartender looked up when I entered and followed me to Thomas's table. He set a clean glass on the wood surface as though he'd been expecting my arrival, and then retreated behind the bar again.

I slid into the chair across from Thomas and he slowly raised his head. Dress shirt unbuttoned at the collar, tie loosened, and suit wrinkled, he appeared years older than the last time I'd seen him. That was several weeks ago, when he'd come to the café for coffee. The lines on his face had deepened. He poured several fingers into the empty glass. Amber liquid splashed around the base.

"He loved you very much. Both of my brothers and I cared for you, in our own demented ways," he said wryly.

I inhaled a sharp breath.

He gave his head a slow shake. "No more secrets."

That's not my family's crest. It's Claire's.

Something shifted inside me, bringing clarity. "Phil's your brother."

"Uncle Grant's son and Mom's. She and her brother Grant were very close before he hired Dad and Mom fell in love with him. Dad took her surname when they married. I think it helped in his position as president of Donato."

No wonder James kept so much about his family from me. He must have been ashamed about his mother and her own brother. And Phil was a product of that union. The Donato family hid that secret well.

I dropped my gaze to the table, considered the whiskey in the glass, then looked back at him. He was right. No more secrets. "I don't believe for a moment Phil cared about me. He attacked me the day James proposed."

Thomas lurched back. "Fuck, Aimee. I didn't know." He looked away from me, staring off into the corner. "It all makes sense now. Why James was hell-bent on getting rid of him."

"Where is he?"

He turned back to me. "Phil? He won't bother you again."

His words sounded final.

"What happened to James? Why did you lie to us?" Nineteen months of pain and loss poured out with those questions. Salty tears beaded in my eyes.

"I was protecting him from Phil, who was trade-based laundering, using Donato Enterprises as cover. He'd purchase our furniture with drug money and arrange for it to be exported to Mexico. The cartel then sold the furniture for pesos, thus getting their money back into the banking system," he explained in a gravelly tone. "Phil wanted to ruin us. Uncle Grant left Donato to my father, and my father gave it to me, not Phil. Phil felt entitled to the business."

They've taken everything from me. Phil's words came rushing back. I'd thought him insane.

"Dad and I were cooperating with the DEA, who were after bigger fish than Phil. We had to pretend we didn't know what he was doing so he'd keep his operations going until the DEA got what, and who, they were after. The people Phil worked for? They wouldn't hesitate killing anyone who found out what Phil was doing."

I remembered James and Thomas arguing. James had wanted to bring in the DEA, but Thomas had already been working with them.

"James didn't know the DEA was involved," I surmised.

Thomas shook his head. "Dad and I agreed the fewer who knew what was going on, the less risk to us and the company. In retrospect, I should have told James. He's whip-smart. He did our finances and discovered pretty quickly what Phil was doing."

"And you didn't do anything about it when James told you," I guessed.

"I couldn't. There was already a plan in place. But James grew impatient with my lack of action and interest. He took off to Mexico on his own and confronted Phil. Now that I know what Phil did to you, I think James had a lot of pent-up rage inside him."

He did. James had gone ballistic when I'd wanted to take down the painting of our meadow. "We will not let that sick fuck control our lives," he'd told me.

"I have no idea what happened when James met up with Phil," Thomas was saying. "We may never know unless he remembers. Phil said they went fishing and that James fell overboard, so that's the story I went with. I think Phil tried to kill him."

Words failed me. It was too much. All the issues with his family James had been struggling with while trying to protect me.

"Because of the DEA case, I had to let everyone believe James had died. They needed to keep Phil engaged in his activities, not running off on a manhunt if he learned James was still alive. James might not have survived another attempt on his life. And if the Mexican cartel knocked off Phil, there went the DEA case." He thumbed his chest. "I kept James hidden to protect him."

"But you left him here," I cried.

"He was only supposed to stay hidden a few weeks, three months tops. But the weeks turned into months, soon a year. The DEA took longer to do what they needed to get done. By then, James was heavily entrenched in his new life as Carlos."

"He'd met his wife."

"He was already married with a kid on the way. He fell hard and fast for Raquel."

Thomas tossed back my whiskey since I hadn't touched it, then stared into the empty glass. "I thought for sure you'd find out sooner. Your PI almost bled me dry. He threatened to tell you where James was. I had to pay him off to shut him up."

Like he'd paid off Imelda. He'd paid me off, too.

This was too much to digest. Besides, I'd heard enough. It was time to go home. I stood and smoothed my skirt.

Thomas's head snapped up. He snagged my wrist. "I'm sorry, Aimee."

My gaze slowly rose from his fingers clasped around my wrist to his face. "I'm not the one who needs your apology."

"How is James? Is he coming home?"

"No. He's needed here, but he has questions. Make sure you see him before you leave."

"What about you? Are you going home?"

"That's where I belong. My café—"

His grip tightened. "I knew you could do it. I'd told Joe—" I stiffened and Thomas grinned. "It was me. I covered your lease during build-out. It was the only way I could get Joe to agree—"

I yanked my arm from his grip.

"Yeah, well . . . I wanted to help." He dragged himself out of the chair and stumbled toward the bar, collapsing on a stool.

I turned to leave, but stopped. "Did James really go to Cancún?"

Thomas shook his head. "He wanted us to think he was there and not chasing Phil."

"And the casket. What was inside?"

He gave me an empty look.

"James's funeral," I explained. "What was inside his casket?"

"Sandbags." He shrugged like it was of little consequence.

I briefly glanced away and momentarily closed my eyes. When I looked back, Thomas faced the bar, head supported in his hands.

Without a backward glance, or word of good-bye, I walked out of the bar, and out of the lives of the Donato family.

CHAPTER 30

"Open up, Aimee!" came Ian's muffled yell. He banged hard on the door.

I tossed aside a shirt into the opened suitcase and rushed over before other guests stirred. It was only five-thirty in the morning.

I yanked open the door and he blazed inside.

"Christ! I've been calling all night. Where've you been?"

"With Carlos."

He visibly swallowed. "You should have told me. I was worried."

"I left my phone here by accident. I didn't expect to be gone all night. I'm sorry."

"So, you talked with Imelda?"

I nodded. "Carlos, too. He came to my room and we went to dinner. After we—"

"Did you sleep with him?" he demanded in a strained voice.

"No! Nothing happened." I moved closer and he lurched back. I stopped. "We talked. That's all."

"Is he coming home with you?"

I shook my head. From habit, I went to stroke the ring on my finger until I remembered it was gone. The fluttery movement caught

Ian's attention. His gaze dropped to my hand, then jumped to my face. "Where's your ring?"

"I gave it back to him."

Ian realigned his body so he fully faced me. His eyes traveled my entire length. I forced myself to relax, even smile a little. His brows bunched. "How are you holding up?"

"I'm doing . . . all right," I offered with a smile. I wished he'd say something about "us." "So . . . we're good?" I motioned between us.

He spied my roller bag. A single brow arched. "You're packing?"

"There's no reason for me to stay." I moved to the dresser.

"Not any?" he asked sourly.

"Nope. Time for me to move on." I scooped up a pile of dirty clothes. "If you pack quickly, we should make the first flight out today."

Ian didn't move as I dumped the dirty clothes in the case. I retreated to the bathroom and gathered my toiletries and cosmetics. After a quick glance around, I returned to the room. Ian stood by the balcony doors, hands on hips. He gazed at the early morning sky. My eyes darted from him to the suitcase. "Aren't you going to go pack?"

He shook his head. "Imelda's promised to help me find Laney. I'll fly home tomorrow as planned."

I inhaled swiftly through my nose, biting my lower lip. I'd forgotten about his interest in Laney-Lacy. Dumping the toiletries in the case, I tugged at my naked finger. "Do you want my help?"

He watched me for a long moment before he shook his head.

My chest constricted. "Um . . . OK. I'll see you at the café on Wednesday then?"

He gave me a level look. "I quit. Remember?"

"Oh yeah. That's right." I wilted. "Well, good luck. I hope you find your mother. If there's any way I can help . . . well, you'll let me know, OK?"

Ian slowly nodded and turned back toward the balcony. It was only a slight repositioning of his head, but the movement put miles between us. He didn't want me to stay with him so I resisted the urge to ask about us again. He hadn't said anything, so it was probably too late to fix the damage I'd done to our friendship. He'd opened his heart and I'd walked away, leaving him alone in his bed. Then I told him what happened between us never should have happened. It was the worst thing I could have done. He only wanted to help me because he loved me.

I resumed packing and closed the lid, swearing when the zipper snagged on my clothes.

"Here, let me." Ian gently pushed my hands aside and fixed the jam, zipping the case closed. Then he turned to me and brushed the back of his fingers against my cheek. I sucked in a breath. He lowered his arm and hauled the roller bag off the bed. "I'll walk you to your cab."

At the curb, he hugged me good-bye. There were no kisses or promises to meet later. He paid the cab driver my fare and closed the door after I was seated. I opened the rear window. "Ian," I anxiously called as he retreated. "When will I see you again?"

His expression was guarded as he roughly combed fingers through his mussed hair. "You know where to find me."

Wendy's gallery, at his next showing. Where we would be polite and professional toward each other. I inwardly winced.

The cab pulled from the curb and I leaned out the window, watching Ian until we turned on to the road and he disappeared from view. It wasn't until I'd reached the airport I understood I'd let go of more than my hold on James. I'd let Ian go, too.

My flight landed in San Jose nineteen hours and two layovers later, very late at night. The terminal was several travelers shy of vacant as I stood alone in baggage claim, waiting for my luggage. I shivered, bundling my coat tighter over my sundress, and stared at the rain-drenched windows. The baggage carousel rotated and several moments later, my roller appeared, toppling forward on the ramp. I hauled it over and bumped into Nadia.

She grunted, grasping my shoulders. "Welcome back."

"How—?"

"Ian called." She wrapped an arm around my waist. "Come, let's get you home. You look like shit."

"Gee, thanks." I followed her to the parking garage.

As Nadia drove, I told her about James's condition, Thomas's confession, Ian's admission of love, and how I'd left all three behind.

"Holy shit," she said, her gaze on the road ahead. She stole a glance at me. "You've had one wild weekend. So James is really gone? There's nothing left of him? What a trip."

"Carlos is his own man with kids and career. It took me a couple days to accept James wasn't himself anymore. On some level I understood something was different about him. His touch didn't feel right. It's James's body, but it isn't James inside. Does that make sense?"

Her brows arched high. "In an odd sort of way, it does. That's crazy, girl. You're OK without him?"

I squeezed her hand. "Aside from losing his wife, he's happy in Mexico. I found it much easier to let him go than I'd thought."

She gave me a girlfriend smile. "I think you got the closure you were looking for. Promise you'll call if you need to talk? I know you. You'll mull the last few days over and over in your head. Don't bury this. Talk it out. I'm here for you."

"Promise." I squeezed her hand again. I was done burying my past.

In front of my house, Nadia kept the motor running as I hefted my luggage from the rear seat. "What are you going to do about Ian?"

My mouth angled downward. "Nothing. I hurt him. He's not interested in me."

"Trust me. The man's more than interested. He was very concerned when he called, and it doesn't take an idiot to realize he's crazy mad in love with you. He's already told you he loves you. You of all people should understand you can't fall out of love in an instant." She snapped her fingers. "Don't get in the habit of letting go too easily. Give the guy another chance."

"We'll see." I shrugged and shut the door.

Nadia drove off once I let myself into the house. A house that hadn't changed or been updated since the day James left almost two years ago. I wheeled the case into the bedroom and opened the beveled closet doors. His clothes stared back at me. I trailed my fingers across the clothing and lifted a sleeve. Pressing my face into the material, I inhaled. My nose tickled. Nothing but dust.

I grabbed a handful of hangers and removed James's clothes from the closet, carrying them into the guest room, where I laid them on the bed. Tomorrow I would box everything for Thomas to pick up. He could decide what to do with James's belongings.

On the way back to my room, the framed pictures on the sideboard stopped me. There were four photos of James. Snapping up each one, I added them to the clothes pile. Thomas could send the pictures to Carlos.

For the next hour, I transferred James's belongings to the guest bedroom. Paintings, art supplies, clothes, and pictures. I allowed myself one small photo, a snapshot of us leaning against James's old BMW, which I would keep on my desk.

When everything had been moved, I collapsed onto the chenille couch James and I had purchased together. Running my fingers over the worn fibers, I decided the couch should also go. One day.

Soon, my eyelids grew heavy and I lay on my side, tucking a cushion under my head. Then I drifted to sleep. And dreamed.

Several weeks later, at the end of the day, I was cleaning fingerprints from the café's food display case when the door jingled, cold air blasting inside. Feet shuffled behind me. "We're closed," I said without looking.

"It's just me," Nadia said.

I faced her, rag and cleaner in hand. She wore a burgundy cocktail dress under a wool coat. Her hair was pinned up and loosely coifed, lips painted, and cheeks reddened from the frigid air. "Where are you going tonight?"

She grinned. "I have a date with Mark."

"Really?" I absently rubbed at a stubborn smear on the glass. "What changed your mind about him?"

"You," she said. I straightened and she walked farther into the café, propping a hip against the counter. "I have a tendency to let go of men too easily. Mark's a sweet guy, and he's no longer attached to his wife. I wanted to give him another chance."

My brows lifted. "You really like him."

"I do."

I folded the soiled cloth. "Where are you going tonight?"

"Dinner, and afterward"—she retrieved a postcard from her clutch, sliding it toward me across the countertop—"we are going to Ian's exhibit."

I looked at the card with Ian's name boldly printed underneath Wendy's logo. Featured on the front were two images I hadn't seen in Ian's collection, but I'd been there when he took the pictures. They were from Puerto Escondido. I skimmed my fingertips across an image of two men smoking cigars in a storefront. "There are people in his photos," I murmured to myself.

"You should go. Give him another chance."

I shook my head.

"Have you seen him since you left Mexico?"

"No."

"Have you called him?"

"He hasn't called me."

"You already know how he feels. Have you told him yet you love him?"

"Not yet," I said without thinking.

Nadia flashed a grin. "I knew you loved him."

I moistened my lips and studied the postcard.

"I have to go. Try to meet up with us at the gallery. Kristen and Nick will be there."

"I'm not sure . . ." My voice trailed, and I slid the card into my apron pocket. "I have shelves to stock."

She buttoned her coat. "The shelves aren't going anywhere."

But someone else might.

She let the unspoken words hover, and then she kissed my cheek. "I'll see you tonight," she called, backing out the door. A discerning smile touched her bright lips.

I locked the door behind her, then went back to cleaning. I scrubbed the counter harder, put another load in the dishwasher, and unpacked several boxes of supplies. It wasn't until I started straightening the newspapers and magazines on the community reading rack I realized I was stalling.

I looked at the postcard again. His images were beautiful and I wanted to see them. What had changed his mind about his photos?

I also wanted to see Ian. I missed him.

So, what was I waiting for?

My clothes were rumpled and my hair a mess, but if I went home to change, I would find an excuse to bail. So I turned off the lights, armed the alarm, and left the café, walking the two blocks to Wendy's gallery.

As with his previous showings, the gallery was crowded. I recognized many faces. Ian's adoring fans. Unlike before, there wasn't a mix of photos from different expeditions. Every picture displayed was from Puerto Escondido.

I stared transfixed, slowly moving through the main room. Banner-size portraits depicting a millisecond of life reached from floor to ceiling. Surfers barreling through harrowing water tubes. Couples embracing, silhouettes against the sunset. Carlos leaning against a palm, staring off toward the ocean's horizon.

Carlos.

I touched my stomach. No nerves or anxiety. No sense of anticipation or loss. I glanced at my toes before looking back at the picture. A hint of a smile tugged the corners of my mouth as I realized it was Carlos I saw in the portrait. Not James.

All the pictures were dazzling, making the room blaze with an array of color. It was unlike anything I'd seen from Ian.

"Strange, isn't it?" Nick said from beside me. "I see James, but the eyes are different. Then I don't see him and it's someone else."

I thought of Ian and how he'd described the pictures he took of his mother when Jackie was the dominant identity. "His name is Carlos," I murmured. "Jaime Carlos Dominguez."

"Can I visit him?"

I looked at Nick. "He wouldn't know you."

His gaze darkened. "Thomas had us all fooled." Then his expression turned apologetic. "Sorry about Ray." He swore. "I can't get ahold of the bastard."

I smirked. "I doubt you'll hear from him again." Thanks to Thomas, Ray, the PI Nick had recommended I hire to find James, was probably on a small island drinking margaritas, sitting on a small fortune.

In the rear, a small crowd circled around a picture. Shades of yellow and gold peeked over their heads. I excused myself from Nick and moved closer, pushing through the gathering. Then I stilled. It was a picture of me, and I stared as though seeing myself for the first time.

Ian had caught me dancing at Casa del sol. I had let go, feeling the music.

My Caribbean-blue eyes framed in ebony lashes had been sharpened so you couldn't help but stare into their depths. A mass of brunette curls haloed my head and appeared to dance in the twinkle lights. They sparkled like fireflies and gold dust.

Was this how Ian saw me? The portrait was moving, taken by an artist who didn't just love the subject of his work. He was *in love* with her. I wanted to weep.

I sensed Ian beside me before I felt him brush against my arm. "She's beautiful," he murmured just loud enough for me to hear.

"Ian . . . ," I started.

"You're beautiful," he whispered in my ear, making my pulse quicken. "I've missed you."

My eyes stung. "Your pictures are . . ." I shook my head, unable to find words to describe how magnificent his photo work was at this showing. "There are people in your pictures."

He shifted beside me. "Someone once told me I have a gift. Apparently I'm skilled at capturing the good side of people. I guess I had to accept not everyone has something ugly to hide." I felt his gaze on me. "You were afraid to let James go, but you did, and I'm willing to bet you're a stronger person because of it. I went with you to Mexico scared I'd lose you to him. You'd never know how much I loved you. I still—" He stalled, going quiet.

I blindly reached for his hand. He twined his fingers with mine. "Come with me," he said, and tugged me to a corner, away from the crowd.

"I've missed you. I'm sorry I didn't stay with you in Mexico," I said the moment we were alone.

He wrapped his arms around me. "I understand, Aims. You needed some distance after all you'd been through and I gave you that space, hoping you'd find your way back to me." His voice caressed my ear. He brushed his lips against the sensitive lobe. Tingles pranced across my skin.

"Laney? Did you find her?" I asked, using the name Ian referred to Lacy. "Any word about your mother?"

"No."

My face fell. "I'm sorry."

"Don't be. If she's alive, I'll find her. One day."

"I love you, Ian." I couldn't hold the words inside any longer. "I should have told you before—"

He kissed me.

"I love you," I whispered against his mouth. "But I do have a question."

He broke off the kiss. "What's that?" he asked warily.

"Will you have dinner with me?"

He grinned, slow and sexy. "Are you asking me out on a date?"

"Why, yes, I am." I grinned.

"Well, in that case, it's a yes. I'll have dinner with you, and breakfast the next morning," he promised as his lips brushed mine. "And every morning that follows." He kissed me hard, giving me a taste of the future ahead of us. It was the future I wanted.

EPILOGUE

FIVE YEARS LATER

He dreamed about her again. Blue eyes so bright and hot they branded his soul. Waves of brunette curls stroked his chest as she moved over him, kissing his heated skin. They'd be married in two months. He couldn't wait to wake up with her each morning and love her as his wife, exactly how she was loving him now.

There was something important he had to tell her. Something urgent he had to do. Whatever it was remained elusive on the foggy edges of his mind. He narrowed his focus, honing on the thought until he could . . .

Protect her.

He had to protect his fiancée. His brother had assaulted her. He'd hurt her again.

He saw his brother, the conviction in his expression. It bordered on insanity. They were on a boat. He had a gun and was making threats. His brother pointed the gun at him and wouldn't hesitate to shoot, so he dove into the water. The ocean was wild, dragging him under. He felt himself sinking. Bullets sprayed the surface and shot past his head and torso, narrowly missing their mark.

He swam hard and fast, his lungs burning, propelled by the greatest fear he'd ever known. He had to protect her.

Large, powerful waves tossed him against rocky cliffs. Searing pain tore at his face and limbs. The ocean wanted him, but his will to protect the love of his life was stronger. He had to get to her before his brother touched her. The current sucked him below the surface. He floated, drifted. Back and forth, up and down. Then darkness came.

"¡Papá! ¡Papá!" a small voice squealed.

His eyes shot open. A small child jumped over him, messing the sheets. He looked at the boy, giggling as he leaped around the bed.

"¡Despiértate, papá! Tengo hambre."

The child spoke Spanish. He racked his brain, delving back to his college Spanish courses. The kid was hungry, and he'd called him "dad."

Where the hell was he?

He shot upright and backpedaled, slamming against the headboard. He was in a bedroom surrounded by framed pictures. He saw himself in many of the photos but had no memory of them being taken. To his right, windows overlooked a balcony and the ocean beyond. *What the fuck?*

He felt the blood leave his face. His body broke out in a cold sweat. The child jumped closer, spinning full circles when he launched in the air. *"¡Quiero el desayuno! ¡Quiero el desayuno!"* the boy chanted.

"Stop jumping," he croaked, holding up his hands to ward off the boy getting too close to him. He was disoriented. Fingers of panic slithered around his throat. "Stop it!" he yelled.

The child froze. Wide-eyed, he stared at him for two heartbeats. Then he flew off the bed and out of the room.

He squeezed his eyes shut and counted to ten. Everything would return to normal when he opened his eyes. He was stressed—work, the wedding, dealing with his brothers. That had to be the reason. This was only a dream.

He opened his eyes. Nothing had changed. Labored breaths blasted from his lungs. This wasn't a dream. It was a nightmare, and he was living it.

On the bedside table he spied a mobile phone. He picked it up and launched the screen. His heart stumbled as he read the date. It was supposed to be May. How the hell could it be December . . . six and a half years after his wedding date?

He heard a noise at the door and jerked his head. An older boy stood in the doorway, his espresso face pasty. *"Papá?"*

He sat up straighter. "Who are you? Where am I? What is this place?"

His questions seemed to frighten the boy, but he didn't leave the room. Instead, he dragged a chair to the closet. He climbed atop and retrieved a metal box from the upper shelf. The older boy brought the box to him and punched a four-digit code on the keypad. The box's latch popped open. The boy lifted the lid, then slowly backed from the room, tears streaming down his face.

Inside the metal box were legal documents—passports, birth certificates, a marriage license, along with a death certificate for a Raquel Celina Dominguez. Thumb drives and several data storage discs were tucked at the bottom, along with an engagement ring. He knew this ring. She wore this ring. He held it to the light, staring, uncomprehending. Why wasn't she wearing his ring?

He returned the ring to the metal box and an envelope caught his attention. It was addressed to him. James. He ripped the envelope open and extracted a letter.

I write this on borrowed time. I fear the day's coming I'll remember who I was and forget who I am. My name is Jaime Carlos Dominguez.

I was once known as James Charles Donato. If I'm reading this note without any recollection of writing it, know one thing:

I AM YOU.

ACKNOWLEDGMENTS

Like Aimee's journey in *Everything We Keep*, my own journey to publishing has been full of twists and turns. It's been a crazy, exhilarating ride that has brought some of the most incredible people into my life. Thanks to their enthusiasm and expertise and the ongoing support of family and friends, I have the privilege of sharing Aimee's story with my readers.

I have much appreciation for my agent, Gordon Warnock of Fuse Literary Agency, for taking the time to listen, for his encouragement, and for not giving up. Most of all, I am thankful he found *Everything We Keep* a home. And for Jen Karsbaek, who plucked my manuscript from the slush pile. Thank you for loving Aimee's story as much as I do.

The entire Lake Union Publishing team has been amazing, especially Danielle Marshall and my editor, Kelli Martin. Thank you for everything you've done to make this story shine. I am tremendously grateful. It's a joy working with you.

Everything We Keep wouldn't be the story it is today without my first readers—Elizabeth Allen, Bonnie Dodge, Vicky Gresham, Addison James, and Orly Konig-Lopez—who patiently read revision after revision. Your honest feedback helped make me a better storyteller and writer. And while all this writing was happening, someone had the crazy notion of launching an association. To my cofounders of the Women's Fiction Writers Association, you are my inspiration! We can write books and build a national organization. How fabulous is that?

I have to recognize my parents, Bill and Phyllis Hall. They've been my biggest champions since day one, when I announced all those years ago I planned to write a book. Thanks for showing a girl how to dream big.

To my children, Evan and Brenna, thank you for always asking about my books. Don't ever lose that inquisitiveness. I love to write, but I love being your mother more.

And finally, to my best friend and most patient, adoring husband, Henry, I have so much appreciation for you and everything you do. Thank you for being you.

BOOK CLUB DISCUSSION QUESTIONS

1. Aimee is caught off guard when Lacy approaches at James's funeral. Initially, she doesn't believe Lacy. How would you have reacted in a similar situation?
2. On several occasions, Kristen encourages Aimee to open up about her emotions, to talk to someone. Do you think she sensed Aimee was hiding something? Did you suspect Aimee was hiding something?
3. Per James's request, Aimee doesn't take down the meadow painting, her and James's special place and the site of Phil's assault. What does this say about Aimee? Do you think her inability to discuss the incident ran deeper than keeping her promise to James?
4. Had James not disappeared, do you think Aimee would have gone through with the wedding? Would their relationship have lasted or would the incident with Phil have come between them?
5. What do you think helped Aimee more with her healing? Opening her café or searching for James?
6. Imelda describes Lacy as an "enigma." She remains a mystery to the very end. Both Ian and Aimee interacted with her in their own way. How do you think Lacy connected them in their quest pursuing lost loved ones?

7. What was your view of James before the flashback to Phil's assault? Did it change once you learned how he reacted after the assault?
8. What do you make of Thomas's confession? Were his revelations surprising? Did he really have James's best interests at heart?
9. Do you agree with Aimee that James kept the truth about his relation to Phil secret because he was ashamed? How do you think Aimee would have reacted had James been honest with her from the beginning? Do you think a relationship can last when one person has a deep, dark secret?
10. This story has many themes: letting go, healing, forgiveness, and love. Which theme resonated the most with you? Which theme had more impact on the story?
11. Until the end, Aimee never removes her engagement ring. What symbolic role does the ring play? How does it connect to the story's themes?
12. The story ends with James coming out of the fugue state. What do you think happens next?
13. Aimee's life changes in many ways she didn't anticipate—losing her fiancé, opening her café without him, then traveling thousands of miles to find him only to leave him behind—but her journey is internal. How is she different at the end of the story?

ABOUT THE AUTHOR

Photo © 2013 Deene Souza Photography

Kerry Lonsdale believes life is more exciting with twists and turns, which may be why she enjoys dropping her characters into unexpected scenarios and foreign settings. She graduated from California Polytechnic State University, San Luis Obispo, and is a founder of the Women's Fiction Writers Association, an online community of authors located across the globe. She resides in Northern California with her husband, two children, and an aging golden retriever who's convinced she's still a puppy. *Everything We Keep* is Kerry's first novel. Connect with her at www.kerrylonsdale.com.